SEEKING
REDEMPTION

Curses & Secrets Book Three
A novel by Elisabeth Zguta

BOOK SERIES

EZ-INDIE-PUBLISHING.COM

Curses & Secrets

Other Books
by Elisabeth Zguta

BREAKING CURSED BONDS
EXPOSING SECRET SINS

Check out the newest Mystery Thriller -
IN THE WOODS–
Murder In The North East Kingdom

"...the book took off in so many directions that it kept me interested through to the end. I really enjoyed this book. Although a crime thriller, the threads woven through of love, friendship, family, nature and heritage created a rich fabric of which the main character, Samantha Tremblay, was the strongest thread running through it. Well told and well-shaped,  Elisabeth Zguta is an author that I look forward to following and reading more of her work."

COPYRIGHT

2016, 2021

Cover design and book formatting by EZ Indie Design

Editor: Richard Thomas

CHAPTER 1

Shadows

Robert de Gourgues stared into the black night; a chorus of frogs and locust drowned his thoughts. He raked his fingers through his dark wavy hair, tugging at it, inflicting some pain upon himself which he no doubt deserved. Movement at the far end of the portico caught his attention. He squinted. A stranger stood in the darkness, obscured in the far corner of the long front porch that ran along the facade of the family's Memphis mansion. The glow from his cigarette lent a brief glimpse of his outline—a man, tall, thin, and wearing a fedora. The stranger tossed the butt to the porch floor and snuffed it out with the toe of his shoe. Slow and deliberate, he walked toward Robert, passing the wicker furniture until he stood just a few feet from him, but remained curtained in the shadows.

Robert's pulse quickened, and a shiver slithered down his back. He rubbed his clammy hands against his trouser leg. *Is this retribution? Does this stranger intend to harm me?* Thoughts of the shady things he had done and gotten away with in the past flashed in his mind—embezzling money from his father's company. Worse, he had poisoned Pierre, his father. Done to make him appear unbalanced and delude others into thinking that Pierre was unfit to steer the business—so that Robert could gain control of the company. All his plans, the hoaxing and backstabbing, had failed.

Robert stood on the porch, in pitch blackness, waiting for the next catastrophe. Much had happened in the past year, and he'd never be able to atone for the injustice he inflicted on his family. Robert accepted that he deserved to be humiliated in public, sent to prison even. Whatever punishment his family wished upon him was valid. Still, deep inside, he wanted another chance to prove himself. He hoped that there was a path to forgiveness. He wanted to live and prayed that this stranger hadn't been sent to kill him.

Not long ago, Robert would have done anything to gain more money and power. It was like a sickness inside of him, a deep craving for more. Still, no matter how much wealth he managed to accumulate, no matter how many cars and things he acquired, it never filled the emptiness inside. Robert socialized with other men like himself—wealthy and willing to take advantage of others. He lived on the edge. He conspired with Tom Bennett, his business mentor, and the leader of a powerful secret society. Robert craved beyond anything else in this world to be a member of the elite group—the Black Wolf Society.

Yesterday changed all that. Everything was different now that Tom Bennett was dead. *Is this revenge?*

Robert swallowed back his fear and prepared for the worst. The man's shadow moved closer. Robert knew that the man was a member of the Black Wolf Society, sent to silence him, and Robert's time on earth would end in seconds. *Would they care that it was self-defense?* No, how could they have known that Tom Bennett had already been a dead man, a monster? No one would believe the story. It was better this way—let him shoulder all the blame, and keep any mention of his family out of the recent events.

A timbre voice with a French accent broke the eerie quiet.

"Mr. de Gourgues, you've been through a lot in recent days. As I see it, you could use some assistance. You don't know us yet, but we can do business together. Take a few days of rest, collect your thoughts, and then, *mon ami*, I will approach you again. I can help you, and you help me. How you say it, one hand washes the other? *Non?* We'll be in touch."

The man disappeared, slipped into the cool darkness. A

2

noise startled Robert. He turned to his right. A second person had been standing there in the shadows, listening to the brief one-sided conversation. The mysterious person slinked away unseen. Robert could only hear the trailing sound of footfalls against the crushed stones that lined the path.

The night was still again. Only the rattling of dried leaves against the walk sounded as the cool autumn wind blew across the almost bare trees.

Robert didn't have enough energy or the courage to follow the strangers. Confused about the proposed business liaison, at the same time, he was relieved that no one knew what they had done to Tom Bennett. All that mattered now was his family. He understood why they were furious with his recent shenanigans. His sisters had been traumatized and physically hurt by Bennett, who had gone too far. Of course, they were disappointed in their brother for being friends with the man. *But he wasn't a man–Bennett was a monster.* Still, after everything Robert had done, Michelle and Emilie remained concerned about him. He was thankful that his sisters were blind to the worst of his actions. They didn't know how far off the edge of decency he had fallen. Somehow, he had to redeem himself and make it up to them. There was no time to worry about strangers in the dark.

The stranger hadn't actually threatened him, though Robert was sure the man represented the Black Wolf Society. The thing Robert had desired most—to be one of them—was now his worst fear. Following the mysterious visitor would have been another rabbit hole that he'd rather not fall into. He decided at that moment that he didn't care about anything else except how to get his life back on track. No more chasing after money. He vowed to find a way to make it up to his sisters, Emilie and Michelle. And to his new wife, Rachael, as well. His only hope was that it wasn't too late.

Robert turned and went back into the house.

Standing in the foyer, Robert listened to the laughter that drifted from the front parlor. The family appeared to be enjoying themselves. He wasn't needed...they were better off without him. If only he dared to end his charade, to leave them and continue on his own, alone. But of course, he couldn't, he wouldn't. He needed them, not the other way around.

Staring at himself in the mirror, which hung above a Louis XVI marble-top console table, he straightened out his disheveled hair. Touching his face, he gently ran his finger along his new scar, inspecting. He winced—a sore spot. The disfigurement would be a constant reminder of what happened up in Boston, a badge he wished he didn't wear. The raw, pink, jagged scab made him look all the meaner, and stronger paired up with his square jaw. He turned sideways and approved of his tall, slim figure. He liked staying in shape. His stance was just like father's had been. There had been many occasions when young climbing socialites craving a good catch, told him that he carried himself well. Easy enough when you can wear tailored clothing, he supposed. Otherwise, he didn't look special.

Besides, the joke was on them, because he wanted the same thing, a good catch. That's why he married Rachael, convincing her to run off and elope with him. He had loved the chase, the courtship, and appealing to her better sensibilities. Just when he thought it was a hopeless game, Rachael had agreed to marry him, and they eloped. He was still excited about her, but now for reasons other than money.

Just a day ago, he and his sisters were tormented by Tom Bennett. Throughout the entire ordeal, all Robert had thought of was getting home to Rachael—for one more chance to hold her in his arms—to kiss her. Her influence over him at times smothered him, at the same time filled him with happiness.

Looking at his reflection, he straightened his collar and tie, then practiced his customary confident smile. *Everyone will be scrutinizing my every move.* He might explode at any moment, like a pressure cooker set on high.

"Boom!"

Robert made a crazy face into the mirror, then turned around and stepped into the parlor.

"Robert, there you are. We were wondering what happened to you," Michelle said. She walked to meet him and slipped her skinny arm in his. She wore a black A-line silk dress designed by Marc Jacobs, business dress meets grunge. He appreciated her seamless individualism.

Michelle had always been a friend to him. He kicked himself for being such an ass to her in return. She gazed up with her big blue eyes, her small face framed with dark hair like his, styled short and sassy. He'd ignored her ever since father's funeral. That was when he found out that he didn't inherit the family business. Truth be told, he *did* resent her for being the person in charge of things. Michelle was the youngest, after all. He assumed that managing the business would have been his role after Pierre died. But he knew it was his own fault that he'd lost that chance. *I wish she didn't remind me of that fact so often.* He quickly chastised himself for that fleeting thought, afraid of reverting back to his old self. He can't allow himself to slip into cynicism, not even for a second. He squeezed her arm.

"I'm fine, Chelle, no need to worry. I just needed some fresh air to calm my nerves for a bit." He grinned, half-heartily.

"Robert, we're in this together," Michelle said. "We all experienced horrific things, and we survived by sticking together."

She batted her dark eyelashes, done as a sign of comfort, and then smiled as if she understood. Michelle was smart, but he hoped with all his heart that she didn't know the depth he had fallen. Now that she ran things, she knew some painful truths, like how he had conducted business behind father's back. He hoped she didn't know everything.

There was a rattling sound, and Robert turned his attention to Aunt Victoria, who had put down her bone china teacup. It was the cup with the vibrant blue birds painted on the side, two of them standing on a branch of cherry blossoms. It was so delicate. He looked up at Victoria; her whimsical appearance stunned him. She wore a bright ensemble of yesteryear's design, which reminded him of fairy tales, except with tall people instead of pixies. She had soft blonde hair like Mother used to wear. However, Victoria stood almost a half foot taller than their mother had ever been. He never met a more determined woman and thought that maybe Aunt Victoria was a bad influence over Michelle. When they spent time together, their wills turned to solid stone.

"Please don't blame yourself for any of it, Robert." Victoria blurted out. "We understand the wickedness of Tom Bennett and the deep power he used to coerce you. He was evil."

"Please—let's not even mention the name." Robert felt his face heat up.

Victoria nodded and placed her hand on his shoulder. Robert pulled himself tight. She dropped her hand and then walked away. Victoria sat on the elaborate, gold velvet sofa next to his other sister, Emilie.

Em was the steadiest person he knew, despite the struggle with her clairvoyant gift. She claimed it was a burden, but lately, it had been a lifesaver for them all. Emilie sat quiet, smiling, looking so calm and relaxed. No one would guess the power she yielded. Her long brown hair fell gently over her shoulders, which were covered with a pink angora sweater. He watched as she pulled a strand of hair back behind her ear; she was nervous about something. Who knew which person's emotions she was experiencing right now? That was her burden to bear. She wore a simple dress without any bling accessories, except for that engagement ring on her left ring finger. The sight of the two of them, Em and Aunt Victoria, sitting together, gave Robert a glimmer of years ago. Mother used to sit beside Emilie, their heads bent toward each other, contriving stories before bedtime.

Robert turned around and swallowed a lump that had emerged in his throat. He needed a drink to stop his hands from shaking. The others in the room pretended not to watch him, but as he headed to the bar table, their gaze burned his back. All of their empathy and pity directed toward him was too much to swallow right now.

The past few days had been confusing, to say the least. To think that his friend and mentor, Tom Bennett, hadn't even been human. Thank God they had put the monster or whatever he was to rest, permanently.

Robert's soon-to-be brother-in-law, Jeremy Laughton, was a hero after delivering the final blow. Robert turned and watched Jeremy sitting near Emilie. The man's skin was bronzed from hours in the sun, his body mass firm and strong. His ash hair was combed back naturally. It must have taken great pains for this nature-loving man to actually kill someone. No, something. Robert behaved badly toward Jeremy, another regret to add to the pile.

Since Jeremy had stepped into Emilie's life, Robert had taunted him, making fun of his English accent, his easy-going nature, and old-fashioned morality. Tonight Robert understood that he owed the man his life. If anything, Robert should feel gratitude just to be alive. Still, his horror trumped every other emotion he should have felt.

The image of Tom's dead body, lying at his feet, shook him.

He remembered the warm spray of blood sticking against his skin, covering him from head to toe. His clothes, soaked after the beheading while standing right in front of him. Robert shuddered. He sucked in a deep breath and let it out slowly. That memory would never be erased, no matter how much he scrubbed himself.

An emotional spike ran through him, and in a split moment, everything tumbled together in his brain. His heart began to melt. His sisters, Emilie and Michelle, still wanted to save him from himself. To keep him in their lives. *How could that be*? The protective wall surrounding his heart crumbled a little and cleared a path for his family to enter.

A tear stung the corner of his eye. He wiped it with the back of his hand and poured himself a drink. He didn't dare express his feelings, worried that everything would free-fall over the dam, knocking down all the self-preservation he'd built up over the years.

Things needed to get straightened in his head. Painful memories of his mother's death haunted Robert more than they should after all these years. His father's rejection when growing up still stung, despite recent revelations of his true affection. The worse hurt was knowing that the one man he admired most, and to whom he had given all his faith, had been nothing more than a creature of the dark. When Robert watched Bennett turn from a man into a dark wolfish-creature—he thought he had gone mad. And when he had morphed back, and spoke to him in his human voice, appealing for mercy . . . it broke his heart and any sensibility that remained. All he had thought of was Rachael.

He noticed his wife was missing and became uneasy. "Where has Rachael gone? I hope she didn't sneak off to her father's house."

"She was just here a moment ago," Michelle said.

"Here I am, darling." She entered the room. "I was freshening up."

She smiled at Robert seductively. A spark throbbed through his body, his pulse rushed. Rachael had curves and knew how to move them. Her hair flowed down her back in an auburn blaze. A memory ignited—the first time he noticed Rachael. It had been at her father's home during a business gathering. She stood across the room, the bright lights reflecting off the marble floors, encircling her in a warm glow. He met her gaze; Rachael's green eyes intoxicated him. She walked toward him as if in slow motion. Her little black dress hugged her hips; her mouth was slathered with a dark crimson lipstick. He swore she was tempting him, sliding her tongue against her soft lips. Maybe he had imagined it. When she reached him and finally stood close, he whiffed her perfume. A deep sultry Patchouli undertone filled his nose. Then the exotic combination of jasmine and orange flower overtone lingered and roused his primal instincts. Spellbound, he diligently worked to gain her confidence. How lucky he was despite himself.

"Robert, maybe we should share what happened up in Boston with Father Eddie and Rachael?"

He turned abruptly, his thoughts jarred, and realized it was Michelle speaking.

"We need them to know just in case the police or anyone comes snooping around, asking questions."

"Do they really need to know? I mean, can't the lawyers handle these things? I want to be honest, of course, but I certainly don't want to scare my wife to death with such an ugly story."

"Now I'm intrigued. Be honest—tell me what's going on." Rachael nudged Robert in the arm.

"Thanks a lot, Michelle."

Emilie stood and walked to her sister's side. "Michelle's

right. Everyone should know the truth. It's better if they understand what you're going through—I mean, what all of us are
dealing with—after everything that's happened. We're bound
to be off our game for a bit. It's a horrible story, yes, but it
wasn't our fault. We only did what we had to do."

"What do you mean? Please—just come out with it."
Rachael said.

Victoria cleared her throat. "Tom Bennett has been a thorn
in our family's side for years. It started years ago, back in college, when he stalked my sister—I mean, your mother. He
ended up harassing both of your parents."

Gasps filled the room.

"What are you talking about?" Robert said. "I wasn't aware
of that. You must be mistaken."

Victoria and Father Eddie exchanged knowing glances. Father Eddie, their father's confidant and keeper of secrets. Larger
than life, he was dynamic and loved by many. A big man, Father Eddie always dressed in his church garb, dark hair going
gray with age, and dark sage eyes. Despite his forceful presence, his voice gave away his true benevolent personality.

"Emilie, did you know about this?" Robert glared at her.

"No, it's news to me, too. It explains a lot. Aunt Victoria,
why didn't we know about this before now?"

Aunt Victoria stepped closer. Her long, lean frame almost
glided across the room. Her face looked like their mother's, fair-
skinned, freckled, with blonde hair that framed it like a soft pil-
low. "Your parents never wanted you, children, to know, and I
wish you didn't have to know now, but it's relevant to what
happened. Just a few days ago, I told Michelle some of the details. She was determined to learn the truth about the vendetta
Bennett held against her parents. I owe you the truth as well.
It's only right that you all understand what lit up this fiasco."

"For chrissake!" Robert raked his fingers through his hair

and pulled at his strands until his roots stung in pain. It felt good to feel real pain instead of just hurt feelings.

Jeremy snapped his fingers. "So that must be why Bennett ended up at the Blackfeet Reservation. He must have been running away from trouble all those years ago."

"I seem to be missing quite a few pieces to this puzzle," Robert said. "I want to know everything else, the entire story. What's this about the Blackfeet Reservation?"

Victoria picked up the story. "Your father's family made sure Bennett was kicked out of Harvard. They've always had political pull, you know. And I personally reported him to the Cambridge police; he was wanted for questioning. That, and being kicked out of school, made him eligible for the draft. Not a good thing back then. So he fled to Montana to hide, like a coward. Your mother and father went on and lived happily ever after, and Bennett . . . well, he chose a life fringed on revenge. He resented them, their life together, and over the years, he tried to hurt your parents. But they created a safety net of security, or so they thought." Victoria hung her head.

Michelle stepped closer and placed her hand on their aunt's shoulder. She turned and shot Robert a glance, her eyes harsh.

"Of course, that security was sabotaged when Robert became friends with the monster," Michelle said. "As soon as he realized who you were, Bennett used you to weave a plot of revenge against all of us."

"I feel sick." Robert doubled over and sat down in a nearby chair.

"I'm so sorry, Rob, " Michelle said. "Oh no, he's turning green. He's going to vomit."

"Please, I'm fine." He raised his hand. After a deep breath, he said, "Continue."

Emilie picked up the story. "Jeremy and I learned that when Bennett fled Boston in 1972, he hid at a reservation in

Montana. The chief realized that Bennett was troubled and encouraged him to do a sweat lodge, you know, to clean his spirit. Of course, he never walked away healed. Bennett was filled with so much hate. While searching for his spirit familiar to guide him, he wound up connecting with an evil spirit from the other side of the veil. I know it sounds bizarre, but that's how he became the wolfish-creature we all saw. According to Chief Flying Crow, something happened back in '72 that changed Bennett's spirit. He became possessed and turned into a creature they call skinwalker. I wouldn't have believed it myself if I hadn't seen him and felt the evil inside. Don't you get it—we killed a killer. We did the world a favor," she said.

"Wait a minute. You killed Tom Bennett?" Rachael's voice trailed. "Robert, what have you done?"

Robert noticed a look of panic on Rachael's face. He'd never seen her *afraid* before and regretted they had shared their nightmare with her. It shouldn't have been her burden to bear.

"Rachael, it's all right. I promise everything will be okay."

"Wait. It wasn't Robert. We all took a shot at Bennett but it wasn't what you think." Michelle's voice was firm and unyielding. "He attacked us and was going to kill us all. It was self-defense. Besides, it wasn't Robert's shots that did the monster in—"

"It was me," Jeremy blurted out. "I killed him in the end."

Emilie went to Jeremy's side. She tenderly looked at him, as if she were embracing his every thought. Robert wished his wife would look at him like that, he needed her support.

"I think that's enough information for today. Come on, Jeremy. It's been a long day, let's go up to bed. We can finish this conversation tomorrow with cooler heads."

Emilie and Jeremy left the room. Everyone else remained quiet. Robert waited for Rachael to ask more questions, but she never did. He wondered what was going on in her pretty head.

He watched her as she sat on the gold velvet sofa, her long auburn hair rested softly against the pillows. Her eyes were wide open, but not another word uttered through those soft lips until she said, "I'm going up as well."

Robert knew he needed to explain more to her, so she'd understand if she was ever going to trust him again.

CHAPTER 2

Anxiety

Everyone wandered out of the parlor, leaving only Robert and Father Eddie. Robert swilled down the last of his drink.

"Father, you want a round?"

"Sure, I'd be happy to join you."

The large framed priest got up from the sofa and joined Robert near the bar table. Robert noticed a bead of sweat on his brow. This man was an enigma.

"Father Eddie, you claim to be a man of faith, yet you went along with my father's superstitious beliefs, right until the end."

"Do you have a question, Robert? Something concerning you?" Eddie took the offered drink and went back to sit, this time choosing an armchair.

"Well, Eddie, what's it all about? Are you after money from the family? I hear you fellows have a quota you need to bring in these days, like ordinary salesmen. My father left the church a bundle when he died, so you must be the number one employee by now." Robert raised his voice a pitch, trying to get a rise from Eddie.

There was a moment of silence. Eddie stared across the room at the fireplace on the opposite wall.

"Okay, I give up." Robert raised his hands then sat down in a matching chair beside the priest. "I know you've been good to the family, and after Rachael and I eloped, you took the time to counsel us. I appreciate your efforts."

"Thank you for that, Robert."

Eddie gazed off at nothing. Is he aware of regrets that Rachael might have?

"So Eddie, what do you think of all this? I mean, this story we told is bizarre, to say the least. I mean, we killed a monster."

The priest squeezed his eyes. "It's all very...unfortunate."

"You knew already, didn't you?"

Father Eddie nodded. "Yes, unfortunately, I knew some of it."

"Tell me, did you know Tom Bennett was a real monster?"

"No, that's news to me. I knew the man was evil, knew the harm he had caused your parents, and knew of a rape incident up in Montana. But no, I didn't know about him being influenced by an evil spirit." Eddie downed his drink, wiped his mouth, and stood up.

Robert remained seated and stared into the air while clutching his glass.

"Evil spirit, my ass! It was horrible. You should have seen it. The man I thought I knew turned into some kind of wolfish animal right in front of us. It seems impossible, but yet I know what I saw. He was a shapeshifter, skinwalker, or whatever the Blackfeet want to call it. I heard his bones pop and saw his face morph into some dark creature that drooled. It was horrible."

Father Eddie paced, stopped a second and leaned on the mantel, then paced again.

"Unfortunately, not only good crosses over. Evil creatures creep over that veil, too," he said.

"How do you know of such things? Aren't priests supposed to believe in the goodness of God?"

Father Eddie sat back in the chair and turned to face Robert. "Yes, of course, we do. I do. But there is also hell to consider. Something from that realm slipped into ours. I can't explain it all. I don't want to believe anything so heinous could exist—yet you saw it with your own eyes."

The two men remained quiet for a moment.

Robert drew in a deep breath and exhaled, slow.

"That's not the part I dreaded the most. Yes, I was hurt to know I had put my faith in a monster. That's going to be hard to live down, but the harder thing to understand is my sister's powers."

"You mean Emilie's clairvoyant gift?" Father Eddie shifted his weight.

"Yes, but I wouldn't exactly call *it* a gift. My God, she had light beaming out of her hands. She pushed her power toward the monster. It was like watching some old movie about a fire-breathing dragon or a sorcerer that could zap out magic power. Except this was my sister. I'm afraid for her. What does this all mean?"

Eddie smiled. "It means she has a special gift. Mind you, a gift that saved your life."

"Yes. Don't think I'm not grateful."

Another awkward silence lasted too long for comfort.

"Robert, I need to talk to you. After you left for Boston, in the middle of the night like that, well . . . Rachael came to me. She has more reservations about staying with you."

"I thought everything was fine—we're planning the party to announce our marriage to the world."

"It seems her father isn't all that accepting of you for his son-in-law. He's been putting pressure on her. Trying to get her to change her mind. Of course, she claims she hasn't, but she looks up to her father, so this is causing some discomfort for her."

"I'll talk with him. You'll see, I'll win him over just like I did Rachael."

Father Eddie patted him on the back. "That's a good idea. I think you need to keep at it. Now, go to your wife. Make her feel safe, and let her know you'll never take off like that again. Trust is the cornerstone to any marriage."

Robert put down his glass, shook Father Eddie's hand, and

headed for the stairway. As he climbed the stairs, he wondered what he should say to Rachael to gain her confidence again. *The truth, you moron, be honest with her.* He wondered if he remembered how to be honest.

Robert tiptoed into the bedroom. It was dark except for a sliver of light coming from the adjoining bathroom. He undressed, went to the bathroom, washed, and brushed his teeth. He returned to the dark bedroom and slipped under the covers.

She was sleeping. He watched her chest rising and falling in a steady rhythm. He found her beautiful, like a princess in a fairytale. A smile was born, as he realized he loved her. He turned on his side and let her sleep. Closing his eyes, he joined her, feeling at peace for the first time in a long time.

CHAPTER 3

Decisions

Robert awoke with a start, unnerved by a dream. The early morning sun flowing into the room was warm and cleared away the dark shadows of his bad dreams. He turned and saw Rachael by the window, opening the drapes, wearing only a skimpy nightie.

"Good morning, sleepyhead," she said.

He yawned and stretched his muscles.

"Good morning. How about you come back to bed. I'll give you a proper morning kiss." He patted the mattress beside him.

She smiled and joined him in bed, slipping between the sheets and snuggling up to him.

"When I came to bed last night, you were out like a light."

"Yes, I was exhausted," she said. "I've been so busy making plans for the reception."

"I'm sorry I haven't helped more." Robert closed his eyes and wished he could be a better man for her. Rachael wasn't only sensuous, but she was also undemanding. That's a rare quality, hardly ever found in a wealthy woman's personality. He nuzzled her a little closer and wished he knew how to make her happy to the point of never wanting to go back to her father's house again.

"Rachael, whatever still needs to be done, I'm your man."

"You certainly are my man."

She turned up her head and pressed her mouth against his with a playful kiss. The plump softness of her lips touched his. Her gentle embrace soon accelerated into a more heated exchange. She pulled Robert on top of her. He didn't remember her ever being aggressive, but he liked it.

He smothered her neck with light kisses. The string straps of her nightie fell off her shoulders. His hand pushed down the silky top as his lips roamed down to her breasts, kissing her skin. His tongue reached out and licked her nipples. She moaned. Slowly he moved one hand down to her nightgown and pulled it away, entirely. He cupped her breast with his left hand, and the other groped her rump and then massaged her supple skin like an artist forming clay.

His actions stirred a response, and Rachael doubled his verve. She rolled him over with an urgent roughness. Her fingers traced the contours of his chest muscles, then wandered down to his belly, and then further still. Her eager touch thrilled his hardened flesh. The sensation from her fingers sent shivers throughout Robert's body. She licked her lips. Nothing else mattered to him except Rachael.

It was his turn to moan as she slipped herself onto him. The heat intensified. It was so natural between the two of them, fitted pieces to a puzzle. Together they moved their hips in synchronized rhythm. He looked up into her green eyes, watched as they rolled back into her head, and he hoped that his hardness would last as long as she needed him. He traced a line down her sides with his fingers. She moaned, deeper and deeper. Her moans and the heat between them ignited frenzy within him. Robert arched his body upward and pushed until he heard her sighs of satisfaction, and she succumbed to an orgasm. Then he flipped her off him, took the top position, and continued to push himself into her until his body followed with a climax.

He collapsed, on top of her, satisfied. After a moment, she flung him off and spread out her arms and legs as if to cool.

"Are you all right?" he said.

"Hmm."

She turned and cuddled next to him. They rested in each

other's arms in silence. He inhaled her perfume which lingered on her skin. It was *Jasmine or maybe orange blossom.* He liked that she always smelled of exotic jungle flowers. His finger twirled a strand of her hair. He noticed how the sunbeam escaping between the drape folds made her red hair shine as if each strand was plated with gold.

"Robert, I've come to a decision."

He froze.

Her voice sounded determined, and he worried about what she would say. He hoped that she wasn't planning on leaving him. After swallowing, he asked. "What about?"

She pulled herself up on the bed and looked down at him with a big smile on her face. He noted a sparkle in her green eyes, not love or playfulness—something else. She was about to instigate trouble.

"I decided that I don't want to wait another half a year for the reception. The lead-time for the hall we rented is too long. I want to announce our wedding right now, without any delays. We've been married for six months already. It's about time we go public. The other day after you left, I was so angry. Then I was worried when you didn't answer your phone. If anything had happened to you . . ."

He sat up. "I'm so sorry, Rachael. I promise that I'll never do that again," he said.

"I believe you. When you finally called, I realized something horrific had happened. I heard it in your voice. I thought about how difficult it would be to live without you around. Robert, more than anything in this world, I want to share our news. I want to announce to the world that we belong to each other and then begin our legacy."

Robert wrapped his arms around her.

"Yes, of course. I'll find someplace that we can use right away."

She pushed herself away, smiling.

"I already have. We'll have the reception at my father's house. It's big enough, and it will feel comfortable being home."

Robert was surprised. It was her home, not his, but then he saw the amusement on her face. "Yes. It will suit us just fine, as long as your father is willing for us to abuse his house."

"You know perfectly well he hosts parties at the mansion all the time. This will be his favorite for sure. After all, it's not every day you publicly announce your daughter's marriage."

"He does realize we're already married. It's too late to run me out."

Rachael nudged his arm. "Behave, rich boy. I know my father is odd at times, but I love him dearly."

"Yes, we all know. He spoils you to death."

"As any good father should." She kissed his nose and moved off the bed. "Okay, rich boy. Time for breakfast. I need my strength."

Robert watched Rachael flitter towards the bathroom. Relieved and feeling rather lucky, he figured he could stand her father for her sake. Mr. La France was nothing like his own father. They were both stern businessmen, but that's where similarities ended. When it came to Rachael, Mr. La France was putty in her hands.

After they had eloped, her father refused to speak to him for weeks and treated Robert like a piece of furniture. Maybe having the reception at his house would go far to smooth things out between them. It certainly couldn't hurt.

◻◈◇◈◻

Later that morning, they drove to the La France mansion. It loomed ahead of them, a colossal fashionable home of the new Mid-south. Built of brick with French design, sporting massive rooflines, copper details, beams, shutters, and lancet windows pointed at the top, as if they belonged in a Gothic church. He parked his silver Jaguar under the carport, got out, and opened the door for Rachael.

They stepped into her father's house—a Memphis mansion with a grand foyer tiled with marble, the floors gleaming. A marble staircase, detailed with a wrought iron railing of intricate rosettes and ivy design, protruded into the entry.

"My God, this place is a palace. I don't remember it being so large."

"That's because you always saw it filled with people. This will be perfect for the party, with enough room for everyone, and I think we'll have the ceremony in the backyard—in the garden. It will add, you know, ambiance for when we recite of our vows officially for your priest."

"That sounds romantic." Robert was about to kiss Rachael when he heard the heavy office door slam closed. Mr. La France's office was just off the hallway from the foyer. His father-in-law's footsteps echoed as he drew closer, the sound building up intensity like in the old movies, waiting for the bad guy to appear.

Mr. La France noticed them and came to stand beside his daughter. He was medium height, not much taller than Rachael. His white hairline receded, his eyes were true blue, deep in color to the point of eeriness. His nose looked pasted on and too large for his face. Dressed in a finely tailored suit, he looked polished and ready to step into a boardroom. Robert thought him stuffy and a bit over the top. Even his own father had dressed more casually when at home.

One thing Robert did admire about her father was his keen business sense. A man who knew how to generate tons of money, he was a King Midas. However, today Robert noticed something else about Mr. La France. *Why hadn't he noticed it before?*—the way the man's eyes looked right through your body as if you weren't there. He leaned his body backward, angled away from you as if inspecting every inch of the floor between himself and others. *Creepy.*

A cold sweat chased down Robert's back, and he suddenly felt clammy. Creepy or not, Robert needed to walk the thin line drawn. He'd do anything for Rachael, even make small talk with his father-in-law.

"Good morning, Robert. Welcome. I suppose you agreed to have the reception here, in my house, as Rachael wants?"

"Yes, sir, if that's agreeable with you. She seems to have her heart set."

"Yes, it seems that's what she wants." Mr. La France turned his attention toward her. "Whatever you want Rachael, you shall have."

"Thank you, Daddy." She kissed his cheek mechanically.

Despite his misgivings about her father, Robert could never deny her.

"I took the liberty of having my social planner here. He can go over his suggestions with you and take care of getting the invitations out, even at such short notice."

Robert detected a little bit of snark.

"Oh, Daddy, I don't want this to be a business thing. I only want close family and friends."

"Of course, whatever you wish." He patted her hand. "All I ask is that you go over his list. He's quite thorough and even checked into the de Gourgues family tree to ensure everyone was included. It was odd; he couldn't locate any living relatives. I hope we haven't missed any extension of the family line."

"Thank you, sir. Unfortunately, we are a small family."

"That will change one day," Rachael said.

She turned and walked toward her father's office. Robert followed, wondering what she had meant. *Did she want a large family?* They never discussed having children before.

Robert stepped into another big room. Bookshelves lined the walls filled with tomes. In between the heavy wooden cases was hung art. Every inch of wall space was covered. One painting caught his interest. It was a dark subject, maybe a Francisco Goya knockoff. A dark horned figure was painted in the foreground, standing in front of a group of grotesque people, their faces mangled and distorted. Robert shivered.

A large, heavy walnut table occupied the center of the room. It was oval with a carved center post with a geometric design of old Bavarian influence. Mismatched wooden chairs scattered about, some ladder-back, some Windsor. A tall thread-like man stood beside the table examining swatches and color wheels. His dark hair was cut in a scissored work of art. Dressed vogue, his professional attire popped with a pink bow tie accessory.

"Hello, my dear Rachael."

He walked over to them.

"Sergio, this is my husband, Robert. Robert, our designer, Sergio."

"Delighted, sir. Think of me as your wedding planner."

Robert shook the hand extended to him.

They went straight to work. Rachael chose the color scheme and flower choice, both already dreamed up in her head after picking Michelle and Emilie's brains for weeks. Then it came time to review the guest list, which was too long in Robert's opinion. He didn't recognize most of the names on the list. Rachael looked it over and asked for a few to be scratched out.

"Robert, do you want anyone added?"

He looked over the names again, checking them to ensure his family was there. Aunt Victoria, old schoolmates from Harvard, even Jackson Bennett made the list. Some of the business people he knew, the top men whom he used to work with; now they dealt with Michelle.

"Dear, do we need so many business associates to attend? I thought we were keeping it to close friends."

"Okay then, who do you want to delete?" she asked.

A trick question. "I guess it's fine as is. I don't want to cause any problems with your father."

"Great! So we're on. Sergio, how soon can we expect this setup? I want it as soon as possible."

"My dear Rachael, we could have it this weekend and I promise, people will come. It is, after all, you and Robert. No one will want to miss this special day."

"Fine, this weekend it is."

Robert rubbed the back of his neck, kneading the knots in his muscles. All of a sudden, everything in his life felt so finite and controlled.

CHAPTER 4

The Future

Later in the afternoon, Robert stood alone on the back porch, his glass of Highland Park scotch in hand. They had returned home from her father's house then Rachael left again. She drove Aunt Victoria to her businesswoman's function. His aunt had promised to speak to the women's club about her book. Emilie and Michelle left for the office to check on things. Robert imagined his sisters wouldn't be home until late, dealing with the many issues after being away.

It seems odd to be alone. Robert took a sip and looked out across the backyard. His spirits lifted when he spied Jeremy's tall frame walking up from the woods. His boots were covered with mud. The man must have been inspecting the river's flood plain in the tree line at the back of the property. *He's a true nature boy.* Robert wondered why his sister was so taken with the man. Jeremy was ordinary. Yes tanned and handsome, but no money or prestigious English title. The complete opposite of Robert, Jeremy was laid back about most things and never ruffled. He annoyed Robert with his pleasantness—always smiling and seeing the best in life. Oddly enough, Robert hoped Jeremy was coming to talk with him. For some reason, Robert felt uncomfortable drinking alone. He didn't want to be by himself any longer.

Robert called out, "Have a drink with me."

Jeremy quickened his pace and joined him on the porch.

"What's your poison?"

"Water is fine, for now," Jeremy said. He took the bottle offered and drank half in a gulp. He wiped his mouth with the back of his hand, then smiled.

"How long have you been out there?" Robert asked.

"All afternoon. Even though it's fall, the afternoon sun still drains you."

"So did you hear the news then? We've moved the reception up to this weekend."

"Really? What's the rush? I thought you two planned a huge gala six months from now?"

"Well for some reason it's important to Rachael to have it now. She doesn't want to wait."

"Excuse me for asking, but is Rachael pregnant?" Jeremy asked.

Robert jerked his head back a tic.

"Not that I know of. Is the father usually the last to know?"

"In my experience, he's usually the first, sometimes the father knows even before the mother does."

"Now you're poking fun. How could that be?"

"I'm serious. Men know their own wives' bodies. I think if she were expecting, then you would have noticed a change in her."

Robert thought about that a moment. He didn't notice much lately. He'd been so blinded by his own twisted need for money. He had missed a lot of things that had been going on with his family...things that should have been evident to him.

"Well, if we are pregnant, then I'm the idiot for not knowing."

There was an awkward silence. Jeremy finished his water and asked for another drink, something stronger this time.

"Glad to have a drinking partner." Robert handed him a glass of scotch. "So Jeremy, how are you doing?"

"Thanks for asking. To tell the truth, not so well. I keep seeing that monster in my head. When I close my eyes, I can feel the blade in my hands, and its weight straining my muscles. I relive the thrust and the feel of the resistance . . ." Jeremy shook his head. "I would have never dreamed in a million years that I could've cut off its head, or done such violence."

"You had no choice. You were protecting my sister. You love Emilie—you had to do it."

Jeremy harrumphed.

"I'm not joking, old sport."

"Not so long ago you accused me of going after Emilie's money."

"Sorry. I wasn't in my right frame of mind. My better judgment was clouded at the time."

"Understandable. I hope you aren't being too hard on yourself."

Robert laughed aloud.

"What's funny?" Jeremy put his drink down.

"You above all people know how horrible I behaved. I regret many things and on the top of the list, I regret being implicit in the burglary that hurt your uncle. I apologize for having his book stolen. If I could do things over again, I would."

"I have to be honest. I'll never be completely over the loss of my uncle. Uncle Thaddeus was my best friend. No, more like a second father figure." Jeremy's face reddened. "Let's try to move on. We need to for everyone's sake."

"You mean for Emilie's sake," Robert said.

"Yes." Jeremy agreed. "The rest of the family's sake, too."

Robert nodded. "You're right of course. I'll take care of Rachael and you take care of yourself for my sister's peace of mind. Lord knows she has a lot of weird stuff to deal with and she needs you by her side. I don't think there's another person in this entire world who would've stood by her with all that mojo going on."

They looked out across the yard. It was serene as the sunset cast a pink hue over the horizon. Robert gazed over to the wooded area behind the pond and noticed movement. He leaned his body forward and stared.

"What is it?" Jeremy asked.

"I thought I saw someone in the woods. Did you notice anything odd back there today?"

"Nothing odd. There were some paths with the brush pushed aside, but it could've been from anyone riding the horses. I know your stable kids take the horses back there to keep them exercised."

They both turned around at the sound of the others jabbering away. Rachael and Victoria stepped onto the porch.

"There you are." Rachael kissed Robert's cheek. "Your Aunt is divine. Everyone at the luncheon devoured her every word. I never knew your family had so much spunk."

"Just what exactly did you talk about, Aunt Victoria?"

"Oh, little anecdotes, you know personal stories about this and that, being a woman and having to deal with the ole' boys club while trying to grow a business. Growing up in Massachusetts and bargaining with all the Yankee horse traders," she laughed.

Robert poured the ladies a drink and they chatted about the plans for the weekend. Rachael glowed. He recalled Jeremy's words. *Was she pregnant? If so, why not tell him?* He tried to think of the last time they had had sex, before this morning. Was it days, weeks? Could she have been pregnant for a while already? Robert started getting suspicious, then caught himself. *Stop being so cynical!*

"Robert, you are so lucky to have this wonderful woman by your side."

"Yes, I am, Aunt Victoria."

A half-hour later, they went upstairs to freshen up for dinner. Robert watched Rachael as she changed her clothes. *Did her body look and feel different?* He stepped closer to her and wrapped his arms around her waist. *Skinny as ever.* He breathed in and noticed her smell—jasmine. He buried his face into her neckline and drew in another deep breath while holding her tight from behind. He was the luckiest man in the world with Rachael by his side, the most beautiful woman alive.

"I'm so happy you're my wife," he murmured.

She turned around and smiled, then kissed his forehead. "Prove it, Mr. de Gourgues, and have your way with me right now." She unbuttoned her blouse and slowly pulled it away to expose her black lace demi-bra. Her skin was soft and lily-white.

Robert touched her arm, closed his eyes, and let his hand travel up to her shoulder. Opening his eyes, he recognized her desire. He lifted her into his arms and carried her to the bed. "You asked for it," he said.

Rachael took control. She kissed his body as she pulled his clothes off. Her lips felt hot and wet against his skin, sending waves of delight throughout his body. He went to a corner of his mind where worldly things were forgotten. The two of them were soon lost in the fury of lovemaking. Any thought, other than her, abandoned.

They spent the next hour together. Finally, exhausted they fell into each other's arms and rested. Robert heard the grandfather clock chime.

"Almost dinner time," he said, then gently kissed the top of her head.

🔳◈ ◈ ◈🔳

In the evening hours, the entire family met up in the parlor. As expected, Emilie and Michelle arrived late.

"Tough day at the office?" Robert called out from across the room. "A drink is in order."

He poured two wines, handed each one glass, and looked them in the eye. He noticed their fatigue and wondered if it was business trouble or just residual anguish from the experience they all had just endured.

"You know, if you need help with anything, you can ask for my assistance. I don't mean I'd go to the office, of course, but I'm just a call away if you need advice."

Michelle scrunched up her nose and darted him *a look*.

"That's very generous of you Robert. Things are running smoothly. It's just that we still haven't really been able to wrap our heads around everything that happened."

Robert understood that sentiment. He nodded and let the subject die.

Rachael made the announcement. "Robert and I moved the reception date to this weekend. So, clear your calendars."

Everyone's disposition changed immediately. The smiles delighted Robert, and he realized this party was going to be the medicine they all needed to get their heads back to some degree of normalcy.

"Family, I want to express my gratitude for your acceptance. It's important to Rachael and me, and with your support, we'll live a long and happy life together. Thank you all for being here for us."

He raised his glass. "To our future."

"To your future," they all toasted.

CHAPTER 5

Visitor

Two days passed. Thursday morning arrived and everyone left the house early to go to work or do last-minute errands for the big party. Robert sat alone in the kitchen, finishing up the last cup of coffee. He had been spending too much time alone the past couple of days, and what he really needed was a friend.

"Can I get you anythin' before I takes off?" Nina smiled, but he saw concern in her dark jeweled eyes. He knew the trusted cook and caretaker worried about him even though no wrinkles showed on her brown plump face. Over the years, she had guarded him just as well as any mother would have, though he didn't deserve the cook's attention. He was glib with her and too often mocking.

"I'm fine, thanks, Nina. You go on now, get your shopping done for dinner tonight. I have things I need to do to get ready for my bride."

"If you need anythin' just call out to Mr. Evans. He can carry you to the store or whatnot. Seems like he's gotz nothin' to do round here since your daddy died. All he does is hangs around, eavesdropping on conversations."

"I'll be fine, Nina."

She nodded, but her eyes never left his face until she was out the door.

"Evans," he yelled out.

The stiff-looking man entered the kitchen. "Can I help you, Robert?"

"Yes. Take the day off. I want to be alone. Now."

The house manager nodded and left without another word.

Robert immediately felt better. He hated how the man was always underfoot.

Robert rose from the kitchen chair and walked down the hallway to his father's library. He opened the large double doors and stepped into the room. The air was stuffy after being closed up for weeks, the room smelled of lemon cleaning oils and old books. He crossed the spacious room and pulled open the lengthy heavy Jacquard drapery. Sunlight streamed into the room's space, brightening things a bit. His father's antique desk almost gleamed, the wood mellow with age. Varied book jackets colored the shelves, and the chairs near the hearth looked inviting. He went to the fireplace, opened the flue, struck a match, and lit the fire logs that sat on the iron grate. In minutes, a fire blazed as the dried kiln popped in the heated flames.

Robert turned his attention back to the walls lined with books. His parents had been avid readers, and the volumes on the shelves covered many genres. He walked over to the shelf nearest the French doors and pulled out a random book. He leafed through the pages, stopped at a page, and read:

"No! My life was getting impossible. And I couldn't keep the secret of what I had seen. I couldn't go on living like everyone else, with the fear that this sort of thing might begin again at any moment."

He raised his hand to his chest. The words touched upon his fears. Robert turned back the pages to find the name of the author, who knew his own mind so well. The short story was named "Who Knows," written by Guy de Maupassant, one of many included in a book of classic stories of the macabre chosen by the master of horror, H.P. Lovecraft. *Is this what my life has become, the macabre?* Robert continued reading. Immersed in the story about a man going mad, he hadn't noticed when the French door opened until Robert felt a cold draft sweep into the room from the exposed back porch.

"Excuse me."

The unfamiliar voice startled Robert. He slammed the book closed, spun around, and inspected the stranger standing in the doorway. Early thirties, short brown hair slicked back, thin, and wearing a cheap suit. The expression worn on his face was as cold as the draft that blew in from outside—a serious man.

"Who are you?"

"I'm Agent Sloan." He flashed a badge and shiny shield, then slid it back into his jacket inner pocket.

"Do you make a habit of breaking into people's homes, Agent Sloan?"

"No, sir. Sorry for the intrusion, but I need to speak with you concerning urgent matters."

"Urgent? Hmm. Well, you can call my attorney, Agent Sloan."

"Mr. de Gourgues, may I call you Robert?" He took a step forward. "Robert, I believe you'd rather speak with me directly. It would be in your best interest."

"It would? And why should I speak with you, especially after you entered into my home through the back door, without an invitation?"

"Robert, I thought that perhaps speaking here at your home in private would be more agreeable. I hoped we might come to terms and avoid any unpleasantness—for example, you being arrested. But, if you prefer, I can get a warrant and drag you to the nearest Federal Bureau—"

"Arrested. What are you talking about?"

Robert worried they had connected him to the death of Tom Bennett. This was just the beginning. The nightmare would never end. He watched as the agent slid his right foot back and forth against the wood floor as if tracing the wood-grain with his toe.

"Well, for starters, you were the last person to see Mr. Pierce alive at the Peabody a few months ago." The agent waved his hands down to calm anticipated protests. "I know you answered questions and the locals seem pretty sure you have an alibi. But the thing is . . . " Agent Sloan smiled and waited a second. "The truth of the matter is, we had been following Mr. Pierce. You see, he was a man of interest in an open case we've been working. So we know, Robert—we know everything."

A thick silence hung in the air and lasted forever. Robert heard the grandfather clock tick in the hallway, as he digested every word the agent had said. Pierce, that man had been a pariah and still haunted him from the grave. He should have felt guilty about killing the man, even though he was a low life, but instead, he only felt fear of being caught.

"Then top things off with your involvement with Tom Bennett . . . "

Robert swallowed hard. His heart pounded against his ribs. The room felt a hundred degrees Fahrenheit. *What does this man really know?* He wiped his wet brow, then absently played with his cuffs, while trying to think of some witty retort. He had nothing.

"Now that's something interesting, don't you think? So, Robert, are you ready to have a serious conversation with me yet?"

Robert waved his arm toward the set of chairs near the fireplace. He closed the glass door, turned, and walked across the room, seating himself down.

"Just exactly what do you want, Agent Sloan?"

"Here's the thing." The agent walked into the room. "Like I said, there's an ongoing investigation. The FATF has been following the money, so to speak."

"Excuse me, what money are we talking about?"

The agent smiled. "Well, quite a bit of money. What tipped us off about you, Robert were the funds you funneled from your family's enterprise to Tom Bennett's offshore accounts. Please, let me start over and give you an official introduction. My name is Agent Jeffrey Sloan and I work for the Bureau of Investigation. Currently, I'm assigned to a special task force with Fin CEN and a FATF task force."

"Am I supposed to know who that is?"

"Robert, I would've thought you heard of them by now. Your accountants have been required to file BSA reports ever since the Bank Security Act in 1990. FATF, the Financial Action Task Force fights financial terrorism. We follow the money internationally and fight crime by revealing, arresting, and prosecuting money launderers and worse. The FATF operates under the direction of the Financial Crimes Enforcement Network, alias Fin CEN, who in turn reports directly to the United States Treasury Department."

Robert shook his head. "Hold on one minute. There was nothing dirty about the money I invested with Tom Bennett."

The Agent laughed aloud. "Investment. That's what you call it?"

"I paid my taxes on that money—it was clean. Not drug money, or anything illegal to get the gains." Robert said in a huff of indignation.

"Robert, it's not your money's origin that's the problem. It's where it went and what they're using it for. I know you've heard of the Black Wolf Society. Need I say more?"

Another moment of silence.

The Agent walked closer and sat in the armchair across from Robert.

"Please, let's discuss things like two reasonable men."

Robert drew in a deep breath and exhaled. He knew he was backed into a corner, and needed to hear what this agent had to say. "Very well. Continue, Agent Sloan, you have my full attention."

"The Black Wolf Society is responsible for various terrorist acts all across the world. They use the ill-gotten funds to back crooked government officials, buy warheads and ammunition to fund guerrilla armies and similar activities. Their sole goal is to create chaos in the world so they can manipulate governments, businesses, and basically control the markets and money."

"Sounds like a big conspiracy." Robert cringed. He had no idea the Black Wolf Society existed worldwide and so entrenched in politics. Hopes of staying away from them shrunk to improbable. Robert had a sinking feeling that he was going to become more involved than ever.

"No, it's not a conspiracy, it's a terrorist network, Robert. And we plan to shut them down by following the money. Your help will be invaluable."

"I don't believe in such nonsense." Robert didn't want to believe. He closed his eyes and wished this man away. Of course, Agent Sloan was still there when he opened his eyes again.

"No, Robert, from what I've witnessed of you and your activities, you don't believe in much, except yourself. This might be your chance to prove me wrong."

Robert's face burned. "Just what, exactly, are you holding over me? I want specifics."

"Well, for starters, the room in which Mr. Pierce lodged was bugged. We heard everything you said when you were in the room. The man's death was recorded. Next, we have surveillance of you with Tom Bennett the night before he disappeared. There was a live camera recording the four of you arranging to have a warehouse torched, and planting evidence against a political candidate. So that leads us, and by us, I mean the FATF—

to the conclusion that Tom Bennett is not only missing, but dead, and that you know something about that. Of course, nobody was found, only lots of blood left behind at the scene. The entire warehouse looked a mess when we got there. The locals couldn't stomach it—they had no problem letting our task force take control of the crime scene." The agent paused a few moments.

Robert adjusted his weight in the armchair but stopped cold when he noticed the agent's stare at him. He was scrutinizing Robert and his reaction.

"That was some bloody mess the other day, up in that warehouse in Boston. Disgusting really. We questioned Detective Ramsey, but he wasn't able to say much, what with being in intensive care and all. But he did murmur your name, over and over again."

"You plan to extort me as well?"

"No, Robert, nothing like that. That's your game, not ours. We're giving you another chance here, to wipe the slate clean. We'll lose the tapes from Pierce's room and forget about your involvement as an embezzler if you agree to help us with our investigation."

"You mean, you want me to spy for you? Put my life and my family's lives on the line?"

Agent Sloan nodded. "I don't see it quite that way. Robert, I'm giving you a chance to help your country. To right your wrongs. To find some sort of redemption for your past indiscretions. Hell, I'm absolving you, almost like a priest."

"Yeah, you're some saint."

The fire crackled. Robert turned and watched the flames, thinking of everything he had done. Agent Sloan was right about one thing, he needed a way to make up for his jaded past. He had done horrible things: made decisions that hurt people's livelihoods, bullied businesses for a better bottom line, agreed to hurt people and put out contracts . . . those were the least of his bad deeds. He tormented his father with knowledge of the curse, even slipped a hallucinogenic drug into his coffee. Then Robert stole his family's money, had killed a man even. He saw the truth, if he had kept on the same path with Tom Bennett leading the way, he would have fallen into a dark world of evil—consorting with gruesome murderers and monsters, just like Tom Bennett himself.

"Let me get this straight. If I agree to help you with your investigation, any previous infringement of mine against the law goes away? In writing?"

"That's the deal." Agent Sloan crossed his heart and smiled.

"So, what exactly do you want from me? What do I have to do to get this special consideration?"

"We need you to infiltrate the Black Wolf Society. We know Tom Bennett had already suggested you as a candidate. We want you to pursue it as if nothing else had happened. When the time is right you'll need to go along for the ride, and hopefully lead us to the main headquarters of the society."

"Oh, is that all." Robert gave a disingenuous grin. "What about Sturbridge? If you know about Bennett you obviously know about the secret hideaway there."

"That was just a local faction run by Bennett. He reported to a larger syndicate. We're aware that they keep the organization's helm someplace in Belgium, but we don't have an exact location. We need you to lead us there."

"Belgium." Humph. "And what do I do, fly over there and just walk around hoping someone will see me and make contact? Should I take out an ad?"

"Robert, don't take the task force for fools. You were already contacted, right here, the other night when you returned home."

"You mean the shadow man in the fedora, out there on the

porch. Listen, he didn't leave his name or calling card. I have no way to connect with him again."

"He'll contact you. I believe that's how he left things. The Society wants you to join their merry group for some reason. We still haven't figured out what else you could offer them, but you have something they want."

"Good to know."

"Yes, good. So it's a deal?"

"Deal. Don't I have to sign something? I want my surety in writing."

Agent Sloan pulled some paperwork from his inside suit jacket pocket. He unrolled the papers and handed them to Robert. After Robert read the fine print, which clearly stated that in return for his cooperation, he had full immunity from any previous crimes, he signed the agreement. A weight lifted off his shoulders.

"You understand that I have a big wedding reception on Saturday?"

"Yes, and please can you slip an invitation to me? I want to attend, just in case someone contacts you there."

"It's mostly family and business associates, I highly doubt anyone from the Black Wolf Society would be there."

"We suspect that the local representative of the Black Wolf Society, the equivalent to Tom Bennett, is someone involved in your business. Or maybe someone who's privy to your financial information, or at least has access in some way. We wouldn't be surprised. So be on guard from this point foreword."

Robert believed the agent was trying to scare him now, but he went too far.

"Agent Sloan, I had a thorough background check done on all the people I dealt with, before ever associating with them. I can't imagine any of them have the gumption to be involved in such an intensely unscrupulous group. Hell, that's one of the reasons I wanted to join, to be the first. Of course, that was until I learned the truth, and the evil behind them."

"That's the point, Robert. It will be the person you least expect. Someone who passed all your sniff tests with flying colors. A person trusted in your household and at the office. That's how they operate without ever being suspected. They are so ground in, more so than the best Russian spies. Don't underestimate this group. The Black Wolf Society has been around for thousands of years, morphing, changing their name whenever needed to escape detection. That has been our biggest concern. We're afraid that they'll go under and create a new alias, leaving our investigation with a dead end."

"Okay, I'll play along. Just make sure I'm not turned into a dead end."

"We'll watch your back, every step of the way. So give me an invite or two and we'll get things started."

Agent Sloan handed Robert a simple flip phone.

"You're kidding?" Robert said. "I didn't think these existed anymore. Okay, I get it. No photos or online media."

"After you're contacted by someone from the society, find a private place where you can talk, and call the second number programmed into that phone. Tell us what happened, then keep the phone hidden but accessible."

The agent got up from the chair, crossed the room, and exited the same way he entered.

Robert followed, but when he reached the door to look out, the man was already out of sight.

A harsh autumn wind rushed across the patio, swirling dried leaves into the air until they fell into the corner of the house. The brisk coolness sent a shiver up Robert's back. He knew in his heart that he had just taken on more than he should.

He thought of his parents, wishing they were there to show him the way.

He was on his own. No one could help him now.

CHAPTER 6

Past Troubles

Robert spent the rest of the afternoon in deep thought, sitting by the fireplace. He thought of the days when he was young and still happy. He had pushed those memories away for such a long time. Now it took him hours for them to resurface to a point where he actually remembered the warm gentleness of family love. Suddenly he wept, like a child relieving himself of the horrid fears. The vision of the monster still lingered in his mind's eye. He prayed and asked for God's forgiveness, hoping his mother and father could protect him, somehow from above. He was thankful that they escaped the wrath of the evil man, who he had once called a mentor.

A noise from behind startled him. Leaning forward, he turned around in the chair. Father Eddie s

tood by his side like a statue.

"I beg your pardon," he said. "I didn't mean to disturb you, Robert."

Robert cleared his throat. "No problem, Father Eddie. Come join me, please."

He motioned to the chair near him.

"Thank you." Father Eddie slipped into the chair, his deep brown eyes on Robert the entire time, inquiring with concern.

"Don't worry about me, Father. Everything will be fine."

"I hear the party is moved up to this Saturday. You should be on cloud nine, but instead, you look like you just saw a ghost."

"Not a ghost, Eddie, a monster. We all saw a monster the other day. The day before we came back to the house."

"You need to talk about it?"

"Talk? Unfortunately, talk can't take away the ugliness I see in my head."

"Now I'm curious."

"You know what they say about the curious cat, Father."

They smiled at each other, but it wasn't enough to lift the heaviness that Robert felt.

"Do you believe in second chances?" Robert asked.

Eddie chortled. "Of course. That's what my business is all about."

"You were there for my parents, weren't you? Did they confess their secrets to you?"

Father Eddie's face turned pink. He dropped his eyes to the floor.

"Okay, enough evasion. I think you need to fill me in—spill, Eddie. What were my parents hiding from us? I know there's more to this story. No point in protecting them now. Besides, I'm sure, under the circumstances and recent events that my parents would want us to know the truth. It was mentioned that you shared a secret with our mother. Something about a trip to Montana . . . "

Robert watched Eddie, his expression revealing his internal conflicts.

"Eddie, we were in big trouble the other day. My sister performed some bizarre acts, using her powers to take control of a monster. That's right, a monster. He stood and morphed into some kind of animal familiar with teeth. And my sister, Emilie, matched his power with her own. Beams of light shot out. I still can't believe what I witnessed."

Father Eddie's head shot up. "I hope she's all right."

"You saw her. Emilie is fine. I hate to admit it, but Jeremy is a god-send for her. He stood by her side the entire time of that nightmare, and he protected her when she needed to be saved."

Eddie nodded his head.

"So, spill, I mean it. What the hell could we still be up against?"

"I hope nothing. I'll speak with Emilie and find out what she knows. Maybe she learned something from their recent trip up to Montana."

"In the meantime, how about filling me in? I'm concerned about more than Tom Bennett."

"I gave your parents my word to protect you all from the truth."

"We need to arm ourselves with the truth, for God's sake. Besides, you heard Victoria. She filled Michelle in on the details."

A few seconds passed, they both stared at the fire. Robert stood and picked up the poker, jabbed the log, and sparks leaped up.

"See Eddie, just like the flame rises up with my poking, the same happened when Emilie and the rest of us faced that monster. We had no idea what we were dealing with, but we sure as hell could have used some insight that day. The more frightened we became the stronger it grew! I hope you're right and that nothing will happen again, but just in case, well forewarned and all that."

"Point taken, Robert." He sighed. "It was years ago, when your parents were still in college, that some unfortunate events happened."

"I have a feeling it was more than unfortunate events."

The priest blurted aloud. "Tom Bennett raped your mother."

Robert dropped the poker, the clang rung in his ears. Hoping he had misheard Father Eddie, he turned and noticed the grave expression on Eddie's face. He spoke the truth. A sick feeling overwhelmed him, and Robert slumped back into the chair.

"It was a horrible time, but your father helped Bethany, your mother, come back into the light. Together they healed."

Robert spoke softly, his energy drained, sinking through to the floorboards. "I didn't know. Oh my God, that beast hurt my mother." He shot off his seat, stumbled to the nearest bathroom, and threw up the rancid vomit. He rinsed his mouth and looked up at his reflection in the mirror. *How could I have been so close to Tom Bennett, the monster who hurt my mother?*

Robert returned to the library and slouched back into the chair.

"Are you all right, son?"

"Eddie, I'm the biggest ass in the world. I don't deserve to live, yet I'm hosting the biggest party of my life to celebrate my marriage to the most wonderful woman in the world. Eddie, I don't deserve her."

A large hand rested on his shoulder. A warm peacefulness filled him.

"Thank you for being here with me."

"I will always support you, Robert. Don't forget that I'm here for you, whenever you need me."

Robert nodded. Somehow he knew it to be true, but it didn't make him feel any better about himself. This sage knew more, but Robert couldn't take any more bad news, no matter how long ago it had happened. Still, he was curious about one thing.

"Father, did Emilie inherit her powers from my mother?"

Eddie nodded.

"I thought so. Never believed they were real until the other day. Now I know better. Maybe you can tell me more about them, but not today. I think I've heard enough. I can't wrap my head around any of this right now."

"I'll be here when you need me—just call."

The priest left the room as stealthily as he had arrived. Robert was alone again with his thoughts. He stared at the fire, trying hard to forget what the priest had said. His regrets were killing him inside.

CHAPTER 7

Making Contact

It was Friday, the day before the party and everyone was out of the house doing last-minute errands, again. The silence was too much for Robert to bear—he didn't want to spend another minute alone in the house. It had been months since his last visit to the Alchemy, or any other restaurant or bar he used to frequent. He'd stopped going to his old haunts after he eloped with Rachael. But today, he needed a short belt of nostalgia. He checked his watch. The Alchemy should be opening the doors in just about the time it would take him to drive to South Cooper.

Thirty minutes later, Robert parked his Jag and went in before he melted in the hot afternoon sun. There were a few warm days left, mixed in between the nippy days this time of year. The weather in autumn always confused Robert. When he dressed in the morning he wore long sleeves, only to roll them up while things got toasty later in the afternoon.

The Alchemy was eerily quiet for a Friday, only a few patrons sat at the bar, their elbows bent, supporting themselves by leaning on the polished black marble top. The restaurant would open to serve dinner in another hour or so, but the food was the last thing on Robert's mind. He walked deeper into the bar area, its décor was modern and fresh. It was the cosmopolitan place to go, especially on Friday. Still early in the day for this place. The doors were always open for Robert no matter what time he arrived—the owner liked him and his money. That was one of the reasons he frequented this place, that and because they had a great scotch menu. He walked to the end of the bar away from the other patrons and sat down on a black wooden stool with a grid back.

"Hello stranger," the barkeep said.

"I'll take my usual."

"Liquid Gold, coming up." The bartender grabbed a glass and filled it with scotch, then placed it in front of Robert. "So, where have you been? We've missed your business the past couple of months." He smiled.

"Has it been that long? Oh, I've been around, just not here." Robert cringed his brow.

"Well, glad you're here today."

The bartender left and attended to another man on the other side of the bar. Robert was relieved; he didn't want to talk to anyone. He only wanted to feel like himself again, find his funk. The past few days had changed him, made him more afraid, and yet responsible in a major way. Hell, the incident up in Boston scared him straight. He felt uneasy as if another big shift was coming—and he had no choice but to play along like a good boy.

Set up as a patsy for the Feds' purposes, the chance of getting stuck between the two forces of good and evil, scared him shitless. He took a sip of his scotch and let it slide down his throat slowly. He savored the malt flavor, then the burning sensation. It was a familiar feeling, and a comfort to him now. He was at the lowest point of his entire life. He should have been brimming with happiness, getting married to Rachael, but something was still twisted inside of him. He was anxious about something else, other than the agent, or the Black Wolf. There was something else he feared, but he couldn't name it.

Going along with any plan conceived by the Black Wolf Society made him nervous, and Robert had so much to lose now. He thought about what Jeremy had said. *Was Rachael pregnant?* That would explain her strange moods lately. All she wanted was sex. Not usually a problem, but Robert also noticed her aversion to discussing anything important. Rachael ran out of the house with Aunt Victoria yesterday, and today she was out shopping with his sisters. The past few days she had been too busy to inquire about his trip to Boston. In a way, it was a blessing because he didn't want to explain Tom Bennett's demise. Odd though, she hadn't asked even once.

Robert felt uneasy. He looked up and saw a man standing across the room, glaring at him. Robert's throat tightened, so he tugged at his shirt collar and undid the top button. He closed his eyes and then looked across the room again.

The man sauntered toward him.

Robert took a swig, finished his drink, and tapped the glass on the bar. Nodding for the bartender to fill it again, the bartender poured it pronto. "Thanks."

The man stood beside him. "Mind if we talk, Mr. de Gourgues?" He sat in the bar chair next to Robert without waiting for an answer. "I'll have a double," the stranger said. He took a sip, then turned his head to face Robert.

The man had blond hair, cut short, neat under his fedora. He dressed in designer clothes and looked like a professional from Generation Z. His eyes were gray-blue and reminded Robert of steel. He envisioned the man had a lining of rust.

"Well, what do you want to say?" Robert said. He swirled his drink around and then took another sip, not bothering to look at the man.

"I like a man who gets right to the point, don't you Mr. de Gourgues? We met the other night, on your front porch, non?"

"I'd hardly call that a meeting. Never did catch your name."

"And you never will." The man took another sip. "We have business that needs attention. I was sent here to make contact with you. Tom Bennett has vanished. We wonder if you have any idea of his whereabouts."

Robert turned to face the stranger, taking care not to give

away any emotional response.

"In my experience, when someone vanishes, it's usually because they don't want to be found or have met their demise. Last time I saw Tom he was quite himself," he said. He smiled at his own words. *Yes, Tom was himself all right, dead as can be. The man who mentored him had been a dead man all those years.* His face tightened into a scowl. Robert shook his head and tried his best to get those thoughts out of his head. He had new business to concentrate on and he didn't want to mess things up.

"I agree, and that's why I'm here. We can't wait for Mr. Bennett to resurface. The Black Wolf Society wants to meet you."

"Me? Why?"

"We have an empty chair without Bennett. Some suggested that with your ruthlessness, and money ties, that well, maybe you'd be a good fit. How about a go?"

The stranger's words stung. Yes, Robert had been ruthless, but he didn't want to play that role anymore. Inside himself, a battle raged. "I'll have to think about it."

"No. You see, Robert, it's not the usual type of request. It's the kind you can't refuse, like a Beneficial Act."

"Yes, well, that's all well and good, except that I was never initiated. I'm not obliged to perform a Beneficial Act. Not yet anyway," Robert replied.

"I think that's all a matter of interpretation. Since you know so much about our group already, well, let's say we're protecting our anonymity. The last we heard from Bennett, you had requested a meeting with the head council as soon as possible. That meant immediately—"

"I have a big reception this weekend that I can't miss without causing suspicion."

"We know all about it, and we like the fact that Miss La France will be publicly regarded as your wife. She's an heiress to a large fortune, non. Which, of course, interests us. We always encourage more funding for our cause. I meant immediately after the big party, of course. Come on." He nudged him. "We know you're dying to join the Society."

Robert looked away. His face burned up. He drew in a deep breath, thinking about how he was putting his wife in jeopardy. He had to comply. *Come on, you've got this. You're the master of disguises.*

"Okay, you made your point. Where do I need to go? Maybe I can arrange something for the near future."

"Oh, you will. We need you in Belgium. I suggest you take the new wife on a honeymoon. You'll find it's romantic in Brussels this time of year. The streets are already beginning to look like the holidays."

The stranger got up. "I'll be in touch with the specifics. Check your phone for a text message from STRANGER. That's my user name. The address, date, and time will be there. Au revoir." He nodded his head and then walked to the door without looking back.

How am I going to pull this off? Robert pulled out his phone and started surfing the web. Yes, Brussels would make a lovely vacation spot to take Rachael. All he had to do was convince her of it as well.

CHAPTER 8

Before the Party

Saturday morning everyone woke up early. Robert heard the excited chatter all the way up the stairs. *Of course, the morning of the reception.* He stumbled down to the kitchen and grabbed a cup of coffee. Nina gave him a look as if he was missing his head. Ignoring her, he sipped his coffee. When he heard Rachael's voice his attention awakened.

"Thank you so much for your help, Aunt Victoria."

Rachael and his sisters were talking in the morning room. He decided to leave them alone, but leaned back against the kitchen cabinet and listened to their conversation. Emilie and Michelle fussed over Rachael, insisting she eats a good breakfast.

"We know that you eloped and technically you're married, but it's important to have your marriage blessed, Rachael. This is a big deal. You'll recite the vows in front of all our family and friends," Emilie said. "The holy sacrament sanctioned by the Church is important. You're so lucky Father Eddie will be able to do the blessing right there in your father's home and forgo the big church scene."

"He said he just needs to bring the sacred Mass stone with him. Sounds a bit superstitious to me," Michelle chimed in.

"Dear, do you have all the usual things? Something borrowed, something new, something old, and something blue?" Aunt Victoria had been a great help to Rachael the past couple of days. Together they had shopped for the personal things Rachael needed for today. She helped Rachael pack for the surprise trip that he had arranged. A last-minute honeymoon in

Brussels. So far things were falling into place but Robert remained cautious.

"Auntie, are you sure that's how the saying goes?" Michelle spoke in between bites of cereal.

"It doesn't matter. I'm not superstitious. Let's not talk about the ceremony any longer, you're all making me nervous," Rachael almost sounded huffy.

"Rachael, are you feeling anxious?" Emilie asked.

"Em. Why don't you just sneak yourself in her head and find out for yourself?" Michelle snapped the remark without thinking, as usual, and Robert could hear her slapping her own mouth to cover it up with her hand. "I'm sorry. I didn't mean . . ."

"It's okay, Chelle. I could do that I suppose if I wanted to. But I make a point of not spying on my family's emotions. Helps me keep my own feelings in check."

Robert ducked into the room. He saw Emilie smiling and hoped that Rachael believed Em, today of all days, no one needed to be probed with her magic mojo.

"Good morning, ladies."

"Robert, you're not supposed to see Rachael before the ceremony," Michelle crowed.

"No worries, she's not in her dress yet. Besides we're already married."

He leaned over and kissed Rachael's forehead.

"Good morning sweet thing."

"Good morning Robert. Are you as excited as I am?"

He nodded. "Of course, maybe more."

Rachael smiled. "Well, I'm finished eating for now. Girls, please give me half an hour to myself, then come on up and help me get ready if that's okay." She rose and headed upstairs.

"It's your day princess. Whatever you command we obey," Victoria called out to her as she left the room.

"My Lordy, I can't believe his majesty is really married," Nina said as she entered the breakfast room to gather the dishes. "It'll be official today with the good Lord's blessing." Nina picked up the plates from the table. Tears welled from her eyes.

Robert reached out and grabbed Nina and gave her a big bear hug, patting her on the back. "All your work on me paid off."

"Nina, I think they've already tied the knot if you know what I mean—they consummated the marriage months ago." Michelle laughed to herself. "Did you hear them going at it last night?"

"Michelle, really."

"What? Auntie, you must have heard them too. Hell, the entire house was a shaking," she laughed.

"I can always count on you, Michelle, to keep me an honest man."

"Yes, Rob, you can." Michelle got up gave Robert a hug and left the room.

"Well, it's time for all of us to start getting ready for the big event," Victoria said. She went upstairs as well.

It was just Emilie and Robert.

"I hope you find happiness. Enough to erase all the bad in your world." She raised herself on her toes and kissed his cheek.

"I love you Em," he replied.

Later, while they spent hours in the bedroom combing Rachael's hair, and helping her dress into a lovely gown, Robert kept himself busy. Banished from his own room, Robert took up temporary residence in one of the guest rooms. His laptop hummed as he surfed sites. Finally, he called a travel agent to make arrangements for him and Rachael. They would fly on the family jet and stay at Hotel Metropole in the European

Quarter, not far from the Grand Place in the historical district. Has a bar for me and a salon where Rachael can read, "Great," he said aloud. With that squared away came some relief. He would surprise Rachael with the trip's final arrangements all set, how could she refuse.

◻◆◇◆◻

To Emilie, Rachael had always been one of the family. They had been best of friends years ago, but over the years their paths strayed from each other. Today was a great turning point that would bond them together as sisters forever. Michelle and Emilie were doing their best to make Rachael feel like she belonged in the family.

While talking and fussing with her hair, every once in a while, Emilie perceived a strange feeling. She was curious but had promised herself to stay out of other family member's heads. Well not their heads really, just the emotions they emanated. Some days she couldn't help feeling them blaring at her, and it always made her feel as if she was invading their privacy.

They had no clue how many of their emotions radiated to her. Her clairvoyant gift picked up other's emotions like radar. Today of all days, Rachael deserved to have her privacy. *Having your own feelings wasn't the same as keeping secrets, after all.*

"Here, just let me move it to the side a bit more." Michelle placed the hair comb studded with diamonds at the perfect angle.

"I love it," Rachael said.

"Are we ready for the photographer?" Emilie asked.

Rachael nodded and Emilie went to the door. "We're ready for a few pictures before the ceremony." She opened the door wider so Susan, a local photographer famous for her organic style of photojournalism, could enter. A professional Canon was strapped around her neck, ready for business. They were posed and the shutter clicked.

Everything flowed smoothly, that was until Emilie started feeling odd vibes emanating from Rachael. At first, she assumed her friend might be nervous, but the emotion soon became angry and volatile. Emilie watched Rachael's face, *picture-perfect*. She wore a subdued smile like a blushing bride should. *An act?* Emilie hated to think of her friend capable of hiding her true feelings so covertly. Normal, happy people didn't do that kind of thing. She decided to break her own rule and dig deeper into Rachael's emotions.

Emilie unhinged the barrier she had in place to shield others' emotions from slipping into her world and allowed her gift to spread out and sense the vibes around her. Michelle was excited, *check*. Emilie was glad her sister was so happy and relieved to know that her empathy power worked correctly. Having sensed her sister's emotions beforehand and comparing them to what she sensed now verified that she was correct. She turned her attention to Susan, who was excited as well but with an edge of nervousness. Plausible of course, the woman was dedicated and wanted to do a good job on the shoot. These pictures were bound to be all over social media and would give her business a big boost.

Her clairvoyant gift roamed the room, searching for Rachael's feelings. A shroud of anger formed a wall, partially blocking the intensity. Emilie had much experience with this and recognized it at once. A darker mood, almost sinister in nature, stood behind the facade. She looked across the room and studied Rachael's face, looking for a trace of where this hostility originated, but Rachael looked like the fairy princess.

Rachael glanced up, their eyes met, and she matched Emilie's concentration.

"Rachael, you look so beautiful." Emilie managed to cover up for her stare.

"Thank you, Em, your vote of confidence means a lot to

me."

"Okay, everyone, I'd like to take a few shots of the bride alone," Susan said.

Gathering their things, they left the room to Rachael and Susan.

"Try a few shots outside on the lawn . . . and on the porch as well," Victoria called out as she trailed down the hallway.

Emilie heard the photographer call back, "Yes, that's a definite. It's a gorgeous day out today."

◻◈◇◈◻

Emilie hurried to her own bedroom and closed the door.

"What's going on?" Jeremy said. He was doing up his tie, standing in front of the mirror.

"Need help?" she asked.

"Your help, always."

Emilie smiled and went over to him and started tugging at the tie.

"Do you know what you're doing?" he asked.

"Of course." She tugged at the tie to straighten it, then flipped and tightened.

"So, are you going to tell me what's on your mind? How's Rachael holding up? She already feels like one of the family. She fits in well, don't you think?" He took hold of Emilie's hands and grabbed her attention. "Em, tell me what's going on in your lovely little head."

"Before you pass judgment, I want to say I couldn't help it."

"Explain, please."

"Well, we were getting ready, having fun doing up her hair and all . . ."

"Yes, and then . . . he rolled his hand trying to pull the words from her mouth.

"Then I felt something odd, something that didn't belong

in the room. I searched and realized it came from Rachael."

"You did your thing and brain scanned her?"

"No, it's not like that. But yes, I let down my usual barrier and allowed her emotions to be felt. Just remember, she's the one feeling them, I'm just an antenna picking up her vibe."

"Well, it must have been revealing because you are obviously upset over it. Do you want to share?"

"No, I don't want to, I'd like to think I can use discretion in these matters, but this time it may not be wise."

"Stop skirting the issue. Tell me what she was sending out."

"A dark malicious mood, sinister and ready to explode. It definitely wasn't what a woman in love should be feeling. I've felt that kind of rancor before."

"When?"

"The other day in the warehouse—coming from Bennett." Her words hung in the air a minute. Emilie regretted her words as soon as spoken. She knew that Jeremy relived that nightmare in his head every day, and who could blame him. It was the most horrifying experience any of them had lived through—and yes, Rachael's darkness felt like the close cousin to the emotive mix that had stewed in Tom Bennett. The shadow sensed wasn't Emilie's imagination—it was a warning.

Finally, Jeremy said, "We have to keep an eye out."

"Keep an eye out for what?" Michelle had walked into the room without the two of them noticing her.

"Nothing, Michelle, we're just talking," Emilie said.

"Come on guys, you both look like you saw a ghost." Michelle smiled. "Kidding. Lighten up you two. What's going on? And please, no lies. We promised to tell each other the truth, remember?"

"You're right, Michelle. I was just saying that something feels off with Rachael. She is sending out some bad feelings."

"Well, I agree we should watch out for anything strange,"

Michelle said, "and believe me, I don't take your talent for granted, Emilie. But maybe this time your instinct is off a tad. Rachael seems just fine to me, glowing even."

"Yes, maybe she's carrying? Women get all kinds of emotional turmoil when their hormones are off. I remember from when my mother carried my little brother, William."

"Is she pregnant?" Michelle's eyes opened wide. "Tell me."

"Sorry," Jeremy said. "Not that I know of, and I don't want to start a rumor or anything, but you never know. Em, maybe it's something like that?"

Emilie shook her head. "I know what I felt. She's off the chart, like deeply angry about something. I know it seems wrong, I admit she looks beautiful but . . . just promise you'll keep an eye out for anything weird. If you see something odd, tell me right away."

"Okay I'll text you if anything looks wrong," Michelle said.

"We better get going, girls." Jeremy handed Emilie her purse and they went downstairs and joined the others in the foyer. Only Rachael was missing, she had gone on ahead of them to finish up photos at her father's mansion, and to make sure Robert didn't see her before the ceremony.

"Oh, I almost forgot." Emilie snapped her fingers. "I wanted to wear a bracelet of mother's. I believe it's in father's desk in a drawer."

"Really, Em. You don't need it," Michelle said.

"I do, for good luck. It will be a piece of Mother with us."

"You're so superstitious."

Emilie hurried to the library, Jeremy followed. She went to her father's desk and rummaged around, searching for the piece of jewelry. "There you are." Emilie retrieved a shiny object from a small desk drawer and latched the ruby bracelet around her wrist.

Emilie heard Jeremy behind her, as he pulled and pushed

books about on the shelves looking for something. "What are you doing?"

"Oh no, it's gone." Jeremy pulled out a blue-spined book, then put it back into place and pulled out another. He had already rummaged through half the shelf. "Bloody hell," he said.

"What's wrong?" she said.

"The book. It's gone. My uncle's ancient journal, it's missing." Jeremy's voice sounded frantic, his face red.

Emilie knew how important that book was to him, it had been the last great discovery by his Uncle Thaddeus before he died. "Let me help. Someone must have moved it, that's all," she comforted.

They searched the shelves but there was no trace of the old tome.

"Jeremy, I'm so sorry. We'll get to the bottom of this, I promise. But right now, we have to go."

He looked down at Emilie and nodded.

Michelle breezed into the room. "You guys, come on. The car is here, we have to go." She looked around the room. "What gives?"

"You're not going to believe this." Emilie headed for the door.

"The book—my uncle's journal—is gone." Jeremy passed by Michelle as well.

"As soon as we get home I'll help you two look for it," Michelle said as she closed the doors behind them.

The three of them met the others in the front hall.

"Robert insists on taking his car," Nina said. "Too good to sit with the likes of his family."

"Young Robert needs his car at the mansion for their departure after the party, Miss Nina." Evans sounded reticent.

"Ah huh, sure."

"Let me escort you." Jeremy stood beside Nina and took

her arm, a giant next to Lil' Kim, and he escorted her to the limousine. They all followed then were driven to the La France mansion, nestled in a new subdivision of prestigious homes that were hidden behind electronic gates manned by real people.

Inside the car during the trip, the subject of the old book was dropped. Instead, they chattered about the day's festivities and the guest list. Emilie noticed Jeremy's anxiety. It matched her own.

CHAPTER 9

The Reception

Robert flew past the Beamers, Caddies, and Mercedes that lined the driveway. Stopping quickly, he parked his Rhodium Silver Jaguar F-Type under the carport. A valet was quick to claim Robert's keys.

"Don't worry, sir, I'll be real careful of her. She looks so aerodynamic."

Robert smiled at the young attendant's eagerness. His car was over the top, a chance to park his vehicle was a treat for anyone.

"It's a high-performance vehicle, for sure. When I get her over 60 MPH the spoiler deploys automatically. Then she flies with the wind."

"Wow."

"I trust you'll take good care of her without going over fifteen," Robert said.

He laughed as he entered the house through the side door and climbed the back stairway, two steps at a time. He felt perky, just like that kid outside, jubilant about life's possibilities. Whistling, he walked to the room assigned to him by Sergio, the wedding planner. As soon as he opened the door he was greeted by friends.

"There you are, I was getting worried you'd miss your own party," Sergio said.

"Not a chance. I've been waiting for this day." Robert smiled.

His mood was uplifted. He had yearned to have his marriage with Rachael blessed by the Church ever since they had eloped. For him, it meant that it was real. Suddenly his insecurities broke into his thoughts. An internal voice arose from nowhere, telling himself that he was a fake, an impostor, and didn't deserve to live happily ever after. How could he after everything he had done to dishonor his family? And now planning to deceive his wife as well?

No. He decided he had to make things work out for everyone's sake. Today would change things. The marriage would be officially recognized by the laws of the Church, they'd be tied to each other for life. Robert owed it to Rachael to be completely honest with her about everything. He wondered if he could. Sweat ran down his back. The door opened.

"Finally, the best man has arrived," Sergio called out.

Jeremy walked over to Robert. "Are you sure, you want me for the job?"

Robert nodded. "Jackson wasn't able to come. Besides, as far as I'm concerned, you're my brother already."

"Thank you."

Jeremy appeared pulled together even though he had freely admitted that he still struggled with the horrific incident in the warehouse. He always acted so sure of himself and Robert admired him for that, and for the gentle care that he showed his sister. He hoped he could do the same for Rachael and that someday he might be worthy to have the affection returned.

"Soon it will be you and Emilie tying the knot on your wedding day. Maybe things are turning around for the family. Starting a good streak." *A good streak will truly begin once I get this charade over with and the Black Wolf Society is out of the picture for good.* "From today forward I plan on taking care of the family properly and concentrate on starting another generation."

"That's great news, Robert. So then, is Rachael pregnant?"

"No, but soon enough, old sport."

He thought of what Jeremy said, and part of him hoped it

was so, but she gave no indication, not a word spoken of children. Still, there was plenty of time to start their family.

"You're up, Robert. You ready for this?" Jeremy sounded sincere as he tapped his shoulder.

"Yes. I'm ready. After today there's no turning back."

Robert took the lead and walked down the stairs. Together he and Jeremy marched through the open French doors, across the lawn, to the arbor set in the middle of the flower garden, the spot they would recite their wedding vows.

Father Eddie stood in place by a thin podium, prayer book in hand, and he nodded as Robert drew close. "Good to see you so happy, Robert."

"Thank you, dear friend. Let's hope we can keep this good fortune rolling." He winked at Eddie. Despite his words of confidence, he knew there was still a lot of turbulence to deal with, but today felt right.

He loved Rachael. She was the most beautiful woman he had ever encountered. She remained mysterious, always kept him wanting more, yet so open to his affections.

He took his place under the white arch covered in red roses. Robert breathed in the fragrance that floated in the air. He felt euphoric. He looked toward the crowd. The guests were seated in the rows of chairs set up, a space left for an aisle. A red carpet had been rolled out and strewn with white flower petals. Music began to play.

Robert watched the wall of glass doors open wide and he saw her standing at the top of the staircase. Rachael, ravishing in her off-white gown made of delicate lace that gently flowed to the ground. She held red roses in her arms, a huge bundle that trailed down the front of her dress. Her hair glowed more lovely than the hue of the bouquet. She had strands of hair pulled up with lengths of pearls woven throughout her loose curls that brushed against her alabaster skin.

Mr. La France slowly escorted her down the stairs. Robert stood mesmerized as they marched closer to where he stood. He only saw her face, radiating as she came toward him.

He stepped forward to meet them and took her arm offered and walked with her the rest of the way. They stood in front of Father Eddie, who waved his hand in the air making the sign of the cross. The marriage ceremony began. Robert couldn't stop himself from looking at her, even when she lowered her head in prayerful reflection. He couldn't stop himself from being hopeful for a promising future.

"Robert, do you take Rachael . . ." He heard the words, but Robert felt he was on cloud nine, looking down. When the words stopped, he instinctively said, "I do."

He kissed Rachael and turned around to face the crowd. They were married, legally, and blessed by the Church — bonded for life. Jeremy's hand weighed down his shoulder. He looked up to a face that wore a happy smile, but it didn't reach his eyes. Robert turned and noticed his sister, standing on the other side of his bride. Emilie too displayed a disingenuous smile. *Something is off.*

Robert got pulled around. "Let me be the first to congratulate you, Mr. and Mrs. Robert de Gourgues." Father Eddie hugged him.

It was as if a big bear was squeezing the air out of him, and Robert loved it. He saw his wife, smiling, looking the happiest he had ever seen her. *You should be happy as well, you're entitled to some good things in life,* he told himself. The concern over his sister's odd expression was forgotten and Robert began celebrating with the guests.

They marched back into the house and the party began. Drinks were poured and toasts were spoken. Gaiety filled the house and garden. A band played music, some brave guests took to the dance floor and moved their feet to the beat. The crowd enjoyed the party. Laughter rose above all the other sounds.

Robert felt his front trouser pocket vibrate. He pulled out the phone and saw a flash message—a text from STRANGER. He slid his phone open and read the message: GRAND PLACE FRONT SPIRE MONDAY 3 PM. The place and time he was supposed to hook up with someone from the Black Wolf. He looked around the room, checking to see if the stranger was nearby. The man with the fedora was nowhere to be seen.

Now that the Black Wolf Society had made contact, he needed to find Agent Sloan or look for a quiet place to call him. He searched the great room hoping to see the agent, since he had an invitation, he might be close by. People were loitering and laughing in every corner. Robert made his way through the crowd. People approached him offering their congratulations; he shook their hands and nodded but continued to cross the floor. He exited the room down the small hallway that led toward the back of the house. Earlier, he had noticed a small closet under the back stairway when he came through the side entrance. *The perfect place to make a secret call.* He felt like a Hardy boy. The hallway was just off the kitchen area. There were servers and cooks in the bustling kitchen but all too busy to notice him. Robert opened the closet door and walked into a pantry, closing the door behind him.

He pulled out the old flip phone and pressed *2. On the second ring, Agent Sloan picked up.

"Robert, congratulations. It was a lovely service."

"This isn't a social call, Sloan."

"Of course not. What do you have for me?"

"A text message from the Society's contact. It reads Grand Place front spire Monday 3 pm. That's all they sent, so I assume that's where I'm supposed to be to meet up with them."

"Good. They want you, Robert." After a second, Agent Sloan said, "Yes, go there and do your best to play the part. It's a busy place, especially with the holidays near, and out in the open. Don't worry, we'll have you covered from all directions. Be assured we will be following your every move."

"I certainly hope so. Sloan, I know I've done horrible things, but I don't intend on getting my absolution from playing hero against this group. Promise me things will run safely. Not for my sake, but for my wife."

"We'll have your back, promise. Now off with you. Go enjoy the party with your lovely new wife. Oh, and keep the phone near you at all times, just in case some other message comes through. No worries, we'll follow you to Belgium and you won't even see us."

The line clicked off. Robert slipped the phone into his pocket and opened the door a crack. No one was nearby. He went back toward the great room being used as the banquet hall, the same way he had come. He glanced down the other end of the hallway and saw his father-in-law walking in his direction.

Robert hoped to avoid him, so he slipped to the side and hid in a doorway jamb. After a moment he peeked around the corner. Mr. La France hadn't noticed him. His father-in-law ducked into his office and within seconds was followed by two other men, both identities unknown to Robert. What he witnessed looked odd; a strange feeling turned his stomach and caught his breath.

Robert had suspicions concerning Mr. La France and from what he discerned, the mysterious man hid much, even from his daughter. No one knew exactly how he managed to accumulate so much wealth in his lifetime. Some speculated he washed money, but his impression imparted a man too strait-laced for anything that volatile. Other rumors said the family had old money, traced back to the days when men made fortunes from the cotton exchange. Robert bought into that theory more easily, his family also made a ton of money back then. He mused how he knew more about the history of his family's money than he did his ancestors.

It was a shame the de Gourgues' lineage had been cursed and that the women who married into the family had died, all too young. Over the years, no one had concerned themselves about recording the family's history in an album. Most probably they preferred not to look closely.

He planned to talk with Emilie about it, one day soon. She had researched the family name and uncovered much information about their heritage. He fancied the idea to continue the search and wanted to hear all she had discovered. He hungered to understand where he came from, a desire that festered inside of him. Robert felt it his duty to keep the bloodline alive. He looked out again; no one loitered in the hallway.

Robert came out of hiding and quickened his pace. Reaching the door, he leaned his ear against the wood panel, trying to hear through the thick mass, which proved impossible. He devised a quick plan—the idiot son-in-law card—the sole person lost in the big house. He would feign that he certainly didn't intend on interrupting anyone's private discussions. Maybe he could discover what they were doing and possibly the other two men's identity if his father-in-law was gracious enough to carry out introductions.

His pulse quickened. Clearing his throat, he knocked on the door then walked into the room. It was empty.

CHAPTER 10

After The Vows

Robert stood in the middle of Mr. La France's office and turned around, searching for another exit. There were no doors. The bank of windows were shut and the only other opening on the wall was the fireplace which currently had a blaze roaring.

A click at the door. Robert turned around, his adrenaline rushing through his veins, his throat tight in his neck.

"There you are."

Robert exhaled and smiled. "It's you."

"Yes, it's me. And why are you in here? You left the party."

"I didn't see you, so I started looking around. I thought I saw someone come in here, but as you can see the room's empty."

His face burned but Rachael didn't seem to notice his embarrassment. He couldn't let her know that he suspected her father of foul play. She adored her father. She walked across the room to meet him and wrapped her arms around him. Her dress was lacy and draped her shape, creating a very seductive vision. Robert couldn't resist and kissed her on the lips. First a gentle peck, then another more heated kiss. His lips slid down to kiss her neck, then her shoulder. Rachael moaned.

"Take me now, right here, Mr. de Gourgues."

Robert jerked back. Lately, Rachael's sexual appetite has been more demanding than usual. If she wanted a quickie right then and there, what would happen if her father suddenly reappeared?

"Please, Robert." She bit her lower lip and looked up at him from behind her thick fake lashes.

"My pleasure and honor, Mrs. de Gourgues."

He kissed her again. Together they swayed across the room, dancing without music, and ended up in front of the fireplace. He stopped, turned her around, and carefully undid the long line of satin buttons on the back of her dress. They were delicate, holding together the sheer netting material that was as soft as silk. When the last button was opened, he slid the dress from her shoulders and it fell to the floor. She wore high-heeled white shoes with diamond straps that glistened from the flames, a white lace thong, and a strapless white bra.

She faced him again and unfastened her bra and dropped it to her side. Looking into his eyes the entire time, she reached for his pants, unbuckled his belt, and unzipped his trousers. They fell to the floor. He kicked off his shoes then his clothes and pushed them aside with his feet. He moved closer to her. Her breaths were warm against his face. She wore that exotic perfume he loved so much; he closed his eyes and allowed the jasmine fragrance to engulf his senses.

Robert reached around her in an embrace, but Rachael raised her hands to his chest and stopped him. He dropped his arms. She undid the knot of his tie, unbuttoned his shirt, taking her time while never looking away from his eyes. Her green orbs reflected the gold from the fire's flames. She looked as if the spark of a devil was there, ready to take him to a sinful place.

They stood face to face naked. Seconds felt like an eternity. Robert was in agony and couldn't resist the temptation of her any longer. The danger of the situation excited him. He reached out and pulled her to him. He massaged her body, stroking her soft skin, and felt her shudder when her body rubbed against his hardened flesh. He grabbed her buttocks and raised her up, then pushed himself against her. She accepted his body into hers and moaned.

He let her down. She pulled Robert to the floor, and they

lay next to each other for a moment. He watched the shadow of the flame as it played against her face, reflecting in her eyes. Rachael reached up and kissed him with a fury. She groped him between his legs and stroked her finger back and forth. It drove him mad. He rubbed her breasts, then licked her with his tongue, feeling her nipples harden.

Robert rolled on top of her and surrendered to his pent-up desire. One last thrust and he exploded in ecstasy. Rachael cried out in orgasm just in time to meet his.

Exhausted, he dropped his body to lie next to hers. He opened his eyes and saw her face, smiling with her eyes closed. Rachael looked like a goddess, so beautiful. Her hair was pulled down, the up-do hairdo lost. Long auburn waves flowed around her body, shiny and vibrant. Her face glowed from embers of her arousal. Robert couldn't believe his good fortune and knew he didn't deserve such happiness.

A small voice in his subconscious awoke. *I must protect her from the ugly truth.* He decided to hide the ruse he was about to play with the Black Wolf Society from her. But then he was done, no more lies, no more taking chances. He would live a wholesome life and keep Rachael happy.

Robert rolled onto his back and closed his eyes as well. "You are remarkable," he said.

"Yes, I am." She giggled. "Don't ever forget that. Promise you'll never leave me again, out of the blue, like you did when you took off for Boston the other week."

"Yes, I promise." He said it and meant it, then realized he had just lied. On Monday he would have to leave her again. Robert needed to devise a plausible excuse, he couldn't explain about the secret meeting with the Black Wolf Society and refused to get her involved in this last campaign. To make matters worse, he had no idea how long the meet-up would take, where they would be going. But he was in too deep to get himself out now. It was quicksand, and he was slipping into the deep earth. The good mood evaporated as the reality of his situation crystallized. A shadow of doubt fell across his face.

"Rob, are you all right? You seem too, quiet."

"I was just thinking of how lucky I am—I don't deserve you, but I'm keeping you just the same." Robert smiled, rolled over, and looked down at Rachael. "I love you."

Rachael kissed her finger and placed it up onto his lips, then smiled.

"How about we get back to our guests, now that we've consummated the deal, again."

Robert stood and helped her up.

"Yes, the guests. I wish we were on our trip already, alone."

"Everything in good time," she said.

He watched as Rachael dressed, carefully slipping her gown on. She turned for Robert to button her back up. He gingerly buttoned the back of the dress, gently touching her white flawless skin as he went. Once she was back in order, she turned and kissed him once on the lips, then left the room.

He stood there and wondered why she hadn't waited for him.

🔲◈ ◈ ◈🔲

Robert put his clothes back on while looking around the room. *Her father entered, but how did he leave?* Once dressed, he began to feel the walls, looking for a secret door. Most of the space was covered with bookcases. He stood back and looked for some kind of embellishment on the wooden shelves that could possibly hide a latch to open something.

"There you are." Emilie and Jeremy walked into the room. "I've been looking for you. Jeremy saw Rachael leave this room, and sure enough, here you are. Having a rendezvous?"

Robert smirked. "None of your business. Some things

should remain secret."

"I'll second that," Jeremy said. "I've heard more secrets than I care to know."

Emilie walked up to her brother and slipped her arm in his.

"Speaking of secrets, I need to talk with you," Emilie said.

"I didn't do it, I promise," he said half-jokingly.

"It's not you this time. First, I apologize I even went there but I couldn't block it out."

"Block it out? What are you talking about, Em?" Robert froze. He immediately assumed she had learned something about his meet-up with Agent Sloan or maybe something about the Black Wolf Society, his imagination went wild.

"I'm talking about Rachael," she said.

Silence hung in the air. Bewildered, he wondered where this was heading.

"Well, you have to finish what you started—you can't leave me guessing like this. What on God's green earth are you trying to tell me?"

Jeremy moved to Emilie's side and wrapped his arm around her shoulder, which only worried Robert more. Jeremy had a habit of doing that when Emilie was distraught about something she sensed.

"I was with her this morning, getting ready for the party."

"Yes, so . . ."

"Rachael started giving off all kinds of bad emotions. Like anger and worse. Darkness shrouded her, yet she smiled right at me as if everything was fine."

"Really, Em, you probably misunderstood." Robert started to sweat, and pulled his handkerchief from his pocket, and dabbed his forehead. "You see how happy she is, we are. You're overreaching, Em."

"That would be nice, except I know it streamed from her.

I've had enough practice at this type of thing. Believe me, Robert, I want to be wrong. I didn't ask for this—didn't even want to feel it. I tried to block her out, but it was as if she directed it right at me." Emilie dropped her head and looked at the floor.

Robert could see his sister was upset. "Emilie, I know you'd never make up something like this, but you're mistaken. Believe me, I've learned to respect your gift, but maybe the feeling came from someone else in the room." He thought about how wonderful it had been with Rachael in his arms just minutes ago. *Could she be that clever, to cover up her feelings so well, and was she leading him on? No, there had to be another explanation.* "Maybe something was bothering her. We all have our nervous moments," he said.

"She went to a very dark place. A sinister emotion was coming from her." Emilie stepped back to give Robert some room. "Like the same kind of emotion you sent out when we sat at the dinner table with Father."

Robert stood still, recalling how much he had hated everyone back then. Yes, he had been in a very dark place. Dark enough to commit murder. It didn't compute that Rachael would feel this way too; she appeared so happy. He shook his head.

"Sorry, Em, you're wrong this time. It's more likely that it came from someone else. Maybe Evans was hanging around in the corner like usual. He could have been having a bad day."

"Maybe. I just thought I should tell you." Emilie looked down at the floor again.

"Thank you for facing me with this instead of keeping it a secret," Robert said.

"What secret?" Michelle walked in at the end of the conversation.

"Nothing to worry about," Robert said. "We're all being very cautious about the people around us, even my wife."

Michelle laughed aloud. "She's a sweetheart. Wish all our troubles looked like her."

"Careful what you wish for," Emilie said.

"Wow, I thought you were besties?" Michelle said.

"We were, I mean, we are. It's just that she was emitting some dark stuff this morning."

"I was there and didn't notice anything wrong. Don't worry, Rob. Everything is okay."

Jeremy was quick to Emilie's defense. "Michelle, are you clairvoyant, now too? Or have you developed some other latent talents that read minds?"

"Jeez, Jeremy. Don't get into a huff." Michelle turned away. "Come on, lighten up. This is a celebration."

"You're right," Robert said. "Let's join the party. You go ahead, I'll be right out. I just need to talk with Jeremy a bit."

Emilie walked out with Michelle. "Come on, let the men have their privacy."

Michelle laughed and closed the door behind them.

"Jeremy, I do need your help," Robert said.

"What's going on?"

"I saw Rachael's father enter into this room, then two other men followed him. I got this creepy feeling about it all, they came across off somehow. I'll tell you one thing, I have a lot more respect for Emilie's gift these days. Anyway, so I followed using the same door as you. But when I walked in, no one was in there. The room was empty. I've been looking for some kind of secret entrance."

"Robert, you and Rachael are going out of the country, right?" Jeremy said.

Robert nodded.

"Just be careful and watch your back. If you need any help, call and let us know. With all the craziness that happened the past few weeks—well, you can't be too careful. Seems something odd is going on, still." Jeremy looked sincere, and Robert knew that he was right.

"You think Mr. La France is part of the Black Wolf Society?" Robert asked.

Jeremy raised his shoulders, arms out. "Who knows? I guess it's possible."

"So many weird, unexplained, things happened recently," Robert said. He thought of the family curse that claimed his mother's life, and of the skinwalker who had chosen a monster as his animal familiar and determined to kill his entire family. The list of recent events proved crazy.

"Who would ever believe our stories?" Robert said.

No one could shield him any longer, especially not his sisters. Robert would meet up with the Black Wolf society, help the Feds get the evidence they needed, and get rid of the menacing influence before it was too late. Before they managed to do anything that might hurt his Rachael.

Robert continued searching the room with Jeremy's help.

"I don't see anything that looks like a secret door panel," Jeremy said.

The door opened up behind them. They both turned around, startled. Rachael stood at the entrance. The chatter from the guests in the other room hummed.

"I think you should be with me today, Robert."

Robert's face turned red. He patted Jeremy on the back. "So you'll take care of that little issue for me old sport, right?"

"No worries, Robert. I'm glad to figure it out for you." Jeremy grinned.

"Good, thank you."

"What's going on?" Rachael asked.

"Nothing important, dear. We're talking about property—the backwoods at the house."

Robert fibbed, but managed to keep his cool demeanor. It wasn't exactly a lie, after all. They had talked about the property, a few days ago. He nodded to Jeremy and took Rachael's arm in his. The married couple left the room. Jeremy followed them out, spotted Emilie at the wine table, and walked in that direction.

Robert hoped they would make their way back to Mr. La France's study and figure out what happened to her father. Something weird was going on—people don't disappear into thin air.

◼◈◇◈◼

Robert and Rachael worked the room for an hour or so, they changed into their travel clothes and said goodbye to their guests. Rachael's father showed up, in time to see them off. As the man hugged his daughter, Robert noticed that Mr. La France had dust or dirt of some kind on his jacket. Robert stared at the spot trying to figure out what it was and noticed Mr. La France stared back, then followed Robert's gaze.

Mr. La France quickly brushed off his jacket, his pale face reddened. Robert wondered where the hell he'd been all that time.

The couple left the house and drove to the airport, then took the family's private jet to Brussels.

"Robert, thank you for the lovely party."

"Thank you for gracing me by being my bride. Now it's official to the Church and the world—we are husband and wife." He couldn't suppress his smile. Even knowing about the dark mood Emilie claimed to have felt, he couldn't help but feel like the luckiest man in the world.

"Why was it so important for you to have that priest give us a blessing?" she asked.

"That priest? I thought you liked Father Eddie?"

"I do. I just mean in general. Why is the Church's blessing

so important? Do you believe in heaven and hell?"

Rachael sounded like she was making a joke of his religion, something she had never done before.

"Does it bother you? Would you have preferred a different church, or perhaps you are agnostic altogether?"

Rachael's mouth lifted on one side, a smirk. Why such an odd grin? He had never noticed that cynic expression before.

"I'm agnostic as far as religion goes. We live, we breathe, we die, and we stop breathing." Rachael stared him straight in the eyes, daring him to quarrel.

"Well then, I'm happy you respected me enough to go through with it all. How about all the counseling we've been doing?"

"What do you mean?"

"Did it bother you all this time?"

Rachael shook her head. "It's all for the better good."

"Okay, whatever that means."

Rachael picked up a book and started reading. Robert understood that it meant she had had enough and needed to retreat back to her other world. That's the one thing that never changed with Rachael. She couldn't go an hour without reading something. He smiled at the thought and picked up a book and started reading as well. It didn't take long for Rachael's eyes to close and she drifted off. Robert reclined her seat then watched her as she slept. He brushed back a strand of red hair from her face. She was beautiful, her skin fair, not a scratch on her. Her green eyes melted his heart, but even with them closed, he could feel the power she had over him. He thought to himself that the best he could do for his wife, and his family, was to clean up this mess with the Black Wolf, and then give her the life she deserved.

CHAPTER 11

Later That Night

They watched from a window upstairs as the last car drove away from the house. After the last guest left the La France mansion, Emilie and Jeremy came out of hiding. They had been waiting upstairs in an extra bedroom until the house was empty of people. Noise generated from the kitchen help downstairs could still be heard as they washed up the last of the pans and trays. Emilie felt their weariness while searching for anyone else who might be close by—all was good. No one else was in the house, not even Rachael's father. Emilie wondered where he might have gone after his daughter's wedding.

They crept down the long staircase that swirled in a semicircle and covertly went to Mr. La France's office. Once inside the room, Jeremy snapped on the flashlight of his iPhone. He swiped it up and down the wall, looking for a crack or a lever.

"Wait, turn off the light," Emilie said. "If there's a crack under a secret door somewhere, maybe we'll see light from the other side."

"Great idea."

Jeremy snapped it off. The room was pitch dark.

Emilie scanned up and down the walls. She grabbed his shirt and yanked. "Look, over there."

"Okay, I see it. You don't have to rip my shirt."

She laughed as she made her way across the room. "I like you with your shirt off."

"Yes, you've already managed to rip a few of my sleeves, and I'm running out of proper shirts."

"Poor baby. I'll make it up to you later. Look. Behind the first section of shelves from the outside wall. There. See that sliver of white."

Jeremy went to the far end of the wall. She heard him swipe his hands across the shelves until something clicked. The case swiveled open and amber light flooded the room. They stepped into the passage behind the hidden door, and it closed behind them.

"I feel trapped," she said.

He turned the phone light back on and nodded, then led the way down a narrow passage.

At least the walls aren't crumbling or covered with spiders like in the crypt. Emilie shivered. She remembered when they had been in a tight spot before. When they opened the crypt in France, it had been one of the creepiest experiences in her life, though many more soon followed. Her thoughts were interrupted when the passage turned to the right and descended half a staircase length. They followed a hall space until they were in a room illuminated only by burning white pillar candles.

Emilie choked on the pungent air. The condensed smell of burning sandalwood incense filled the space. The stucco walls were painted a dark crimson. The tiled floor was covered with a deep red area carpet, and in the center was a white marble altar displaying an opened book.

"See that? Another old book. I wonder what this all means," Emilie whispered.

They gravitated toward the altar to inspect the book.

She looked at the opened page. Her presumptions were correct; it was indeed ancient and scripted in Latin, just like the book Jackson Bennett had found in his father's house. *What was with these men—playing with old books written in dead languages?*

"Do you think that Mr. La France is part of the Black Wolf Society?" Jeremy asked.

"I think anything is possible these days. Look, a note." Emilie picked up a plain piece of paper with words scribbled across it. "It's an address for a hotel. Look, 1902 is scribbled under it. Is that a room number, possibly?"

Jeremy placed it back on the altar and snapped a picture with his phone.

A noise sounded from the opposite side of the room. A door pulled open and hit a wall.

They hurried back to the passageway they entered from and hid in the shadows. From their vantage point, they could see two men entering from another doorway.

Men wore dark cloaks tied with rope sashes; the outfits reminded Emilie of a monk's get up. One of them closed the book and took it with him as they exited, putting out the candles, except one. That one remained burning on the center altar.

"That was close." Emilie's heart pounded so loud she thought the men might hear her and return. "Let's get out of here before we're caught."

They left but in the other direction of the mysterious men. Going back through the passageway, Jeremy again used the phone's flashlight. They maneuvered up the steps and hallway and pushed against the wall until it budged open. They slipped out of the secret room and back into the house without being seen.

"Quick, let's get out of here," Jeremy said.

Emilie jogged to the door, peered out, then ran across the great room to exit the mansion. Jeremy was at her heels. Earlier, he had left his truck at the end of the driveway, anticipating that they would need a ride home from the party. He opened the door for Emilie, then he hopped into the driver's seat.

"Does this address look familiar?" he asked as he handed her the phone.

"I think that's the hotel where Robert and Rachael are staying."

"Well, I think we better follow them. If those men we saw

in the underground room were from the Society, they obviously have this address, and it can't be for good reasons. Maybe her father doesn't like Robert after all. Who knows what his plans are?"

"Jeremy, do you really think those men are members of the Black Wolf Society?"

"I don't know, but who else could it be? And why would they have the address for the hotel where your brother will be staying? I'm afraid trouble might be following him."

"You're right. We should follow, to cover his back, just in case. Thank you for caring so much, especially after all the trouble my brother caused for you."

Jeremy smiled. "The trouble wasn't really caused by him, now was it? Seems he was hurt as much as the rest of us. He's your brother, Em. We need to be there for him, he's family."

"I have no idea why you're so good to me." His sincerity comforted Emilie, and she noticed that Jeremy appeared better himself—inside. Seems that when he helped others it healed his wounded subconsciousness.

"You're a good man, Jeremy Laughton."

"I must be because I have the most wonderful woman willing to marry me."

She smiled. "Okay, enough mush. Let's grab a few things, snag a flight, and help out Robert and Rachael."

They drove off and did what needed to be done.

CHAPTER 12

Belgium Honeymoon

They landed nine and a half hours later. Robert reached over and shook Rachael awake. She had drifted off shortly after they were air-bound. He was glad she slept and wished he had been able to as well, but there were too many images invading his mind to find rest.

"Sleepyhead. Wake up." She opened her eyes and smiled when she saw him, which melted his heart. There was no way this woman had dark thoughts. "There's a car waiting to take us to the hotel as soon as we go through customs."

She wiped her eyes. "I hate customs. I'm so tired. That was a long day."

"Yes, it was. Thank goodness you got your sleep during the flight."

She pouted. "I still feel tired."

"We'll get a good cup of espresso to fix you," he said as he gently guided her off the jet.

They were driven to the Hotel Metropole. The bustling street assaulted his ears when they exited the car; he sought refuge in the building marked with a gold M emblem. The lobby soared to the ceiling embellished with gilded leaf design, grounded with gleaming marble floors, flanked with a long bank of deep wood panels, which encompassed the front desk. A wall of windows, arranged in a grid of metal frames, illuminated the great hall.

"Robert, this old-world French architecture is wonderful," Rachael said. Her glance roamed the grandeur, taking in all the eloquence of the royal setting. "You would never guess from the street that there was this much opulence inside."

Relieved that she liked the hotel, Robert chalked up one thing in his favor.

"How about we settle into our room, then we can roam this place and snoop. It has a wonderful room downstairs where I think you would enjoy reading."

She agreed.

He led her across the lobby's red carpets to the marble-floored hallway with the bank of elevators. She looked up. Robert followed her stare to the ceiling. "These windows are something, aren't they?" he said.

"Yes, they are so . . . so . . . French. I didn't expect the influence here in Brussels," she said.

"Haven't you been here before?"

"Yes, but years ago. I have no recollection of the city."

She raised her mouth one-sided, a weird grin or sneer. Robert felt confused. Maybe if he explained, he thought.

"This is an international community with major influences by the French, German, and the Dutch. I think there have been squabbles for years over the language and such things. But overall, tolerance was now achieved with the newest government."

"What do you mean, the newest government," she asked.

"Well, there's been a rocky history here. Back in the '90s, there were trials involving government bribery and sexual innuendos."

Rachael covered her mouth with faked shock.

He laughed. "Nothing like a scandal to pave the way for the new government."

"If you say so. In my opinion, all governments are corrupt and easily bought." She moved in front of Robert as the elevator doors opened. She hurried in. They went up to their suite.

Opening the doors, the first impression of the room was the sea. The decor was a spray of royal blue and silky. The walls were enclosed with a gold rosette wallpaper. The chandelier glimmered, radiating a soft glow within the space.

There was an adjoining sitting room, dining area, and large bath, modernized for comfort.

"Does the room pass expectations?" he said.

"Perfecta. Now, let's search for that coffee you mentioned and a bite to eat as well. I'm famished."

They went back to the main floor and found a nice spot for a mid-day meal. Most of the time together was spent in silence, and Robert worried about what Rachael was thinking. She took small bites, looked around the room as if expecting to see someone, then returned her gaze to her plate. She remained quiet and private. Robert wondered if this was normal. His sisters never behaved this way, always more than willing to speak their minds. He shifted his weight in the chair.

"Rachael, is everything all right?"

"Yes, divine. I like this hotel, good choice. Tomorrow we'll have to go to the old city center if that's agreeable with you."

"Yes, of course. I may have to—"

A waiter stepped forward. "Excuse me. Mademoiselle, phone call for you."

Rachael looked surprised and took the offered device.

"Hello, this is Rachael La France."

Robert's neck tightened, angry that after all these months, she still used her maiden name. He wondered why it was so hard for her to go by Mrs. de Gourgues.

She listened to the person on the other end of the line, staring in the air as if calculating a math problem in her head.

He wondered what was being said.

"Thank you. Yes, another time, perhaps. Enjoy yourself. Good-bye." She finished the call, smiling, without offering any explanations. The waiter retrieved the phone.

"Well," Robert said.

"Well, what? Oh, sorry. That was an old school friend of mine; I haven't seen her in years. She read in the newspaper that we were in Brussels. I guess we made the local social page. Anyway, she wanted to meet with me, maybe do some shopping together at Grand Place. Marcie works here now, for our government on some kind of task force."

Robert jerked his head back. "Oh really. So, when will you be shopping?"

"I told her thanks, but no, of course. I won't leave your side during our trip together."

Robert waited a moment. This was a perfect ruse to get some time away from her, but he didn't want to appear obvious. He stepped into his old familiar persona, ready to stage act and play the scene out.

"Rachael, call her back. Tell her yes, of course, you want to meet up with her. I mean how often are we in Brussels? Your friends are important and I don't want to get in the way of your friendships."

"Really, are you certain?"

"Honey, I can call someone myself. I'll use the time to catch up with an old business acquaintance as well. I'm anticipating that with relations smoothed between my sisters and myself, well, I'm hoping I might get involved in the business again."

"Oh, Robert. That's great news. Are you sure you don't mind?"

"Absolutely not, I insist. Call her back, tell her you'll meet her at Grand Place. I'll go with you. You can introduce her to me, and we'll have lunch. Then you'll go your way and I mine."

She kissed his cheek. "Thank you." She called out, "Waiter."

The waiter brought the phone back. Rachael called and spoke with her friend. Robert sat quietly, his thoughts drifted. *And Marcie just happens to work in Brussels for our government.*

Robert wondered if this was Agents Sloan's help for his cover, so his meeting wouldn't raise suspicions with Rachael. *Maybe it was just a coincidence.* Either way, another weight lifted off his shoulders.

Tomorrow he would be in front of Grand Place on the spire side at three. He still had no idea what he was getting involved with, how deep he'd have to go. Would they keep him at length, or maybe an initiation? Did they expect him to do something wrong, a Beneficial Act, right away to prove himself as one of them? His troubles fast returned and anxiety haunted him.

His fingers played with the napkin that sat on the table. He twisted it unconsciously as thoughts about the sinister things the Black Wolf Society took part in floated in his mind. He regretted accepting the deal with Agent Sloan. Maybe jail time was safer than taking part in anything with this crazy group of fanatics. They might just ask him to do something worse than stealing or planting evidence. This time the stakes could be higher, he knew that. *What if they asked him to kill someone?* What did I get myself into?

"Rob, are you all right?"

He heard Rachael's voice with a strange inflection as if she were judging him. "Of course, I'm fine. I guess a little tired."

"Well, you go upstairs to rest then."

"Trying to get rid of me so soon?" he said. He smiled at her while grabbing her hand, then he kissed it.

Rachael smiled back but it never reflected in her green eyes. She was hiding something, holding back. Robert had no energy to play games right now. He pushed his concerns aside.

"Yes, maybe some rest is in order."

He led the way back to the room. He rested, she read. *Like an old married couple*, he thought as he drifted off.

It was Monday afternoon. Robert had just finished a nice

luncheon with his wife and her old school friend, Marcie. They met at the Aux Armes de Bruxelles, an excellent restaurant close to Grand Place.

The ambiance was bright. The tables were covered in white linen, and light filtered into the room from the exterior walls, which were filled with windows. The bottom glass panels were made of a diamond design with a colored glass crest in the center of the glass frame. The amber color of the glass emblem matched the high-hanging brass chandeliers that were topped with reddish-orange lampshades over the electric candles.

They sat at a table against the far wall, which was paneled with light wood, and gave Robert the vantage of the entire space. He kept watching during their luncheon for any spying strangers. No danger presented itself, and he laughed at himself for being so suspicious.

The women said good-bye and left the table, ready to finish the day with shopping and strolling the nearby museums. Robert wiped his mouth one last time, dropped the napkin on the table, and paid for lunch. He exited the restaurant and strolled two blocks, arriving at Grand Place in four minutes.

He stood in front of the huge spire of Grand Place. The square was bustling with people of all nationalities. The decorations were being strung to get ready for the holidays, which were just around the corner. He heard multiple languages, all chattering at the same time. The voices blended together along with the distant traffic into horrendous noise pollution, distorting in his head. He rubbed his forehead with his cold left hand, trying to calm the tension before a migraine took hold. A man approached him from his right. Robert jumped in alarm.

"Mr. de Gourgues, please accompany me." A strange-looking fellow, a mere toothpick of a man, turned and slipped through the crowd, expecting Robert to follow. He shook himself alert and followed the skinny-bones to a nearby vehicle waiting at the curb of the busy street. The man opened the back door, and Robert got in.

"Move over."

Robert obliged and sat between two men, skinny-bones and his complete opposite, a wide-berth gangster type. The car took off and headed west from the square. A hood suddenly covered Robert's head. He smelled something foul. *Maybe onions? No, something worse.* He sat in the dark with no idea of where they were heading. They turned left, then right, and again right . . . this continued for some time and Robert soon lost hope of remembering the trail. *How the hell am I going to give the location to Agent Sloan if I don't know where the hell I'm going!*

After approximately twenty minutes, the car stopped. Robert jerked forward and turned to his left when he heard voices. It sounded like the driver was speaking to someone outside of the car, through an open window. Then, the car tugged forward again, now going slow, over speed bumps. *A parking lot?* Robert could only guess.

The car pulled to the right and stopped. This time the driver cut the engine. The doors opened and Robert was pulled out, but the hood remained covering his head. He heard cars in the distance, not fast traffic, slow-moving vehicles. The sound of a truck, releasing hydraulic pressure, maybe a dump truck. *A construction site?* He smelled evergreen trees. The hints he recognized didn't make sense together. Robert realized he had no clue of where he was going. He raised his hands to take off the hood and was immediately pushed forward. He stumbled to the ground.

"Come on now, Robert. Be a good boy."

Someone laughed. He got back to his feet and they walked along a dirt path, covered sparsely with loose stones. He almost tripped three times, once on what felt like a tree root, and twice when he stepped into a puddle. His soaked shoes leaked and his socks were drenched. Immediately the cold autumn air froze his toes.

Within ten minutes they were in a building. As soon as the door closed the street sounds disappeared. Footsteps echoed in the place, as he was escorted down a hallway.

"Careful, Mr. de Gourgues. We have a stairway to go down. Mind the treads."

His captors slowed the pace as they descended a long flight of stairs. Robert put out his arm and touched the wall, cold stone. A draft wafted up from the landing below. Once they reached the ground a heavy-sounding door was pushed open and he was led down a series of hallways.

He tried to remember the turns as he was led through a maze. He was so unnerved, and there were so many turns to keep account, that he soon gave up. He'd never find the way back on his own. Robert's fear of what was going to happen to him deepened. A door closed behind him.

"You can take the hood off now," the skinny-bones said.

His entourage of three stood nearby, now all wearing black robes with hoods that covered the top of their heads. Their faces were masked with small swaths of cloth like the Lone Ranger wore on his old television show, long before Robert's time.

"There, on the table. Put on your robe and mask."

Robert did as told, and moved toward the table against the far wall while thinking this scenario was getting more curious by the minute. *How can I identify anyone if they're all cloaked?* He dreaded that if his infiltration into the Society bore fruitless intelligence, that Agent Sloan might not uphold his end of the bargain, and this torture would all be for nothing.

CHAPTER 13

Masked Troublemakers

Robert grabbed the robe and draped it over his clothes. It hung heavy as if made of thick cheviot fabric. The only other item on the table was a rubber mask of a pig.

"This?" he asked as he pointed.

"Put it on, oink oink." The men guffawed.

Robert didn't like what his mask suggested . . . *slaughtered like a pig, squealed like a pig, the three little pigs, and the big bad wolf.* Robert put on the mask and flipped up the hood. An image flashed—Tom Bennett's severed head on the floor. The horrific vision was as real now as it had been just a week ago. How long would it take for that image to erase from his brain?

"Stop wasting time. Move it."

He was nudged back into the dimly lit hall. Robert noticed a strong musty odor that belonged in a wet basement. They walked a short distance to the next door. It opened slowly and creaked as the hoary hinges on the swelled jamb revolted against the movement. Apparently, this passageway wasn't used very often, but the thought gave Robert little comfort.

The room was circular with stone walls that soared up at least three stories, like a castle tower. The floor span of thirty or so feet was made of large stone blocks, and the center of the floor was covered with a scarlet carpet, fringed with gold, knotted tassels. An altar of some sort was the bull's eye. A book lay open on its top.

Across the room's space on the opposite side stood three other Black Wolf members, also robed.

"Thank you brothers," one of the mysterious figures said. "Leave us now. Return when summoned to take the pledge back."

Robert blew out a sigh of relief—*they intend to free me.* He melted to the hard floor, his worries that the group knew of his involvement in the death of Tom Bennett had been unwarranted.

Bennett was held in high esteem by the Black Wolf members, hell, he was damned useful to the group because of his obvious killer nature. Robert understood that now. All the times that Tom had referred to himself as the secret weapon, it all made sense now. This group wouldn't be friends with him if they learned what really happened in Boston. A small voice inside him said, *keep your thoughts quiet, and play the part, you moron.*

No evidence of Tom Bennett's body could be traced back to them. The scene literally had disintegrated into nothing but a pile of hemoglobin mush, which hadn't resembled anything like human blood and guts, if his memory served well. Still, Deputy Detective Ramsey survived that day, and he belonged to the group, too. He might have told on them. No, Agent Sloan said Ramsey had kept quiet, he couldn't have had contacted his group. *Could he?* Then Robert recalled that Ramsey had also tried to shoot Bennett dead. Best guess, he also had every reason to keep his mouth shut. The secret remained safe, he hoped.

"Please come forward." One of the robed figures spoke the words with a heavy French accent.

Robert swallowed back his fear and stepped closer to the center.

"Stop. Close enough."

The three figures walked to the altar and stood not more than ten feet away, just on the other side. They all wore long black robes but theirs were adorned with different designs embroidered at the edges. The member in the middle held a gold staff, curled at the top, and engraved with scrolling designs. It was the kind of staff seen in old paintings, held by bishops of the old Church. Each member wore a unique mask.

"Your mentor told us much about you. Your assistance in attaining funds for the militant coup was appreciated."

"Coup!" Robert said. His surprise was obvious and he internally kicked himself for his reaction.

"Your mentor never filled in the details?" the person in the center asked. His mask was dark gray and resembled the big bad wolf, with mixed DNA of Frankenstein—his mask's facade—sizable and squared.

Robert was compelled to respond. "No, I had no clue what he used the funds for, we kept such information secret, as much as possible. I trusted his judgment and he mine."

"Kept? Past tense," the center speaker said in a tone of disapproval.

Robert swallowed. *Idiot.* The seconds dragged. *Did I give myself away?* Robert shuddered, a cold shiver slid down his spine.

"Well said, good response. The less information known the better," another cloaked member praised after a few moments.

He wore a believable vampire mask and could have been an indie horror film star. Robert grinned at that fleeting thought.

Dracula continued. "This group thrives because of our anonymity. Your mentor is wise to teach you this discipline. Maybe he's more than a mere teacher? Is it possible that you share genes with the great black wolf? Hmm."

Robert nodded but remained confused. *What the hell does share genes mean?*

The member to the left spoke up, using a synthesizer to mask the sound. "Do you know where your mentor is now?" When did you see him last?"

The robotic voice echoed in the open space. *Sinister.* Robert's face burned at the threat. His sweat beaded but was trapped between the rubber and his skin. The perspiration collected on the backside of the mask and dripped down his face. He longed to rip the piggy mask off and wipe his face dry, but he took in a deep breath instead.

"Sorry friends, I have no idea of his whereabouts." Robert swallowed. "I've left him a message to get back to me as soon as possible."

"So, when did you see him last?" the relentless generated voice said.

"About a week ago. We met in a warehouse, in Boston. We were planning—"

"We don't require details about what you were doing, young man." The member to the right had cut in, his arm was held up in the air. His baritone voice lingered like the reverberation of a ringing bell.

Robert worried they already knew that Tom Bennett was dead. *Maybe they are playing games and toying with me?*

"You appear nervous. Look, the pig mask is turning colors." The three figures laughed at him. After a moment the vampire-masked member said, "Please excuse our little attempt at humor."

Pissed that they enjoyed making him squirm, he remained calm. Robert was also scared, confused, and wanted nothing more than to get out of this place, wherever it was located. Taking great pains not to sound frazzled he asked, "Why have you summoned me here today?"

Their gaffs stopped. Silence filled the room for an eternity of seconds ticked. Only a drop of water could be heard coming from somewhere behind him.

"Despite your impertinent behavior, you've been chosen to fill a seat."

The center member waved the golden staff. Robert noticed the chairs lined against the wall, one held a mask of a wolf, which looked just like Tom Bennett's face when transformed into his animal familiar.

"Isn't that Tom's chair? Why would you want anyone else filling his place?" Robert said.

"He wanted you there, by his side. He said you asked for this privilege. Is that wrong?"

"No, it's correct. I requested some time ago for him to pledge me."

"Good. We're assembled to assign your first Beneficial Act. Once you perform it, you can be pledged into our Black Wolf Society as a full brother member. You know what a Beneficial Act is, don't you?"

Robert shifted his weight from one foot to the other.

"Yes," he replied. "I fulfill one request, using any means necessary, and then I can be one with the Society."

"Excellent. Here's your task."

The member in the center took an envelope from the book, walked around the altar, and handed it to Robert. A wave of musky air assaulted his nostrils as the cloak's long sleeve fanned the air. "Can we trust you to perform this?"

"It would be my privilege."

They all laughed together. Robert was about to open the envelope.

"No, not here. Do that in private. Remember, secrecy above all. The less we know of each other's deeds, the better."

Robert nodded. "Of course, forgive me."

"There will be another member assigned to go with you, to verify the deed's accomplished. He'll also watch the newscasts to verify the incident is recorded. You have three days to complete the task."

"But what if—"

"Three days," they said in harmony.

"Drivers," the vampire-masked member called out.

Within seconds his three original companions entered.

"Go now. Do the deed. When you've completed the Act you will return to us and we'll celebrate with a high ceremony."

Robert didn't even want to know what a high ceremony was, he just wanted out. They went back to the original dressing room, disrobed, and then the hood returned over his head.

Half an hour later, Robert was deposited back at the main road nearest Grand Place. The car buzzed away, and Robert didn't even have enough time to catch a good look at it, other than it was a small blue car. He walked back toward the Square. Though it was only early evening, the autumn sky was dark. Robert tore open the envelope and read the instructions. *Kill Jackson Bennett.*

His heart sunk. There's no way he could hurt a hair on his friend's head. Sure, they weren't close like they had been back in college, but the thought that Jackson was in danger at all sickened him. *Why would they want Jackson dead? He's the son of Tom Bennett, the black wolf.* He could never go through with the crazy Act, but this still meant his friend was in the crosshairs of these dangerous people. *If I don't do it, will they have someone else kill him?* A shiver skated down Robert's back. He rubbed his arms, wishing he could get the chillout.

He looked at the slip of paper again, not believing his fate. *This is what the group does—killing people, anyone who gets in the way, even the son of a member?* Up until now, Robert denied this group was pure evil and believed that the Black Wolves only performed white-collar crime, financial in nature. But now, he realized they were murderers and had to be stopped. It wasn't just Tom Bennett who was a monster—the entire organization was corrupt. Agent Sloan was right, the Black Wolf Society had to be exposed for the evildoers they were. It was the only way to keep his family safe, and the world as well.

Robert reached into his pocket and pulled out the flip phone. Just then it occurred to him that they had never searched him, nor questioned his loyalty. That was one lucky break, he thought as he stared at the device. He opened it and pressed *2—time to update Agent Sloan.

CHAPTER 14

Chase In Brussels

Emilie and Jeremy took the earliest commercial flight possible and followed her brother to Brussels. She feared Robert was walking into some kind of trouble, which followed him lately. After sixteen plus hours of travel with changing of planes and delays, they arrived in Brussels. They also booked a room at the Hotel Metropole, hired a car, and drove straight there. They crashed and caught a few hours of needed rest.

"Wake up." Emilie shook Jeremy. "Come on, sleepy-bones. It's afternoon here, we need to find my brother."

Jeremy wiped his eyes and pushed himself up, off the bed.

"I'm ready when you are, Em. Let me just splash some water on my face then we'll go."

Emilie had accepted that Jeremy liked to be prepared, like a good boy scout. She watched as he filled a bag with practical things that would be handy if they caught themselves in a precarious situation while traipsing around Belgium trying to keep her brother safe. Minutes later, the couple grabbed the backpack stuffed with things they might need and took the elevator down to the lobby. The lift doors opened and they made their way to the front of the lobby nearest the street and found a seat, then waited for Robert and Rachael.

"Em, look. They're leaving," Jeremy said as he nodded toward the front entrance.

"Looks like we're taking a stroll."

They followed Robert and Rachael but kept a safe distance so as not to be recognized. Emilie noticed another woman approach them, and yanked on Jeremy's shirt sleeve.

"What?"

"Look, they're meeting with someone."

Rachael hugged the woman and stood back while introducing Robert, who shook the woman's hand. Then they went inside the restaurant Aux Armes de Bruxelles.

"It appears that she's a friend of Rachael's," Jeremy said.

Emilie realized she was hungry. "Meeting her for lunch I suppose."

"That's not a bad idea." Jeremy nudged his head toward the other side of the street. "Let's grab a table there, in the open cafe." The small cafe had tables outside on the sidewalk with a full view of the restaurant's doors. "We can watch and wait for them to leave the restaurant from there."

Emilie nodded. They found a free seat and gave their order to the waiter. Emilie was served a sandwich and ended up drinking two coffees, which helped her feel human again. Jeremy drank extra coffee as well. As he was returning from the restroom, Emilie noticed Rachael and the woman leaving the restaurant.

"Looks like they're splitting up, and the women are going shopping." Jeremy smiled as he stated the obvious, sliding his arm around her.

Emilie laughed. "You're probably right. I might just follow them and do the same."

"Oh no. We have to follow Robert, let's not forget our primary mission."

"Yes, sir." She saluted, then smiled.

Robert exited the restaurant a minute later.

Leaving cash on the table, they left the cafe and followed Robert two blocks to Grand Place. It was easier not to be noticed by him once they reached the Square. They meandered among the other tourists but kept their eyes on her brother's position.

"I wonder what he's doing here. Maybe my brother's a closet shopper," Emilie said.

"Go ahead, poke fun. But right now your brother is talking with a strange-looking man."

Emilie glanced over and saw a thin wisp of a man, leading her brother toward the street on the other side of the market area. "Here we go. They're taking off."

"We need a taxi, quick." Jeremy ran to the curb and looked for an available cab. He spoke with a driver and pointed. The man shook his head and then Jeremy waved for her to join him.

Emilie looked over her shoulder and watched as Robert was ushered into a blue sedan. As they drove away from the curb something was flung over her brother's head.

"Hurry, follow that car. Rob's in trouble, I feel it already."

The taxi followed the blue sedan, and Jeremy leaned forward and gave more instructions to the man, speaking in German.

"I didn't know you spoke German," Emilie said.

"As they say, you learn something new every day." He smiled.

"I'll say." She loved his deep dimples that showed when he smiled, and the way light reflected in his hazel eyes when he was excited. She had fallen in love with this man, and for just a moment, she wanted to bask in that good feeling.

"What other surprises do you have in store for me, handsome? Do you yodel, too?" she said.

"If I tell you all my secrets, there'll be no surprises. I suppose you don't fancy that."

Jeremy was amazingly calm while under pressure. She realized he had become her rock. With so many strange and wicked things happening to her family lately, she needed to find a balance somehow. Her clairvoyant gift soaked up all the traumatic emotions from the people around her. His honest soul was her answer to find equilibrium. Whenever he touched her, she found peace from the chilling emotions that tormented her. Emilie reached over and put her arm in his, and they sat back while the driver followed the blue sedan.

They traveled down many streets, left then right, and the driver made it through the webs of a couple of roundabouts. The blue sedan led them to Avenue Victor Rousseau. The driver said something to Jeremy.

"The cabby said we're in the Vorst district or Forest. Look, over to your left," Jeremy pointed. "That's a soccer stadium, behind the trees and Dudenpark."

Emilie nodded.

After a few minutes, Jeremy pointed to the right. "Look, we're going past National Forest, the music hall."

"How do you know so much, have you been here before?"

Jeremy shifted his body and faced her.

"A few years ago. I brought my younger brother here. We saw a live show with giant puppets. It was fun. Let me think, oh yes, they're named Nele and Pauline. It was some time ago, but I remember it well. Then we went to see *Peter Pan* in the Vorst National, or Forest National Music Hall, over there."

He pointed to a modern-looking music hall. The building's exterior was constructed of gray metal panels arranged vertically. A large window flanked on either side of the gated entrance. Each window was a grid of sixteen smaller panes. Above the central entrance was a large round window that looked back at them like a watchful eye, as they drove past the crowd of people standing in line waiting for a show.

"Wait, yes. I remember Robert talking about a concert he went here, years ago. I think the Eurythmics were playing, but that was ages ago. It was nice of you to take your little brother William to the show. You really love your family, don't you Jeremy."

"Yes, as do you. Look, the car is turning, and heading in a different direction now."

They followed the car down various smaller streets—somehow Victor Rousseau turned into Rue Jean-Baptiste, which turned into Sint Denijsplain until finally, they were on Brits Tweedelgerlaan, which ran alongside a huge Audi manufacturing plant on the left side of the road. They had ended up turned around and were going back in the direction they came from.

"Looks like they're backtracking." Not a second after Jeremy said this, the blue sedan pulled toward the right curb, and slowed. The car pulled into an employee parking lot and stopped. The cab driver went past the lot slowly, and then he started talking fast.

"He said that's for the Audi plant employees only, so he's pulling over just ahead."

The car pulled to the curb and stopped. They turned around and watched from the back window, and witnessed Robert being taken from the sedan and tugged along, still with a hood over his head. They walked through a tree line and across an open area of grass, which led toward the back of an old building.

Jeremy said something to the driver in German and got a response.

"The driver said that's Forest Abbey. If we drive around the bend, there is a street that will take us to the front."

The cab moved ahead and turned right onto Rue des Abbesses, and dropped them off in front of the old building. They got out, paid him, then the cabby drove away. Emilie looked around the street.

"Most of the buildings here are Art Deco. Beautiful, but old looking."

"Not too old. Look." He pointed to a sign in front of a building across the street. CYBER-ESPACE was written on a large white sign with bright red letters.

"Yes, even the oldest of places are exposed to Internet madness," Emilie said.

"Watch out for the barricade," Jeremy said.

They walked around the blue and yellow metal panels set up around the Forest Abbey. The old church relic was undergoing much-needed repair and reconstruction. A clock tower rang. Emilie looked up and inspected the ancient red-bricked church. The building's sides were crumbling; it looked feeble. One of its corners hid an old cross statue, similar to one her family had in their own yard in Memphis. Emilie remembered the small garden shrine, tucked far away from the house, where her mother used to frequent for quiet time. Gone now.

"Come," Jeremy said, as he grabbed her hand. "Let's go to the back."

They circled around the old church and briskly walked down a well-worn dirt path. Three buildings stood in a cluster, backing up to each other creating a small garden section in the back. The lot's outside perimeter was defined by a tree line. She looked for the nestle of trees she thought her brother had been dragged between, but her brother was nowhere in sight.

"Which building do you think he's in?" she said.

"Well, he walked down that path, there—coming from the street. See the car plant?"

She nodded.

"They cut across the grass and must have entered on the other side of that building."

Emilie inspected the long building he pointed to. It was also made of faded, chipped brick with a clock tower of its own. "Yes, let's look behind the building with a clock tower."

They walked under an arched passageway between two of the buildings and headed for the long building on the other side of the center garden. Feeling a tug, Emilie glanced up. Jeremy pointed up. Cut into the slate roof of the old building were smaller windows. The center window was round with framed panels surrounding the center and it looked like a giant eye watching them as they approached.

"This place gives me the creeps," Emilie said.

"Why? It's in the middle of all this Vorst bustle."

"I'm getting a strange feeling, is all. Never mind, forget I said anything."

Jeremy stopped fast and pulled her to him. "I'll never forget anything you say. You don't realize how important you are to me, Em. As soon as this mess gets cleared up, you and I are going to make our plans for our wedding. Only we're going to do it right? A nice Church wedding for you and me."

Emilie rose on her toes and kissed Jeremy. "Okay by me."

"Enough fooling around for now. Your brother has too much of a head start. We have to find him and quick. Who knows what they want with him. Clearly, he's in some sort of distress, what with a bag over his head."

"Right. Thanks for reminding me to worry."

"I didn't mean it like that—he's a big boy and can take care of himself. But just in case . . ."

She grabbed his hand and led him around to the back of the building. They walked its length. The back brick wall contained a bank of windows three floors high. In the far corner, where another section of the building stuck out, there was an old tree, its branches dried and leafless. The boughs reached up toward the sky as if asking for relief from its rooted death. The additional section that jutted out appeared different with a plain design.

"Look for a door." Jeremy sounded serious.

They both spotted the obvious at the same time. The smaller annex shooting out in the opposite direction of the main building exposed a single dark door on the far outside wall. The remaining walls were barren except for one small window about three stories up. No other windows on the sides, just a plain wooden door that looked anything but ordinary. It had a fan design engraved on the top portion, and a tarnished brass doorknob, but no glass windows to spy what might await them on the other side.

They turned and looked at each other, knowing this was the place to look for Robert.

CHAPTER 15

Spying At The Abbey

They hurried. Emilie reached the door first and slowly turned the knob, it turned, but the door only partially opened. Jeremy pushed it with his shoulder, and the wooden door creaked as it cracked open wider. They stepped inside.

"Jeremy, this is the place. I feel it."

"What do you feel?"

"Don't laugh, okay. I feel evil here, and I'm afraid for my brother."

"Please, be a little afraid for us as well."

Emilie grinned to reassure him and took his hand. Together they walked down a dark hall, which led to a staircase. They went down a flight of stairs and reached a landing, which offered them the option of three doorways.

"You've got to be kidding me," he said.

Emilie noticed the muscles on his face twitch.

"No worries. The one in the center," she said.

He squeezed his eyes together, and she nodded. Jeremy reached for the knob and turned it cautiously. It opened.

"I feel like a rat in a trap," he said.

"No, I'm not sensing any threat to us; they don't even know we're here."

"Let's keep it that way."

They entered a foyer-type space, a wood table in the center under a low-hanging chandelier dimly lit by candles. On the far wall was another staircase.

Jeremy bowed and folded out his arm. "Shall we, Madame."

They descended a narrow passage with cement walls and a

rusted iron railing. The winding staircase led them down a spiral of gloom.

It was darkness at the bottom. Jeremy turned on the flashlight on his phone and beamed it on a single wooden door, swollen from the damp cellar ground. The hinged panel fought Jeremy's push. Emilie joined him and thrust her weight against the door to help. It jerked open, inch by inch, scraping and squealing against the hard floor. Finally, enough space opened up for them to slip through. They walked about twenty feet, and then Emilie stopped.

Voices echoed down the hallway. She pulled on his sleeve. "Whoa, slow down."

Jeremy stopped a second, nodded, then started again, but this time crept along more slowly. They walked toward a dim light that shone at the end of the hall. The voices grew louder as they approached. It took half a minute for them to reach the end of the hall. Finally, they could spy into the adjoining room.

The space was an open circular tower, lit only by candles. Three figures stood on one side of a center table, and a lone person stood on the other. All of them donned dark robes and wore distorted ghoulish masks. The shadowy room was mysterious, like an old castle dungeon with chains hanging on the gigantic wall. The floor's carpet was bright as fresh red blood. But nothing gave away the nature of their business, for clearly, they were discussing something.

Emilie closed her eyes and concentrated. She opened herself up, allowing her extrasensory gift to soak in the emotional shroud of the surroundings. Filtering the emotion flowing into her own sensory well, she trembled because of the powerful, dangerous torrent. Immediately she recognized her brother's familiar spirit; he was a strong sender. Opening her eyes, she pointed.

"The lone person on the other side," she mouthed, "is Robert."

Jeremy nodded an acknowledgment.

A door across the way squeaked, and three men, also disguised, entered. They took Robert by his arms and dragged him out of the room.

"We have to get to the other side to help him," Jeremy whispered.

The robed person wearing a vampire mask called out.

"Are we ready yet? Let's get this nasty bit over and quick."

A frenzy began.

"Okay, okay. Be patient, doctor. After all these months of testing, you'd think a few more minutes wouldn't be such a big deal." Those words were spoken by a deeper yet musical voice, coming from behind a different mask.

The same door from which Robert left opened again. Two men, dressed in lab coats and wearing surgical masks, strode in assisting an apparent patient. The body between them staggered as if drugged and unable to walk on his or her own accord. The patient mumbled indecipherable sounds. Emilie got the sense that this patient wasn't a normal person — something was off.

"Bring it here." A voice called out. "Lift it up to the altar."

It? Altar? Emilie's blood rushed, her face burned. *Was this a human sacrifice?*

"Now strap the thing down." One of the robed figures commanded.

They heard straps sliding and locks clicking. One of the robed figures moved closer to the tied-down body and spoke. This voice sounded different, mechanical. *A voice synthesizer?*

"Prepare the final serum." The synthesized voice sounded like the drone of a sci-fi show.

"Yes, grandmaster," said one of the lab assistants. "Roll the generator over," he barked to the other man dressed in lab gear.

The other man wheeled a contraption over and placed it beside the table. It now looked more like an altar for a sacrifice. Emilie studied the sides of the center table. Elaborate designs and symbols were engraved on it, though she couldn't make them out from a distance with accuracy. She stared, thinking she recognized some of the symbols. A memory snapped into place. Those exact symbols were written in the ancient journal that had belonged to Jeremy's Uncle Thaddeus.

Her thoughts were interrupted by a strange hum that filled the room with zaps and sounds of electrical charges, *click, click, tzz, tzz, tzz.* The body lying on the altar jumped into the air, landed back on the table, and bounced, only to rise again. An unearthly sound screeched from the body, *ahhhh, ah-ouch, ah-ouch.* It was the sound of pain.

A flood of energy entered her head. Emilie pushed herself back against the wall and closed her eyes. Her breathing became labored. Her blood burned as if it were boiling under her skin. The searing pain that had just been inducted into the body lying on the table also gripped her. The emotional turmoil of the victim overtook her own senses. She bore the terror that the living thing experienced. Frantic and in self-preservation, Emilie had an urgent need to stop them before it was too late. She refused to allow this torture to continue.

She opened her eyes and looked up at Jeremy. He was close and moved toward her with open arms, ready to embrace her. Emilie ignored his help and stepped away from him. She sprung out from the dark, secluded corner where they hid. She ran toward the altar, screaming aloud. "Stop! Stop this now." She barely heard Jeremy's urgent calls to her.

"No, wait, Emilie. Wait."

Emilie's body surged with adrenaline that pumped

through her veins. The fear that emanated from the creature lying on the altar increased, and she absorbed it all. She channeled the panic and used it to gain momentum. Throughout all of this, Emilie encountered another strange emotion, one that she had never experienced before. It didn't feel human, but most definitely, it was a sense of deep pain. The feelings twisted inside of her and mingled with her own. Like a wounded animal, she hurled out with intentions to do what was necessary. Emilie stood steadfast in front of the group of robed figures.

They froze in place, surprised by her ambush. She heard one of them call out.

"What the hell is happening."

Emilie raised her arms and began her assault against the evil waged. One of them turned and sprinted away toward another side door. *How many doors were there in this old dungeon?* Emilie couldn't afford to pursue the fleeing foe if she wanted to save this poor suffering soul who was lying on the table.

Flinging her arms outstretched toward the others, she focused her energy to align with her vision. Streams of bright light surged from her hands in a rapidly flowing river of power. The force struck them down. The two remaining robed figures and the men in lab coats landed on the hard stone floor and skidded a few feet back. Emilie stepped closer and stood over them. Instinctively, she poured her force over them. Groans of agony cried out as if they were being squeezed with torture. Their bodies popped, one, then another. All of them turned into flying hemoglobin pulp.

Emilie dropped her arms to her side; they felt heavy like lead. She couldn't move. With eyes closed, her only thought was that of relief, now that the evil was exterminated from the room. The hatred had evaporated as well, mere seconds before the strangers' bodies exploded. She opened her eyes and looked down at herself; her clothes were covered in gunk. *Human gunk.*

Jeremy rushed to her side. "Emilie, don't ever do that again."

"Oh my God, what have I done?"

She stood quietly as the globs of flesh dropped off her clothes and stringy tissue dangled. Jeremy grabbed a cloth off the table and handed it to her. She wiped her face and hands, brushed off as many human remains as she could, then turned her attention to the altar.

"Look at the symbols," she said.

There was no response. Jeremy was staring down at the creature, shaking his head. The injured being that she had desperately tried to protect was still. It was dead. Emilie had been too late. She went to his side and together they examined the body on the table. It looked like a lab experiment gone wrong. A Frankenstein of human parts, mixed with animal features, and fur-like skin. It appeared to be male, had one blue eye, one dark eye. Jeremy reached over and gently closed the creature's lids shut.

"Thanks for that," she heard herself say. "What do you think they were doing to this poor creature?"

"Experimenting, what else do evil people do with the helpless? This reminds me of a Dreamtime story I heard once, a long time ago, when I worked a job in the Northern Territory."

"You worked with an Aboriginal tribe?"

"Yes. A government project, far out in the wilderness. The Aboriginal guides showed us the cave drawings of the Dreamtime. We were invited to watch a ceremony. The people had been horribly mistreated . . ."

"Lucky you—I mean to experience the ceremony." Emilie heard her voice but felt removed from the conversation. She stared at the body. *Poor soul.*

"Yes, I am lucky. I found you, Miss Emilie."

She smiled at his gentle words, but she knew full well she had messed up. Her appearance was dreadful, what with pieces of dead members of the Black Wolf Society smeared all over her clothes, and she felt horrid inside. She smelled the foul dead debris. She shuddered throughout her body as the severity of the situation sunk in. She had just killed members of the most hateful group in the world. The Black Wolf Society would surely want her dead, posted on the top of their most-wanted list. *Will this nightmare ever end?*

"We have to leave," Jeremy pleaded. "Now."

Still stunned, Emilie stood there trembling. "I can't for the life of me think of why they would have created this monstrosity?" she said. "The poor thing felt so afraid. Why do you think they were experimenting? Making a hybrid body? It's vicious." She shook her head. "I'm sick of the whole lot of them. The Black Wolf Society can drop dead." Her words sounded harsh to her own ears. Tears ran down her dirty face.

"I have no clue why they did this," Jeremy replied. "But we have got to get out of here before they return. One got away, remember? They will return with more of them any minute."

Jeremy started for the door, but Emilie didn't follow.

"Wait. Look." She pointed to the symbols on the side of the altar, and a book that sat on top, right next to the dead creature's body. Emilie moved the white sheet draped over the creature to the side, revealing more of the book. But it wasn't just any book. It was the ancient journal that had belonged to Jeremy's Uncle Thaddeus. The book that was missing from her father's library—the journal that talked of the curse that had plagued her family—it was here and had the same symbols from the altar drawn on its pages. "What the hell?"

"What is it?" he said. Jeremy reached down and grabbed the book. It was opened to a page.

"Bloody hell, how did they get this?" he said.

"It was in my father's library." Emilie's voice wavered.

"Yes, but you've been away for a while. Someone must have stolen it."

"Or someone gave it to them," she said. "But why? What were they reading from the book?"

They both gazed down to the open page.

"We can't read it here—now," he said. "We don't have time. Just dog-ear it to mark the page."

Emilie took the book with her right hand. "But—"

Jeremy grabbed her left hand. "Let's get out of here, now."

Emilie let go of Jeremy's hand, and folded the page back, closed the book, and handed the tome to Jeremy. "Here, you carry it. It belongs to you. Can we take the creature with us as well?"

Jeremy shook his head and yanked her hand.

"Right, we're hard-pressed as it is. Someone will be coming after us. They know something went wrong."

"You're right, so let's go then."

They retreated the same way they had come in, only this time they fled as fast as possible. Up the spiral stairway, across the room, up the other staircase, again speeding down the hall towards the exit door. By the time Jeremy pulled the door open to the outside, Emilie was out of breath.

"Let's grab a cab," she said.

They stepped outside. Emilie swallowed a mouthful of air and tried to get the smell of guts out of her nasal passage. "I need a shower." She shivered as much from the thought that she wore human tissue as the cold night air.

Jeremy pulled out his phone and tapped the number for the Taxis Bleus, ordering a car to pick them up to bring them back to the hotel. It was early evening. The autumn sky was already dark and the temperature cold. Emilie noticed a mist in the air and felt the dampness rising from the ground.

"I bet it snows soon," she said.

Her voice was drowned out by a lone shot in the dark. The bullet whooshed past her ear. Stunned, she heard more gunshots. She pulled down on Jeremy's hand and they fell to the ground. The cold dirt froze her body and her teeth chattered. Grabbing his arm, she tugged on Jeremy's sleeve. No response. She turned to Jeremy, his face paled.

He moaned and closed his eyes.

She looked down and saw blood everywhere, blood. Jeremy's middle section was covered in a dark wet patch.

She heard a scream. *Is that me screaming?* Her throat tightened, and for a moment, she thought they were both dead. A hand touched her shoulder. Emilie startled, shrugged her arm free, and turned, ready to punch whoever stood there. She looked up and saw a stranger standing over her. He had a good face.

"Hurry," he said. "We have no time to argue. He needs to get to the hospital."

CHAPTER 16

Should Have Run Faster

The stranger yelled for her to hurry. *Hurry where?* She wasn't about to leave Jeremy lying there, bleeding to death, and pulling him up presented another danger. More shots fired into the air. Panic-stricken, Emilie knew they couldn't stay there. She scooped her arm under Jeremy's side and pulled him up to stand. "Lean on me," she said.

Jeremy came to for a moment and managed to hobble alongside Emilie. They followed the stranger into the tree line for cover. An onslaught of bullets fired as they fled. She turned and looked over her shoulder, spotting some men in dark clothes gaining on them. She followed the stranger, as fast as she could. A car waited on the other side of the thicket. The stranger said, "Get in the back."

Emilie did as instructed and the Good Samaritan helped to load Jeremy into the backseat next to her. Emilie held Jeremy close; his eyes were opened but his pupils fading.

"You'll be all right," she said. "Hurry, the nearest hospital."

The car pulled away from the curb and rushed down the street.

"Are you okay back there?" Emilie heard the man call back.

"Not looking well. Please, take us to the closest hospital."

"Exactly where we're heading. What happened back there?" the man asked.

Emilie was dumbfounded and didn't really know herself. She wasn't about to tell this stranger about what they witnessed below, in the Abbey's building.

"I don't know why anyone would shoot at us," she lied. "We were walking about like the other tourists, and someone shot at us. It came from nowhere."

"Here. Use this to compress the wound, maybe it'll hold back the bleeding."

A cloth was handed to her. She put pressure on Jeremy's gut wound. He moaned. She felt his agony and became frantic. She wondered why this man was helping them, then she reasoned it didn't matter, as long as they got Jeremy to help, and quick.

"Did you see who shot at you?" the man asked.

"No, I didn't see, everything happened so fast. Did you see anyone, Mister . . . "

"Mr. Sloan, but please, call me Jeffrey. And no, I couldn't tell who was doing the shooting, but they kept firing, so I figured we should get out of there quick. Your friend needs a doctor."

"Jeremy, please stay awake. Stay with me, honey."

She pleaded but he closed his eyes anyway.

"Please drive faster, Jeffrey. My friend is passing out. He's shot in his abdomen, he bled a lot. It seems to have slowed a bit, but he's lost a lot of blood already. How much longer to a hospital?" Emilie spoke aloud but felt disengaged from her body and functions. She was a robot, doing the necessary things, but inside she was crying, screaming, and weeping for Jeremy. *Nothing bad can happen to him, he's my world*.

"Jeremy. Open your eyes. Please, stay with me, babe."

"Here we are. I'm pulling into the garage, that's where they have the emergency entrance."

Emilie looked out the window and saw the sign for the Clinical De L'europe Sainte-Elisabeth. The car pulled up at the front entrance and then drove into the Accident and Emergency Department. A man rushed towards them, pulling a gurney. The door flew open and another man grabbed Jeremy from her lap and they rushed him into the hospital before she could pull herself from the back seat. Jeffery came around to the side of the car and helped her out. Taking her arm, he escorted her to the Emergency area.

"I must go with him," Emilie called out.

She raced to catch up with the men pushing the gurney. A nurse blocked her way and pointed to the admittance desk.

"Please you must stay out of the way. If you want to help your husband, fill out the paperwork over there. We'll take good care of him."

Emilie went to the desk and tried to fill out the paperwork as requested. All the lines blurred, she kept rubbing her eyes. The nurse offered to help and Emilie gave her Jeremy's passport and medical information. The woman asked a few questions about the nature of the wound, and then Emilie was told to sit in a waiting area. The large space was lined with sofas snug against the wall, very mod-looking. There were few windows. When she looked out of one in the corner, all she saw was darkness and her own reflection on the glass.

The time dragged. It had only been thirty minutes but lingered like hours to Emilie. A nurse walked over and gave her an update.

"Your friend lost a lot of blood. That's his biggest danger. We're giving him some blood now to replenish."

"That's a good thing, right?" Emilie felt a spike of hope.

"The bullet went straight through. We'll have to evaluate the internal damage it caused later. At least now the bleeding is under control, but I'm afraid it's too early to tell how serious of a wound it is. He kept losing consciousness, so we decided to put him out. It's best, for now, so his body can rest and heal. We're monitoring his breathing and vitals. Please don't worry. We are doing our best."

Emilie nodded. "Yes, of course. Merci. Where did the bullet go in?"

She was almost too afraid to ask. Emilie remembered all the blood, there had been so much that she couldn't be sure of where on his body he had actually been shot. She whimpered at the thought of him, in pain, bleeding to death.

"Mr. Laughton was hit in the mid-section, that's why he bled so much, and so quick. The wound is around the liver area, and the bullet came out without hurting anything vital, so that's good news. We will wait to see for sure if any internal damage was done to his organs."

"How long before I can see him?" Emilie asked.

"The doctor will come out later with an update. Right now, sit and rest while you can." The nurse glanced up and down, taking in her appearance.

Emilie nodded but was embarrassed. *Did she realize it was human guts that covered her clothing?* The nurse left and Emilie sat on the sofa, bent forward with her face in her hands. She replayed the incident in her head. With shots fired, surely the police would be involved soon. If they were anything like the police in the U.S., it was mandatory to report a shooting, it would be filed by the hospital as well.

What could she say that would help them find the culprit, without sounding like a nut? And what would they do once they discovered the human remains in the chamber below, and that creature—dead. She thought for a bit and reasoned that no one would find anything. Surely, someone from the Black Wolf Society was already cleaning up the mess they left behind. *Her mess—now she was a killer.*

"There you are. How's your husband?" Jeffery Sloan's voice startled her.

"He's not my—"

"They said at the front desk, you'd be waiting here."

Emilie nodded. "I wish I could see him."

"In good time. Let them do their job."

Emilie nodded again and felt so helpless.

"Thank you for your help, Mr. Sloan," she said.

"No problem, and please, call me Jeffrey. I'm glad I was there and able to help. I can't imagine what would've happened if I hadn't had my car nearby. Those men kept shooting. I think they were after you. And your husband bled so much, so fast."

"I don't know why they were shooting at us," she replied. "And Jeremy and I aren't married, yet."

"Oh. Well then, what were you doing? Maybe that will help us figure this thing out."

"Just walking the area, you know seeing the sights."

"Ah-ha. Are the two of you traveling alone? Maybe a relative or friend nearby can come to sit with you?"

Emilie had to think about that. *Should I call my brother?* Actually, she had forgotten all about Robert. *Did they let him go, or was he still being held a prisoner?* Another rush of adrenaline— and the urgent need to find her brother troubled her. She patted her clothes and checked her pockets, looking for her phone.

"Yes, there's someone," she said. "I want to call my brother."

"Okay, I'll give you some privacy. I'll be back." He nodded and left the area, and Emilie was alone with her thoughts.

◙ ◈ ◈ ◈ ◙

Agent Jeffery Sloan walked away from Miss de Gourgues and turned down a hallway. Now out of Emilie's line of sight, he motioned another agent over.

"I want you to watch over her. Stay in the waiting room, be inconspicuous, and follow her if she leaves. She may be in danger."

The agent nodded and left to stand guard over her in the waiting room. Sloan continued down the hallway and placed a call to Robert de Gourgues.

"Robert, this is Agent Sloan. How are you?" Jeffrey Sloan

tried to make his voice sound positive.

"Agent Sloan. I must say, I've had better days. I was just dropped off, not even fifteen minutes ago, by some Black Wolf members, and I'm walking among the many in the square right now."

Sounds of the crowd muffled in the background confirmed his whereabouts.

"I was briefed about your progress. Well done."

"You mean, someone tailed me? The entire time?" Robert's voice faded. "Excuse me."

He must have bumped into someone, Sloan figured.

"Robert, make sure you're not being followed. If the Black Wolf is tailing you—well, be careful of what you say with people around."

"You think so?" Robert sounded alarmed.

"If they are, my men will spot them and report back. Don't worry, just be careful. I told you, Mr. de Gourgues, we have your back, and the Bureau of Investigation thanks you for your cooperation."

Sloan heard the wind blowing against Robert's phone.

"Tell me, why are you being so nice all of a sudden?" A bell tinkled. "Wait, there I'm inside. I can hear you better. Tell me, what do you want?"

"I have other news to report. It's about your sister's friend, Jeremy Laughton."

"Yeah, what about him?"

"He's in the hospital, here in Brussels."

"What. How the hell did that happen?"

"While we followed you, we noticed that your sister Emilie and Mr. Laughton also followed you, from a cab."

"You're kidding. So how'd Jeremy end up in a hospital? Did you shoot them?"

Sloan shook his head and smiled at the phone. "Of course

not. They followed you down into the basement of that building. Shortly after you left, they resurfaced as well. Unfortunately, they were found out and shots were fired. Luckily, I was there to run out and help them to safety, but your sister's friend was hit. I drove them to the hospital."

"Damn. I need to go to her, right away. Which hospital?"

"No. You wait for Emilie to call you. And when she does, you pretend to be ignorant about all of this. And Robert, no worries. Mr. Laughton will be fine. I assure you. Understood?" Sloan hoped his voice conveyed his confidence. The last thing he needed was for Robert to go rogue on him.

"Listen, Robert, the meet-up tonight was just the beginning. Soon you'll lead us to the entire Black Wolf group. Everything will work out fine if you just stick with the plan."

It was Sloan's job to keep Robert happy, keep him calm, and most of all keep Robert from spilling what he knew. Secrecy was important to make this plan work out. Sloan needed Robert to stay on course.

"You promise with your life that everyone will be safe, Agent Sloan?" Robert's tone sounded harsh.

"Yes, of course. You have nothing—"

The line went dead.

"—to worry about."

After Sloan finished his thought, he realized he was the one worried. Did someone follow them? What if the Black Wolf came back to finish the job in the hospital? Uncertainties aside, he was determined to stay focused. The world depended on him, and loyal public servants like him, to keep the world safe from the likes of manipulators and hate groups like The Black Wolf Society.

CHAPTER 17

Hospital Food

Emilie tried Robert's cell but he didn't answer. She worried he wasn't okay after all. She called the hotel, left an urgent message with the desk, asking them to have him call as soon as possible. Then she tried his cell again, this time he answered.

"Robert. Oh, thank God you're all right."

"Emilie? Hi there. What's up? Everything all right back home?"

She gulped back the saliva built up in her mouth and drew in a breath. *I have to tell the truth.* She exhaled.

"Rob, I'm here, in Brussels and I need your help."

"What? Of course, I'll help. Where are you? Here? What's wrong? I'm in the Square right now, waiting to meet up with Rachael. She met up with an old friend and—"

"Rob, stop. Listen, please. I know where you were this afternoon." She switched hands and wiped her sweaty palm on her filthy pants.

"Em—"

"No, please just listen. I was afraid for you, Robert. So Jeremy and I followed you here. We saw you being kidnapped. We followed you down into that dungeon, at the old Abbey, after they took you away. Well, when they dragged you away, we left too. As we exited the building, someone shot at us." Tears welled in her eyes and burned. It was difficult for her to speak, her words stuck in her throat.

"What! Are you okay, Em? Are you shot?"

"No. I'm fine, but Jeremy . . . he's in the hospital. He was hit by a bullet."

"Where are you? What hospital?"

"Clinical De L'europe Sainte-Elisabeth, it's just east of where you were in Forest."

"Really, Em. I have no clue of where I was, they hooded me. Never mind, I'll GPS it. I'll be there in a few." Robert hung off the call.

Emilie felt better knowing that her brother was on his way to be there with her. She thought about everything that had happened, her brother—dragged out by those cloaked men. *Robert's all right.* What exactly had they seen? Her brother was escorted to the car by a strange man, then a bag over his head. Brought down into the room. Wait, he was dressed in a robe, too. But with a mask. A pig mask. *Was he part of the Society?* Misgivings about her brother brewed.

Maybe the entire thing was some sort of sick ritual. No, he wanted nothing to do with them. Robert's afraid of them as much as I am. If he is involved with them again, I'll kill him. Emilie regretted that thought. It reminded her that she was in fact a killer. Those masked members were dead because of the power she unleashed upon them. She dropped her face into her hands and cried. Once again, she didn't trust her brother, and now she added herself to the list of murderers. How could he, after everything that's happened? He promised . . . She wished she hadn't called him. Emilie didn't want to face him right now until she could manage to wrap her head around what she had done as well.

▣◈◇◈▣

Robert grabbed a cab and went directly to the hospital. He pulled out his phone and called Rachael.

"Rachael, hon, I'll be a bit longer. Don't wait for me. Go ahead back to the hotel and I'll see you there later."

He told her that Jeremy was in the hospital and that he would explain it all when he returned. The entire time his stomach was in knots. He wondered what kind of cover story he could invent to explain why his sister was even in Brussels. He wondered that himself. *Emilie can think of something*, he thought.

Let out at the curb, Robert clipped down the street and entered the building's lobby. On the outside, it looked like an older building, but the entire inside was modernized. An odd modern sculpture of a tuxedo was displayed in the open area. It took him by surprise, looking out of place like it belonged in a restaurant, not a hospital. The entire back stone wall was painted a bright red. *Had he walked into the wrong place?* But then noticed a poster boasting the hospital's newly gotten honor: the "Smiley" award for best food quality and safety. *Good to know, Jeremy will have healthy food to speed his recovery.* On his way to the front desk, he was met by Agent Sloan.

"Did your sister call you?" Sloan asked.

"Yeah, I'm going to her now."

Agent Sloan grabbed Robert's arm. "Maybe it's better if you stay away from her, for now. After all, she's bound to ask you questions that you aren't at liberty to answer. Remember, no one can know the truth."

Robert pulled his arm free. "Agent Sloan, it's been my experience that secrets only lead to trouble."

Sloan smiled. "Yes, it can lead people down dark paths, make them do unspeakable deeds. But this time, it's for everyone's good. If your sister knows the true nature of things, her life will be at risk. You don't want that do you?"

"Ha! I think it's already at risk. They shot at her and Jeremy, for Christ's sake."

Agent Sloan waved his hand and motioned for Robert to lower his voice, then pulled him off to the side. They went into a small room. Robert glared at him, his fists tightened until his knuckles turned white. Agent Sloan spoke in a measured voice.

"Listen, I understand you're upset. But who could've anticipated that your sister would follow you? We're lucky that my men were following, too. They reported back to me that Emilie and Jeremy were at the scene. I went there myself, straight away, with a car waiting. When the ruckus began, I assisted them to safety. Thank goodness we were able to get Jeremy to the hospital quickly, and he didn't bleed out. It could've been so much worse. They both could have been shot, repeatedly. This incident will eventually blow over, but we can't afford for you to muddy the water. Not now, when we're so close. I hope I make myself clear. We need to stick to the plan. We need to stay calm."

Robert unclenched his fists and relaxed a bit. "Clear as a bell. Thank you for being there for my sister."

"My pleasure, your sister is a very nice person."

"Now what? I have to go to her. She's expecting me." Robert clenched his teeth and glared at him.

Agent Sloan raised his hand to his chin, deep in thought. "Five minutes. Just enough time to tell her you're concerned about their safety and working on a plan to get Jeremy home. Safe and sound. Then try to get her to go back to the hotel with you as well. That way I can post a guard without her suspecting anything is wrong."

"Thank you, Agent Sloan. I'll keep my mouth shut," Robert said. "I promise."

Robert went back to the front desk and asked for Jeremy's room. He discovered Emilie in a waiting room. As soon as he saw her, he ran and embraced her. Robert squeezed her tight and kissed the top of her head.

"Emilie, poor baby. What the hell happened? And what the hell are you doing here? My God, what smells? What's all over you, Em?"

She stepped back, wiped her eyes, and turned around.

"Robert, we came here to watch out for you. We discovered a secret room under Mr. La France's study. We thought that

126

maybe he was involved in the Black Wolf and that you were possibly in danger. So we came here to watch over you."

Robert smiled. "Emilie, you're the sweetest sister. I don't deserve such devotion. Still, what the hell happened? Who shot at Jeremy?"

"I'd like to ask you the same question. We saw you getting abducted, at least that's what we thought we saw. As soon as that man put a hood over your head, we worried there was serious trouble, so we followed you. Thinking you were in danger. But then, we saw you wearing a robe and mask, just like the rest of the Black Wolf members." She turned back around and faced him. "Robert, how could you? After everything we went through, how could you join them again?"

Robert felt like shit. The last thing in the world he wanted was for Emilie to lose faith in him. He couldn't tell her the truth—that he was undercover. How the hell was he going to make things right again without divulging the secret?

"Em, you've got the wrong idea. Really, I'm not with them. Believe in me, please. Let's focus right now on what happened to Jeremy. He's the important issue right now."

"He was shot, Robert." Emilie started to cry.

Robert held her in his arms again and patted her back gently.

"It'll be all right, Em, I promise. I'll arrange for Jeremy to be transported back home. He'll get the best of care. Come with me, back to the hotel." He let go of her and took a step back to see her expression. "Look at you, Em. You're a mess. We'll get you cleaned up and arrange for us all to go home where it's safe and sound."

She tightened her lips and wrapped her arms around herself.

"Thanks, but I'm staying right here. He's getting good care, and besides, he can't be moved just yet. Please, just go back to

Rachael. I want to be alone right now, I need to think. I'll see you when we all go back home."

"Emilie, please. You shouldn't be here, alone."

She scoffed. "Didn't you know? I'm never alone. I always have everyone's emotions right here in my head, all of the time, keeping me company. I wish I could be truly alone." After a pause, she said, "Robert, you do need to leave. Go find out what the hell your wife is all about. Like I told you, she's sending out some deep, heavy badness. And right now, so am I."

She turned her back to him.

Robert left the room with regrets that once again, things were bad between them. *When will this bad dream end?* He called for a car and headed back to the hotel, back to Rachael. All he wanted right now was a drink or two. Maybe then things would feel a little bit normal.

🔲◈◈◈🔲

As soon as Robert left, Emilie walked to the nurses' station.

"Excuse me, can I speak to someone about Jeremy Laughton's status?"

A blonde nurse in her late twenties dressed in pink scrubs turned to answer.

"Mr. Laughton was taken out of the ICU a few minutes ago. He's been moved to his own room but he's still unconscious." The nurse covered her mouth. "I'm sorry, that sounded blunt. Please, don't worry. It's for the best so he can rest. How about if you take a few minutes to clean yourself up, then I'll sneak you in to sit with him for a few minutes before I'm off duty?" The young nurse's eyes looked her up and down, taking in her appearance.

Emilie's face burned from embarrassment. She looked down at herself and agreed. She looked gross and smelled, too. "I would like that, and as you can see, I'm still a bit frazzled from our accident."

The nurse pulled her lips tight in a straight line. "Come with me." She got up from the desk and walked around. "I have some clean scrubs in the closet you can change into. My name's Nancy, by the way."

"Hello, Nancy. I'm Emilie. Thank you. You're too kind."

"Don't mention it. We all need to help each other in times like this, right?"

Nancy let out a soft laugh and then led Emilie to an empty patient room.

"Here, no one is using this room. The shower is through that door. Take your time, I'll be back in fifteen minutes to escort you to Mr. Laughton's room."

After Nancy left Emilie sat on the bed for a moment and let out a sigh of relief. She undressed and washed in a small, white tiled shower. She tried not to think about the mess she had caused or the people she managed to blow up with her power. A shiver went through her. She turned off the water and rubbed herself dry, tugging the towel roughly on her skin trying to get the imaginary guts off her until humanized again.

Nancy had left the clean scrubs on the bed. Emilie put them on then toweled her hair dry. Dressed in clean scrubs and smelling fresh, she put her belongings into a plastic bag. She wondered if they had bagged Jeremy's things, then thought about the book. *Where was the book?*

The idea that the old journal could be in the hands of the Black Wolf Society made her angry. Whatever they were using it for, she had no idea, but it wasn't anything good. She grabbed the bag and made her way up to the nurses' station, hoping she wouldn't have to wait to be escorted to Jeremy's assigned room.

"Now there, you look better," Nancy said.

"I feel much better, thank you. Can I see Jeremy now?"

"Visiting hours are over, but I'll make this one exception.

Try to blend in, look like you belong here." The kind nurse escorted her through the unit, and soon Emilie was sitting beside Jeremy.

Jeremy looked pale. An oxygen tube hung under his nose, a drip bag connected to the IV needle plunged into his arm. He had a bag for bodily secretions as well. It scared Emilie to see him so weak and helpless. This wasn't her Jeremy, the strong, healthy, nature boy who was always one step ahead of everyone else. Now he lay there, vulnerable, and it made her angry. There was no way that she would allow the Black Wolf Society to get away with what they've done. Although she didn't believe in revenge, she certainly believed in getting justice.

She reached up to his forehead and brushed his ash hair back with her fingers, then she traced the contours of his face gently with her finger. "Everything will be fine," she whispered near to his ear.

"I can see that you love him by the way you look at him," Nancy said.

Emilie nodded. The nurse finished her last notes and left the room, smiling.

Jeremy slept peacefully, a smile on his face despite the tubes and wires. Emilie lifted the sheet and peeked under the covers. She inspected the bandage that covered his middle area, a thin gauze wrap held gauze pads in place. The sight of blood usually made her feel woozy, but his injury was fully covered thank goodness. Medical care was one area she knew nothing about, so she would sit back and let the professionals take care of him.

The nurse had said they sedated Jeremy, so he'd probably sleep the remaining night hours. Emilie held Jeremy's hand for a few minutes, then feeling exhausted herself, she sat in the chair nearest the bed. She leaned back, closed her eyes, and drifted to sleep.

A noise woke her. Emilie turned her attention to Jeremy. He lay still in the bed, smiling. Probably dreaming of something nice—a good sign, she thought. Looking up at the clock she realized it was early morning. The few hours of needed sleep felt good, she could function like a human again.

An older nurse entered the room. "Good morning," she said.

Emilie nodded and watched as the nurse scanned Jeremy's ID tag, took vitals, and reported it all into a tablet.

"Dear, you shouldn't be in here. The hospital has posted visiting hours. Why don't you go home, freshen up, and come back later? Around noon."

Emilie nodded, pretending not to be upset that she was being thrown out, knowing that she would slip right back in after the nurse left. She gathered her things, bent to kiss Jeremy on the head, and left the room. She needed to stretch her legs anyway. *I need coffee.* She figured the nearest coffee machine should be at the cafeteria on the main floor. She stepped into the elevator and waved at the station nurse as the door closed.

Making her way to find a fresh cup of coffee, Emilie noticed the sign. The Brasserie Europlis, the name of the hospital's award-winning restaurant/cafeteria, wouldn't open until eight in the morning. Glancing at a wall clock she realized it was still a couple hours away. She dug through the plastic bag looking for some money. She found a Euro and a few coins and thought she'd look around for a coffee machine, and hopefully avoid having to leave the building to search for her morning coffee. *Where is Starbucks when you need them?*

She gleaned a shadow in her peripheral vision. A creepy feeling rattled her to the bone. The shadow moved, she turned around. Surprised, she spied a man dressed all in black and wearing a pig mask. *No!* She turned to run, her chest tightened with a grip so strong that she thought surely a heart attack loomed in her near future. Hands lunged forward, she tried to clutch onto anything within reach. Her arm was grabbed tight by the man, as if in a vice. She was swung around. She clawed at his mask, hoping to reveal her attacker or at least inconveniencing him a bit. Maybe show him that she could handle herself if need be, then he'd back off.

The man stepped back and screamed out, "You bitch!"

Someone else grabbed Emilie from behind, placed a cloth over her mouth, then it was lights out.

CHAPTER 18

A Kidnapping

The sun was just beginning to shine, a few rays dared to slip between the cracks of the drapes that hung on the hotel window. Robert opened an eye and tried to make out where the noise was originating. The phone on the desk was ringing off the hook.

"Lord, have mercy," he slurred.

He had overindulged the night before and awoke with a headache. After he left Emilie at the hospital, he was feeling sorry for himself, and a bit afraid, as well. Robert had no idea how to hold all the balls in the air without dropping one. When he returned to the hotel, he told Rachael about Jeremy being in the hospital, and she appeared upset. Realizing there was nothing that they could do so late at night, they consoled each other instead. It turned into a late night with a few too many drinks. Then Rachael wanted plenty of sex. He worried about her becoming so demanding of his attention. He might not be able to keep up his stamina for her demand.

Rachael had whispered into his ear, "This should be our time. Forget the family, if just for the night."

She didn't have to tell Robert twice. In the remaining hours of the night and early morning, he only had eyes for Rachael. After little sleep, the last thing he wanted was to have the hotel ring up a reminder call.

"Did you ask for a wake-up call, Rachael?"

She didn't answer.

Robert sat up on the edge of the bed rubbing his face, slipped on his house shoes, and went to pick up the phone. "This better be important."

"Well, it depends on whether you consider your sister's life important." A deep voice vibrated across the telephone line.

"Who's this?" He said, his attention provoked.

"The relevant question is *what do I want*."

"Is this a sick joke?" Robert felt sick to his stomach.

"Listen to me," an angry voice on the other end of the line bellowed. "You have exactly half an hour to do as I say, or else your dear Emilie will be dead. Do you understand? Yes or no."

"Yes. What do you want?"

"I want something easy, my friend. I want you to send me a wire transfer, one hundred thousand dollars. You got that? Not a million, like I really wish I could ask for. I only want a hundred grand, quick and easy. You make that happen in half an hour and your sister will be released and left in the middle of the Square at Grand Place. You'll be able to get her in two hours, tops."

"What game are you playing?"

"No game. Got a pen?"

"Yes." Robert felt the blood rush to his head and clumsily fumbled on the desk looking for a pen. "Got one."

"Write this down exactly as I say, got it?"

"Shoot." Robert immediately wished he hadn't said that.

"You will be calling Salzburg after you make arrangements with your American bank about a transfer. Call this number exactly, the international code 011 then country code 43, then 662, 5555. When they pick up you say that you wish to use SWIFT. They will connect you to a banker. Give him this Ueberbringer Sparbuch number: 282 dot 778 dot 646 and code KLAUSEL 055. Then Mr. de Gourgues you instruct them to transfer one hundred thousand dollars into the account. Give them your American bank account number. Of course, this is after telling your bank of your intentions so it will go through immediately. Tell the banker to transfer that sum into the Sparbuch account and then for them to convert the funds into shillings. That's it. When you are finished with the transaction, go to your hotel window and open the drapes."

Robert had written it all down but was confused about the instructions. It all appeared to be too simple, too easy. He had been under the impression that Sparbuch accounts were no longer being used.

"How will this be done? I thought they stopped using these types of accounts?"

"They certainly control new accounts, but there's no way to simply make the old accounts disappear, now can they. So mind your own business, kid, and do as you're told. No more, no less. And Mr. de Gourgues, you know not to go to the police, I'm sure there's no need to discuss that. You know what will happen if you do."

He hung up, leaving Robert with a dial tone buzzing in his ear. His headache pounded, and the more he tried to make sense of this, the more confused he became. How did he even know they had Emilie, after all? He snatched up his cell and dialed her number. A man answered.

"Ah, checking I see Mr. de Gourgues. For your benefit, know that this phone will be destroyed as soon as I hang up. Now do as you were told, Mr. de Gourgues, and no more games."

That convinced Robert that Emilie was indeed in harm's way. He dialed Michelle and woke her.

"Robert, what the hell is going on?"

"Michelle, we've got a problem. A serious problem. Some-one kidnapped Emilie, oh and Jeremy is in the hospital."

"No! Rob, this isn't funny."

"You're right, it's not. First things first. I have less than thirty minutes to pay a ransom for Emilie, and I need your help."

Robert explained about the call and restated the easy instructions.

"How do I know you're not tricking me?"

"Chelle, I understand you don't trust me, yet. But we have no time for reassurances now. I have thirty minutes to do this. All they want is a hundred grand, and I say let's give it to them. If need be, I'll sign the deed to the house over to you to cover for it."

"Okay, okay. I get the point. I don't understand, but we have to do this, it's not worth taking a chance with Emilie's life. Grab a pen, here's an account number."

Michelle gave Robert an account number that he could use for the funds, and he promised to call her back as soon as Emilie was safe and sound. Checking the clock, he realized he only had fifteen minutes left. Robert immediately placed the call to the bank, hoping all would go smoothly without any language barriers to waste time. He did exactly as instructed, and with five minutes to spare, the deed was completed.

Robert hung up the receiver and wiped his sweaty palm against his boxer shorts. He walked over to the wall of windows and pulled the drapes open wide.

Rachael protested. "Robert please, I need more sleep. Close the drapes."

Now, it was time to explain it all to Rachael. He walked to her bedside and snuggled near to her. He could still smell her perfume from the night before. She wore an expensive fragrance that had been bottled especially for her, and it suited her well. He cupped her face in his hands and gently kissed her forehead. She opened her eyes. He told her about the kidnapping.

CHAPTER 19

Chains And Darkness

Emilie woke up and opened her eyes. Darkness. A pounding headache. Reaching up, she tried to rub her temples but realized her reach was limited by chains around her wrists and ankles. *What the hell.* Opening her eyes wider, she looked around in the dark, trying to make out shapes in the shadows. She hoped to shed some light on where she was or how she even got there. She drew in a breath and started choking. A horrid reek accosted her sense of smell. It was the odor of death itself. The chain that bound her was attached to a wall. She put her hands out and felt old brick or stone. It crumbled at her touch. She wrapped the chain once around her hand and yanked it away from the wall's plate flange, attempting to pry it loose. The iron holding pin held tight.

She rolled to her side and realized there was enough chain length between her hands and ankles for leeway to stand, but she had no choice but to keep her hands close to the wall, with the little length between them. Her back ached as she stretched erect, her head still throbbed. The small room felt damp, and water dripped on her head from a leak in the ceiling. The only hint of light came from a sliver under a small door. *This must be a closet of some type,* she thought. "How did I get in here," she mumbled aloud.

Emilie tried to remember what happened, and her head pounded more with each stressful thought. She remembered the hospital. Jeremy was there, all alone. Panicked now, she had to find a way out, to get back to him. Her concentration broke when a noise sounded from the other side of the door.

Emilie felt her heart palpitating, small quick beats hitting against her chest. *Should I cry out and try to get free?*

"Help me. I'm in here."

She rattled the chain and made as much noise as she could muster. No one came to open the door. Drawing in a breath, she exhaled, then sat back down on the filthy floor and listened. Her arms raised over her head, unable to move them away from the holding pin. Powerless, she hated not being in control of her own movements.

A few minutes went by and she heard two male voices. One sounded oddly familiar. Emilie tried to remember who it was, but couldn't draw the connection. Then her thoughts of Jeremy flooded. He was in the hospital and she had been at his bedside, waiting for him to wake. The grumpy nurse asked her to leave, instructing Emilie to come back during visiting hours. *That's right, I was going for coffee.* The restaurant at Sainte-Elisabeth hospital was closed. She had gone to the elevator bank in the pursuit of coffee. *Coffee, what I'd do for a cup of strong hot coffee right now.* She bounced her head back against the brick. "Ouch!"

More noises and chains—no keys, rattling. The small door opened.

Emilie protected her eyes as the light blinded her for a second. A tall figure stood in the doorway, then ducked into the cramped space. In a split second, he covered her head with a bag of some sort. It felt rough against her skin and smelled like puke.

"Hey, who are you? Where am I?"

"All things in good time, Miss de Gourgues."

That voice, where did I hear it before?

Someone yanked her to her feet and unlocked the chain from the wall. Unfortunately, the chain between her wrists and ankles was still locked together.

"Follow me."

She was shoved a step forward, her head felt a blow.

"My bad. Please, duck your head, Miss." The voice laughed and was joined by a second person who was laughing as well. *Glad I can make someone's day.*

She stepped out of the small broom closet, or whatever it was, onto a cement floor she presumed based on the feel of it against the bottom of her shoes. Emilie tried to look down to notice anything that might help her identify where she was, but the bag over her head was too snug and left no open areas to peek out. The space around her felt old. She could hear drips of water coming from above, slowly rolling down the walls to either side of her. She reasoned it was a long hallway of sorts, based on reverberations, but at the same time, it felt underground. The echoes muffled. Dampness from the surface below her feet sent chills up her spine. Emilie heard a rattling sound, then realized it was her own teeth, shivering.

One of her captors pushed her again and nudged her down the hall. She carefully stepped, sliding her feet forward to feel in front of her so she wouldn't trip.

"No worries, Miss. We won't let you fall." More laughs on her behalf. Then she received a punch to the side of her head. She stumbled to the floor. "Here, let me help you up."

"Funny," she said. Pulled back to her feet, they poked her in the back.

"Just keep walking."

Emilie felt warmth on the top of her head—then it was gone. It happened again, a brief moment of warmth, then cold. It was like when passing by a sunny window, except this warm spot came from above. This place piqued her curiosity. *Windows above?* In a last attempt to understand where she was, Emilie decided to open up her clairvoyance and feel the emotions of everyone around her. It was all she had left at her disposal. Yet, there was a chance of unforgiving consequences. She would feel the emotions of these two lowlifes, but it was her only option. Emilie took the chance and let the outside emotive wave into her world.

A sudden assault made her buckle over. She held her stomach as a severe pain flowed through her being. A rush of spirits soared through her, overpowering her telepathic channel of empathy. Tears rolled down her face as it all tumbled into her head. Fear, the worst of all emotions, dominated the sensual assault.

"What the hell is the matter with you, Missy?"

A hand grabbed her, snatching the hood up just a bit, along with some of her hair, and pulled her straight up again.

"Let's take her to the Doctor."

She was turned around in the opposite direction. Nausea filled her as if seasick, the various feelings swaying back and forth. The amount of emotion that lingered in the area around her, drained all her energy. A realization struck like lightning, and then she knew where she was—near a graveyard. More probable still, an underground crypt. It explained it all—the dampness, the drips, the volatility of the haunting dead.

Emilie remembered what she had read about the closed crypts in Brussels, that they were long spans of burial crypts, once open to the public. They had been neglected for decades and forced to close. *Could this be the lost crypts?*

More jingling of keys sounded, this time a door opened in front of her, squeaking loudly as if moaning with pain. One more push and she was dumped onto a stool of some type.

"What did you bring her here for? You dopes!" A new voice. It sounded strong and in command, with a French accent.

"We were walking her out when she kinda had a fit of sorts." This was said by the second voice she had heard before.

He had only been laughing before, clearly not a bright individual, but rather childish by the sound of his voice.

"Yes, we thought you might think it interesting." The other voice surmised. "You know, maybe test her or whatnot. This paranormal stuff is right up your alley, is it not?" This was the one she recognized from before if she could only remember where she knew that voice from.

"You two, get out. I don't want her to see your faces. When I'm finished with her I'll call for you to get her again."

She heard the door close then the hood was pulled off of her. She breathed immediate relief and took a gulp of air. The temperature in the room was regulated, with no smell of rot or death, and the atmosphere was steady and less humid. In front of her stood a masked man, wearing the signature black robe and a plain white rubber face. *A member of The Black Wolf Society.*

Fleeting images of the recent meet-up she encountered with the group, then the image of Tom Bennett turned into a wolf monster, flooded her thoughts. A wave of fear engulfed Emilie. Memories of the horrid emotions that spilled from Tom Bennett—that she had felt—sickened her. The things he had done, felt, and seen as a beast—she had endured them all. Now she was face to face with another member of that abominable group. She wondered what secrets of hatred he held below the surface. She refused to open up and feel anything oozing from this crazed man.

The masked doctor raised his hand and slapped her across the face. Something sharp stung her cheek. Drops of blood dripped down her face. Emilie feared for her life. *Will they kill me—inspect me like a lab rat? They had called him Doc and said he liked paranormal stuff? Does that mean me? What does this group want with me?*

"Miss de Gourgues, please forgive me. But the scientist in me likes to experiment and note down people's reactions to pain. Sorry if my ring's setting cut you too deep. You are a marvelous subject. Oh, and I beg your forgiveness for my associates and the barbaric accommodations. I assure you, your stay with us will be brief. The others, they are stupid, non? But, unfortunately, we are a large group, and we need all kinds of members willing to do all kinds of things. On the other hand, there are those like myself. I am one of the more talented, and I'm on a quest, you might say. You see, I enjoy the science of the paranormal. I want nothing more than to test your responses. You are a wonderful specimen, I saw what you are capable of from a videotape from the Abbey. Will you tell me more about your gift? "

Emilie couldn't help her curiosity.

"No. I won't." She leered. "Just what exactly are you doing here? Why am I here, and what exactly is your *quest*?"

"The cat is curious I see," he said. "Miss de Gourgues, I know you are aware of our Society. Lucky for you, we don't feel threatened by this. On the contrary, we find you very interesting. As a matter of fact, your entire family has been of interest to us for many years now."

Emilie twitched involuntarily, having found a new level of discomfort.

"I see you have many questions, as do we. For example, I wonder about the level of your clairvoyance. Your mother had talents, non? I witnessed her, many years ago. But you, my dear, well you leave us spell-bound."

Emilie sat on the stool, looked around the room, and avoided his stare. Dark eyes peered straight through her from the slits of the rubber mask. Uncomfortable being here with this demented doctor, to say the least, her cheek burned. The blood was rushing to the bruise, making it swell. She wiped her brow with the back of her hand.

"You know nothing," she said.

Immediately, she bit her tongue.

"I know much more than you, my dear. I told the others that Tom Bennett is dead, but they didn't believe me. My theory is that you were the end of him. After witnessing the tapes of you doing your thing, well . . ."

Emilie couldn't suppress her smile at his words.

"Ah, you are talented beyond the Black Wolves' comprehension. But, it doesn't matter. Lucky for you, you're off-limits to my experiments. For now, anyway."

"What experiments?"

"Voila!" he said, as he pulled back a curtain, revealing a glass panel separation. On the other side were bodies, lying on tables, connected to all kinds of machines.

"I am gathering data on special people, some like you. You see, they are connected to my machines. I send impulses and then track the reactions."

Emilie got off the stool and hazarded a closer look. The bodies on the other side were laid on gurneys and in a vegetative state. She wondered what exactly she was witnessing, knowing there was more to this story, and didn't want to hear the ending. The exposed parts: faces, arms, legs, and such, looked bruised. Their skin was covered with contusions and burnt marks. The heads had been shaved and odd configured metal probes stuck out of their skulls. *Are they corpses or alive? People? Or creatures, like the one I tried to help?*

"You tortured them?"

"No. I experimented with them, very different."

Emilie felt sick. "Are they dead?"

She reached out, trying to tap into their emotions, but the glass partition somehow blocked her attempts. The masked man drew closer and now stood a few feet away. She sensed his sick amusement.

A phone rang. The man pulled a cell from his pocket, nodded, and then placed it back into his pocket.

"Too bad, time for you to go. I was enjoying our time together, too. I see you have so many questions."

The smelly hood once again was flung over her head. The door creaked open and hands wrapped around her arms. She was led out of the room. Pushed forward and pulled ahead, the other two creeps never spoke to her again, if they were even the same accomplices. Paraded down the hallway, or whatever horrible place this was, she walked for a long time. Then they stopped. She kicked her foot forward and it hit solid. Raising her foot, she noticed she stood in front of the stairs. Raising her right foot she climbed carefully with each step. Pushed from behind she stumbled and hit her shin against the hard cement stair tread. *Bully!* "Okay, I'll go a little faster," she called out. She stood up quickly and hurried the rest of the way up.

After twenty or so steps, Emilie felt as if she was above ground. The air smelled fresher as a breeze crossed her face and managed to penetrate the hood's material a bit. A cool mist touched the skin on her hands. She heard slight drops hitting the cloth over her head. *Rain.* They walked some more in silence. Her shoes soaked up the wet grass. She tripped over a stone of some sort and immediately was pulled up by the chains between her wrists.

She heard the swooshing sound of cars in the distance. Someone grabbed the top of her head and pushed her down, into a seat of a car. The door closed and the car immediately pulled forward. Emilie bent her head down and tried to pull the bag away from her head. From her left side, she was whacked in the head. A bright light filled her vision, despite closed eyes. "Okay, the hood stays on," she yelled in response.

They drove for a long time, maybe close to an hour, she couldn't be sure, she had lost all sense of time and direction.

Every once in a while she heard other cars blaring horns, or revving away from a stoplight, or sign. Too much time was spent in her own thoughts. She worried about Jeremy and wanted to be at his side. Every fiber of her being yearned to see him again, to make sure he was safe and smiling.

She realized nothing of this incident made any sense. Why abduct her, shove her in a cellar of some sort, expose her to their evil mastermind experimentations, warn her about them watching her family—only to drive her away and presumably let her go? If the Black Wolf Society's sole intention was to instill fear, well then, job well done.

The car came to a halt. The shackles around her wrists were unlocked. Emilie felt the weight lift from her arms. The door opened, and she was pulled out by her arm. She heard the car drive away. Led by the arm, they walked fast. A minute later, the hood was pulled off.

The sunlight blinded her. Emilie raised her hands and covered her eyes. After a moment, her eyes adjusted to the sunlight. She looked around, turning in all directions, searching for the person who had just set her free. There were dozens of people walking about, all going in various directions minding their own business. Emilie had no clue which person was the one responsible for leading her here. She didn't care either. She was free.

Happy that she was let go with only a few bruises to show for wear, she decided to contact Robert right away for help. She rummaged through her pockets, no phone. "Dammit." She reached out to a person milling about.

"*Excuse moi. Puis-je emprunter votre téléphone cellulaire un moment?*" Emilie asked. "May I use your cell phone?" she said again in English.

A young woman, maybe mid-twenties, dressed in a camel-hair coat and scarf around her head, turned around and looked at her sympathetically. "Is it local?"

"Yes, I need to call the Hotel Metropole."

"Yes, here I have it on speed dial. I work there. Small world." The woman giggled.

"Indeed." Emilie smiled back. Placing the call, she asked the desk to connect her to Robert's room.

"Emilie! Where are you? Are you all right?" His voice sounded strained from worry.

"Yes, Rob, I'm okay. Please, come get me right away." She leaned toward the woman and asked her, "Where are we?"

"We're in front of Starbucks in the Grand Market Square of course," the woman replied.

Emilie looked up and noticed the sign, *thank you!* "Of course."

"Rob, meet me in Starbucks at Grand Market Square."

"Stay put. I'll be there in five minutes." Her brother sounded in command, protective even. Her heart melted with a glint of Robert's younger, more caring days.

"Thank you," Emilie said as she handed the phone back to the woman. "What's your name, Miss, so I can thank you properly with a few Euros later on?"

"Not necessary. I was already paid." The woman said smiling while looking over her shoulder as she briskly walked away.

Curious. Emilie wasn't going to follow. Instead, she walked into the coffee shop and got in the long line for morning coffee. It would probably take more than five minutes to get to the counter's front, judging by the crowd. A few people stared at her, rolling their eyes up and down, as they waited their turn. She took inventory of herself and realized she still had the scrubs on, but they were dirty beyond acceptance, and she sported a bruised face and must have looked as if she had been in a fight. *Oh well, nothing a good cup of coffee can't cure.*

CHAPTER 20

No Secrets Please

Emilie reached the counter just as Robert wormed his way through the line.

"I'm with her," he said. He squeezed himself between Emilie and the customer next in line, held her close, and hugged her tight. "Thank God! Em, I'm so happy you're okay."

"Hey, if this is a family reunion, get to the end of the line so others can get served," some unruly customer blurted.

She broke the embrace, turned to the attendant, and placed an order, "two Grande black coffee, please. And add a blueberry muffin, too."

Robert paid for the coffee and followed Emilie to a table. "What the hell happened to you, Em?"

She looked across the table and noticed that his face looked pasty. She wondered how long it had been since he slept.

"I really don't know. I was in the hospital and fell asleep. Then the morning nurse kicked me out of Jeremy's room, so I went hunting for a coffee machine. Then some brute grabbed me from behind."

"Who was it, Em? Did you get a good look?"

She shook her head. "No. They put a hood over my head. I'm positive that it was the Black Wolf behind it all."

"How do you know?"

"One of them told me. Robert, what did you get yourself into? You promised all kinds of things, but you were with them yesterday. And now, Jeremy is lying in the hospital, and those goons scared the shit out of me."

Robert took a sip of coffee. "It's not what you think. They hooded me as well, remember."

She nodded and remembered she had felt a threat against him.

"Okay. How about you tell me what's going on then? The truth."

"Em, does anyone really know the truth anymore?"

She let out a heavy sigh and shook her head. Patience spent she didn't care about her brother's hurt feelings anymore. His jokes couldn't change the fact that too much had happened already. She glared at him, her face scowled.

"Okay, okay. Here's the truth. Early this morning I received a call. A man said you were kidnapped, and that they'd release you if we gave them a hundred grand in half an hour. Right away I called Michelle. We did what we were instructed, and they let you go an hour and a half later as agreed. That's God's honest truth. Maybe you should give a statement to the police."

"You called the police?"

"No, of course not. They said for me not to contact the police if we wanted you back."

"Then I'm not calling them to give a statement."

Emilie pulled a piece of the muffin and offered it to Robert.

He waved his hand. "No, thanks. I've totally lost my appetite."

"Well, I'm hungry." She ate a bite and swallowed. "I'm going to the hotel to take a quick shower, then I'm heading back to the hospital."

"You have a blueberry stuck, there, on your front tooth," he said, tapping his own. Robert leaned back in the chair and played with the plastic top on his coffee cup.

"What?" Emilie said.

"Maybe you should have a doctor look at you while you're there as well. You look like hell, Em."

"Thanks." Emilie touched her face. The bruise smarted. "I'll hold off, just a bit. If I can get Jeremy released and back home right away, then I'd rather see our own Doc."

Robert nodded. "Rachael and I have the jet here. You can use it to go home, and we'll fly like the regular people."

"Thanks, that's big of you." Emilie smiled, then stood. "Let's go. I want to see Jeremy as soon as possible."

"Word of advice, take a shower first. I'm just saying . . ."

Emilie looked at herself. "Point taken."

Emilie returned to the hotel with her brother and cleaned up. Then, she went straight to the hospital. It was midafternoon and visiting hours for the intensive care unit had just opened. When she went to the nurse's desk, they told her Jeremy had been moved into a secured room an hour ago. She asked why and they said it was standard procedure, *maybe it was because he was shot?* It didn't matter, he was safe and healing, and she wasn't about to waste any more time. She jogged to his new room, almost running.

A man stood, just outside his room, as if on guard. She nodded at him. He smiled back at her, then turned and walked a few steps away. A slight ping of nervousness fleeted through her. Everything caused her to be suspicious at this point. She wondered if she'd ever trust anyone again.

Emilie flung open the door and saw Jeremy, awake and looking better. The bed was raised up so that he faced her. She was drawn to his smile. His hazel eyes sparkled as the sunlight beamed in from the window.

"There you are. I was worried about you," he said. His smile was infectious. "The nurse rang your phone but no one answered. She said you were here all night but didn't know where you went off to."

"Forget about me, look at you. You look so much better, and have color back in your cheeks."

He stared at her, his eyes pinched.

"What's the matter?" Emilie knew he was worried.

"What happened to you?" he said. "Did you get hurt last night at the shooting, too?"

"No." She hung her head and stared at her hands. "We brought you here, me and that man who helped us, Jeffrey Sloan."

"How did you get that shiner, then?"

"These bruises are from something else, entirely."

The room was quiet. She knew she couldn't lie to him, but she didn't want him to worry either. *Should I keep it a secret?*

"Well, I'm waiting, Emilie. Tell me the entire story. What happened? Where were you?"

"Nothing that can't wait until you're better," she said.

"Remember what happens when secrets are kept, Emilie."

She looked into his eyes and knew she had to tell him. Their entire relationship had been built on trust, and together they had revealed hidden secrets to heal her family. She wasn't going to start new ones.

"You're right. Let me tell you, but promise you won't be upset."

"I think I'm more upset as I sit here and worry about what I don't know."

Emilie smiled at him. "Of course." She explained what happened, leaving out some of the gory details. Instead of describing her fears, she focused the story on how Robert and Michelle paid off the kidnappers, and she was let go right away as promised.

Jeremy listened to her without interrupting. After a moment of digesting the story, he snapped. "That's it—" He reached for the phone. "Let's go back to Memphis right away. At least at the house you'd be surrounded by people you can trust. Okay, maybe not entirely, but at least there you have security."

"Oh, I can hear Nina now. Making a big deal about all this stuff."

Jeremy looked up at her, alarm in his expression. "It is a big deal, Em. You could've been killed. I think we've been taking things too lightly. Better yet, we'll go to my hometown in Surrey. No one will find us there." He moved and winced.

"Should I call for a nurse?"

"No. I don't know."

He was upset. Emilie remained quiet. She held his hand and felt his grip on hers tighten. He turned and faced her, reaching to touch her long brown strand of hair that had covered her eyes. He pulled it back behind her ear. Sighing, he spoke.

"Everything is messed up. In my head," he tapped his forehead. "Obviously, something else we don't understand is still happening. I hoped that after I killed the beast—"

"You mean after we killed Tom Bennett," she said.

"Don't worry, I won't get all depressed. I know we all tried to kill him, but it was me who did the deed. I'm responsible for my actions."

Emilie opened her mouth, ready to console him.

"I know, Em. He was a monster and would have killed us all, I get it. But let's keep things in perspective. I raised the blade and killed him. I cut a man's head off, Emilie. I never thought I'd ever been one to do such violence. I'm no hero."

"Well, you're valiant in my book." She kissed the top of his head. "Jeremy, you saved me, in more ways than you'll ever know."

"I don't feel that way. Seems like since I stepped into your life everything turned lopsided. The danger keeps shadowing us, wherever we go. When will it let up? I want to marry you, so much, but I'm afraid that if I do, I'll end up giving you more bad luck."

"That's nonsense. It's because of you that I can survive all this stuff. You understand how this clairvoyant gift tears me up inside. You saw what kind of things I'm capable of but I will not think of myself as a killer. What happened was justice. The thing you may not realize is that when you touch me, I can find my way back to balance. Jeremy, you save me every day." Emilie wiped the tears that stung the corners of her eyes with the back of her hand.

"Okay, Em. No worries. You're stuck with me, no matter what. I couldn't stay away from you even if I was dragged. I'll always gravitate back to your side. I love you, Emilie de Gourgues."

She leaned forward and kissed him. The warmth of his body, the goodness of his spirit, filled her with deep satisfaction. The turmoil of the morning was all forgotten. All she wanted now was to go home with her love. Opening her eyes, she met his gaze.

"Are we okay?" she asked.

"Yes, we are in heaven right now."

Shaking her head, she affectionately punched his shoulder.

"Ouch," he said, smiling.

"Okay, let's go home then. Robert said we can take the jet back as soon as the hospital releases you."

"All set in that regard. I've already asked for them to get the release paperwork started. The nurse keeps popping her head into the room like a big shadow I can't get rid of. Checking on me a little too much."

"Speaking of shadows, did you notice a man hanging around the entrance of your room? Did the hospital call the police about the shooting?"

"I only woke an hour ago, Em. I saw the doctor briefly and my French isn't that good. Seriously, I was more worried about finding you . . . and getting fed. I was so hungry."

"Too bad Nina isn't with us." She giggled. "You want me to get you something to eat?"

"Emilie, they have great food in this hospital. I ate lunch and I'm stuffed."

She crinkled her brows.

"Really," he said. "I'm not kidding. A nurse told me they won some kind of award for the best food. They're totally into eating healthy."

"Well, it's about time. See, not everything is bad around us." She smiled and hoped they could stay away from any further talk of Tom Bennett's death, or the Black Wolf Society. She was sickened by it all.

"When the doctor comes in, we'll say we're taking you home. Unless you want to stay here for the food?"

They laughed, and Jeremy winced from the pain in his gut. The door swung open as Robert stepped into the room.

"Well, well. You're looking better. Jeremy, I hear you've been playing heroics again."

"Hello, Robert." Jeremy sounded cool as a cucumber. Emilie admired the way he handled himself, always a gentleman, well, almost always.

"Seriously, old sport, I want to thank you for taking one for my sister, again."

"It wasn't like that at all. I was surprised and didn't duck quickly enough. Your sister is faster than me." Jeremy chuckled and winced again, taking hold of his middle.

"Robert, who were those people shooting at us anyway?" she said.

"How should I know? I was taken by two goons and brought down to some secret room with a hood over my head. They said Tom had recommended me to the group, and would I join them, however . . ."

"You won't, will you?"

"Of course not. But things aren't that easy, Emilie. Not with these people. I don't want them to kill me. I might be a bit, what's the word, eccentric, but I'm not stupid."

"Who can we trust? We need to go to the police or someone," Jeremy said.

"Let's not panic just yet," Robert said. "We'll see how things play out. Maybe, now that Tom's not around, they'll forget about us all."

"Humph. I'm not counting on it," Emilie said. "I really didn't appreciate being taken this morning, either. You have no idea how crazy these people are. They're experimenting with telepaths like me, and dead people, too."

She shivered at the thought. Then she looked over at Jeremy, hoping he didn't see her get distressed.

"So, I suppose you told Jeremy all about your morning experience," Robert said.

"Hell yes, of course, I did. I don't keep secrets." Emilie wanted her brother to stop talking. He always made everything feel worse. There was a dark shadow following her brother, and no matter how much she implored him, he never confided in her with the complete truth. She knew it—she felt it.

"Well, let's not get dramatic," Robert said. "You're safe now, that's what counts."

"Thank you, Robert," Jeremy said. "Thanks to your quick action, and of course Michelle for paying the ransom so quickly, Emilie got out of there safe."

"No thanks needed, old sport. I'd do anything for my sisters. I've never wanted Emilie hurt. Now, let's concentrate on important things first. Let's get you released and on the jet homebound. Rachael mentioned she wants to go back with you two if that's okay?"

"Robert, we don't want to spoil your trip," Emilie said.

"Nonsense. The Black Wolf spoiled it, not you. When you

return to Memphis, order up extra security around the house. We'll wait things out. You'll see, everything will work out."

"And what are you planning on doing, Robert?" Jeremy asked.

"I'll be going home as well. But first, I need to make a stop in Boston."

"Why? What are you up to?"

"Emilie, I'm hurt." Robert held his hands to his heart. "Jackson called and asked me to stop by. I figure he must need someone to talk to. Even though it's a blessing his father's dead, I'm sure he's having just as hard a time getting over the whole episode as we are. Maybe more so because he has no one to talk with, so maybe I can help."

"Good. Please give him our best," Jeremy said.

"Maybe you can drag him down to Memphis for a visit." Emilie liked Jackson and was thankful to him for helping Michelle out when she needed a friend.

Robert smiled, kissed her head, then tapped Jeremy lightly on the shoulder. "Get better old sport." Then he turned and left the room.

"Curiouser, and curiouser." Emilie's gaze followed her brother out.

"Yes, I couldn't agree more," Jeremy said.

CHAPTER 21

Make Your Next Move

Robert left Jeremy's room and walked down the hallway to catch the elevator. A hand from behind grabbed his elbow. Robert precipitously turned, ready to slug whoever it was—Sloan. "Where have you been?" he tempered. "There are things we need to discuss."

"Not here, it's too open." The Agent spoke while looking straight ahead as if waiting for the lift with a complete stranger.

"Maybe it's better in the open. Then, we can determine if anyone is eavesdropping."

"No. Set-ups, not my style."

"Since when?" Robert scoffed.

"Take the lift to the third floor. Get off and go right. There's a room marked private lounge. I'll meet you there."

Agent Sloan left and took the stairs. Robert did as told: found the room, knocked, then entered.

Sloan wasted no time. "Robert, tell us, in detail, what happened when you went below at the Abbey."

Robert looked around the room, pale walls, a few pieces of modern poster art on the walls, nothing impressive. The table was modern, matching all the other rooms in the renovated facility. Only Agent Sloan was in the room, and a recording device was centered on the table. Robert grabbed the white chair across from Sloan and sat down, shifting his weight to get comfortable as he began recalling his side of the tale.

"Well, first off, I was surprised as hell when they placed a bag, or hood of some sort, over my head. It smelled disgusting, and I couldn't see a thing. I thought I was going to vomit."

Sloan nodded. "It was done on purpose, first to disorient

you and second to instigate repulsion."

"Worked like a charm. I had no idea where they took me, and I was definitely repulsed. You say it was the Abbey?"

Sloan nodded. "Okay, enough of your rants, tell me something relevant. We know where they took you. The car was followed. As you know, your sister followed you as well."

"Yes, thank you for helping her. I am very grateful. She could have been killed. This is more than I bargained for if you don't mind me saying. You promised my family would be safe."

"We couldn't have possibly anticipated your sister getting involved." Sloan's face reddened.

"Okay. So, they brought me downstairs to a lower basement level."

The Agent nodded his head. "Yes, continue."

"I was given a black robe to put on and a mask, except they gave me a pig face. I didn't like that much, worried like hell about the meaning of it. Anyway, then I was led into a room. It was stonewalled and not very large—maybe thirty, forty feet across tops. I expected a great hall of some sort, I must say I was rather disappointed. I don't think this was the headquarters."

"Yes, well, not every secret society meets in palaces, Robert. The group in Massachusetts met in an old obscure house in the woods. But I agree with your assumption, you weren't taken to the main headquarters. It sounds too small and was also too local. That area has too many tourists during normal hours."

Robert cleared his throat and continued. "The room had an altar in the middle, like a place they might perform ceremonies. There were symbols on the side panels but it wasn't anything I've ever seen in a church."

"Well, that's something to think about. Robert, you need to play along with them. Build up more trust and get invited to a ceremony. That's our best shot to get into the headquarters.

Can you draw the symbols?"

"No." He shook his head. "I can't remember the shapes exactly. But I agree, being at one of their ceremonies might be insightful. For now, we have to settle for what they did instruct me. They want me to do a Beneficial Act. The Society calls favors for another member an Act, and each member is obliged to perform the one assigned, using any means possible. The secret assignment I'm bequeathed—to prove myself worthy to be a member of the Society—I have to kill Jackson Bennett."

"Do you think that they believe Jackson is responsible for the disappearance of his father, Tom Bennett?"

"No, I don't. Emilie had a little chat with a crazed doctor Frankenstein sort, this morning while she was held captive. He eluded to the belief that she had killed Tom Bennett."

"What's this?"

"My sister was kidnapped."

"Fill me in. Tell me exactly, what happened. What did she share with you about her ordeal?"

Robert stood up and paced the room. Moving helped to straighten out his thoughts, but he still couldn't make sense of everything that had happened in the past twenty-four hours. Running his hands through his thick curls, he calmed down and tried to remember the important things. Clues that might unravel this quandary.

"Emilie was kidnapped, from this very hospital, early this morning."

"And why didn't you call me?"

"They said not to call anyone, or else. I wasn't going to take the chance."

Robert ignored Sloan and rolled out the story. "She was hooded, like I was, and taken to a place, she presumed underground. She couldn't positively determine the location, sorry. As I said, some crazy dude, who claimed to be a doctor, spoke to her. He talked about experiments."

"Where were you?"

"I was at the hotel. Early this morning I received a call asking for the ransom. We only had half an hour to complete the transaction, otherwise Emilie . . . her life was in danger. So, of course, we did pay."

"We? Robert, who's we? Did you get someone else involved?" Sloan yanked on Robert's arm. He stopped pacing and sat back down.

"I called my sister, Michelle. There was no choice. I had to tell her about the kidnapping. She agreed with me that we had to pay and she gave me the account information to use. Then I transferred the funds as instructed. The kidnappers let Emilie go, safe but bruised."

Sloan sat quietly for a few minutes, his face tense. Clearly, he was working the information through his own agenda, trying to make sense of things. Robert waited for the barrage of questions, which surely would be onslaught any moment.

"When did this happen?" Sloan asked.

"Early this morning. It happened fast. The entire episode took two and a half hours, tops."

"And how much did you tell your sisters?"

"Nothing. They both already know about the Black Wolf Society. The tactics they used didn't surprise either of them."

"And our secret?"

"I wouldn't compromise our situation. You made it clear that I couldn't tell a soul, so I didn't. The only thing that was weird about this kidnapping deal was the time constraint, and the amount of money."

Agent Sloan looked up. "Yes, and they were . . ."

"I had to make the deal within a half-hour, and it was only a hundred grand. Odd number, why so cheap?"

Agent Sloan stood up and paced. He stopped in his tracks,

stared at the wall while working things out in his head. Turning around, he slapped his hands together and sat back down across from Robert.

"Here's what we're going to do. Number one, I'm increasing surveillance to cover your sisters. Number two, you will go ahead with the job they assigned. Act as if you are willing to kill Jackson Bennett to gain entry into the Society. They'll pick up on our involvement if you hesitate, understand?"

Robert nodded.

"Another agent will contact Jackson ahead of time, and we'll set things up, like in a sting operation."

"I thought you didn't like that sort of thing? Okay, so like I walk in as if nothing is wrong. I'll say hi Jackson, and he'll anticipate everything is okay, and then I shoot my friend. But in reality, what? My bullets won't shoot?"

"Yes, that's it exactly," Sloan confirmed. "Use the gun they give to you, and shoot your friend. We'll make sure the logistics of it all appear true. We'll even announce his death in the press. Yes." Agent Sloan slapped the table. "We'll use the press to legitimize your position. Then they'll have complete faith in you and reveal themselves fully, I hope."

"What about Jackson?" Robert wondered if he was the only one in the room who hadn't lost touch with reality. "If I use a gun and shoot, Jackson will be hurt."

"Don't worry about Jackson, he'll be fine. The Marshall Services will escort him to a temporary safe house until all this business is completed. No worries there." Quiet again, thinking, Agent Sloan snapped his fingers. "Tell me more about the ransom payment."

"Well, first I called my sister for an account number that I could use to make the transfer. Then I called the number they gave me, for a bank in Austria, and gave them the information. It was a very old Sparbuch account."

"Of course. The old accounts aren't subject to modern scrutiny. I told you this group has been around for centuries, morphing itself under many identities. Today the Black Wolf, who knows what they'll call themselves tomorrow. This money transfer is going to be hard to track, but I need the information you have."

Robert took out his phone and scrolled through. "Here, the numbers are listed here in my notes."

Agent Sloan took Robert's device and jotted down the information, folded the notepaper, and slipped it into his inner jacket pocket. He patted his chest. "No worry. Your secrets are safe with me. Now, please call Jackson, and use this phone."

"What if he's bugged?" Robert was nervous about how this plan would play out.

"Here, use this line. " Agent Sloan tossed a nondescript simple phone onto the table. "It will alleviate any issues of call traps if there are any."

He picked up the phone and called Jackson's cell. Robert told him what was going on, asked that he not tell anyone, especially Michelle, for safety's sake. Then together, they discussed the plan. Half an hour later, he walked out of the room and back into the elevator.

Robert stopped by Jeremy's room, said goodbye to his sister and Jeremy. Deep down Robert was a gregarious individual, so playing this lone-ranger, working undercover on his own, went against his nature. He thought he sensed his sister's suspicions, but she never said a word. They agreed to meet in Memphis.

Once he reached the hotel, Robert gathered his things and said goodbye to Rachael. She sat alone, downstairs in the salon, reading in the elaborate room. She looked perfect in the setting, a room filled with deep colors and glittering walls. She was his princess and deserved to be in a castle.

Robert touched her face. She reached up and kissed him goodbye. Her lips were warm, inviting. For a moment, he wanted to drop all plans, abandon them and take her upstairs to ravish her supple body. The thought of her long silky hair, splayed across his stomach, his body covered with the auburn curls, as she played with him. He shook his head. His good sense returned. His duty must come first, so he let go of the fantasy.

"See you soon, beautiful," he said, then left her.

He took a commercial flight, heading for Boston.

CHAPTER 22

Deed Is Done

Robert made it through customs and headed for the baggage area. He had arranged for a car to pick him up and searched for a driver holding a sign that read 'de Gourgues'. His phone buzzed. A text message from STRANGER. CAR CURBSIDE.

Great! Mr. Fedora strikes again. Robert picked up his bag and headed for the exit. He spotted the car right away. The driver opened the door, and Robert slid into the backseat. Once again, he sat face to face with the man who had stood in the shadows at his family's house, shadowing him since. His blond hair was slicked back this time, his eyes as hard as steel and unyielding.

"Well, we meet again."

"Good afternoon Mr. de Gourgues. The Society thought you could use a lift to your friend's home, non? I'm happy to oblige. How do you say, I will be your backup?"

Robert nodded. "Yes, that's it. You can be my Tonto."

The man laughed, but it sounded hollow. He looked like a lost kid, someone who never received a heart when he was born. For a split second, Robert imagined he might have looked lost like this himself, not that long ago. He hated to think of the louse he had been. Now, he was about to kill his own friend. A shiver ran down his spine.

"What's the matter, Robert? Having second thoughts?"

He shook his head and remained silent. He didn't want to appear uncommitted to the Society, but words stuck in his throat.

"Do you have a gun? Or do you plan on using another method—maybe your bare hands." The man with the fedora grinned. His steely gray-blue eyes looked so cold. Robert pulled his coat tighter around him.

"No. I need to buy a gun."

The man tapped on the glass window that separated them from the driver. It opened. "Turn up the heat; my friend is cold. And we need to make a stop, understand?"

The driver nodded and closed the window.

"Not cold feet, I hope."

"No, of course not," Robert said. "I have my orders and will do what it takes, like everyone else in the Society. I can't wait for my official initiation when I get to meet the great master. Will it be at the main headquarters?"

The man laughed. "Tom said you were ambitious, asked a lot of questions, and very anxious to be one of us. Well," he slapped Robert's leg. "He was right. Funny that you'll be taking his place. I bet Tom never saw that coming. Not in a million years. Couldn't have happened more perfect."

"Excuse me?" Robert decided to play dumb. If they thought he knew nothing about Tom, the better.

"Well, just between you and me, Tom Bennett was a bit hard to handle. Always making a mess when he took on his other side. Do you know what I mean?"

Robert shook his head. He didn't want to remember the brutal beast.

"Non. Well, you probably don't know anything about that. Let's just say I enjoy your company better than his. He had a nasty habit of biting those closest to him." The man laughed at his own words.

"Thanks, I think." Robert smiled, then turned and looked out the window. He swallowed back his nervousness. He didn't want the man to see him sweat.

The car pulled to the curb near an old tenement block. The old mill house had been patched up over the years but had seen better days. The building's frame was covered in aluminum siding that had been added decades ago, but now covered with filth. It leaned to one side in defiance of its crumbling foundation.

A young kid stepped toward the car. He wore a dark knit cap pulled over his ears, a plaid hunting jacket, and tight dark jeans. "Got it for you, sir." Steam came out of his mouth as he hurried his words. "Just like you ordered."

The kid's gloved hand held a dark object; he stretched out his arm. The fedora man nodded for Robert to take it. Robert accepted the gun and turned it around in his hands. It felt cold and heavy. The blond man handed the kid an envelope then the window rolled up. The car pulled away. Just like that, he possessed a weapon. Robert felt queasy.

"You all right, *mon ami*?"

"Yes, I'm fine. Let's get this over with, I have things I need to attend to at home. I want to fly down to Memphis later today."

"That's a great idea. I'm heading that way myself. We can travel together, non? Please join me on my plane back. We can sit back and play cards. You play, right?"

Robert nodded, pissed off that he had to endure even more time with this creep. What had he gotten himself into? This cold henchman wanted to play BFFs. Robert looked down at the gun in his hands and checked it out more thoroughly. A compact Glock Parabellum 9mm. He saw that it was loaded with a full clip of 19. *Great.* He wondered if there was a way to empty the clip of bullets without this sicko realizing it. *Fat chance.*

"That gun suits you," the man said.

Robert jerked his head in acknowledgment but couldn't bring himself to utter a word. He knew how to use a gun, but after shooting Bennett . . . well, he'd never forget all that blood. It had splattered everywhere and covered him, head to shoe tip. He could still smell the stench, the rusty smell, and the feel of thick hot hemoglobin, all over him. He'd sworn after that day that he'd never touch a gun again. The thrill was gone. But he knew this charade needed a finale, and he had to shoot one last time. *Play the part,* he reminded himself, though he loathed himself.

They drove toward the Bennett homestead nestled in the outskirts of the city, just north of Cambridge. Robert had spent a lot of time here during his late teen years. Jackson had been his roommate in prep school and college. He had been invited to visit for most holiday weekends. Reflecting back, he realized that it had been Tom Bennett who actually inspired the frequent visits all along. Back then, Robert idolized the man, he had been larger than life and took a shine to him. Since his own father had ignored him, Robert soaked up all the attention offered.

It wasn't until a few weeks ago that he discovered why. Tom Bennett the man, was a myth. In reality, he was literally a beast, a skinwalker, who shifted into a wolf when he needed a fix of fear. He existed only to absorb other people's terror and use it to dominate over them. The most sickening part of the horrid story was that the monster had hurt his mother.

Had Robert known the true nature of Tom Bennett, he would have never entertained a second of his company. Regrets twisted in his heart, knocking against his sensibility, and Robert questioned his own self-worth. How could his family truly forgive him, when he couldn't forgive himself?

The car pulled up the long drive, the stones crunched under the tires. The familiar mansion stood inflexible, a Victorian gem with a grand porch and elegant trim. It was the perfect New England setting, a crisp autumn day despite the sunshine. The leaves had all fallen, but a green backdrop was provided by the dense evergreens in the backwoods. There were local rumors that Tom Bennett had buried his parents in those woods. Some-day it would be considered folklore, but Robert knew it was most probably the truth.

The air was cold. It wasn't far from Thanksgiving. Robert hoped that all this business of engaging with the Black Wolf Society would be behind him soon. Maybe there was a chance that his family could actually mend their relationships this holiday.

"Here we are. How about I go inside with you? Non. Introduce me as Mr. Jones."

"Really?" Robert snapped back. "Why not Mr. Cool?"

The kid put on his fedora and smiled. "As you wish, Robert. It really won't matter five minutes from now, will it?"

A sick feeling overtook Robert's stomach. He prayed that Agent Sloan's plan would work and that the final details had been worked out beforehand between Jackson and the FBI. He forced himself out of the car and trudged up to the house.

◻◈◇◈◻

Robert rang the doorbell.

A servant, wearing pressed Docker pants and a V-neck sweater, answered the door. "May I help you?"

Robert didn't recognize the tall man in his late forties, but hey, he hadn't been there in quite some time. Still, he hazarded a guess that the household help was actually an agent in disguise.

"Yes, is Jackson in? Please tell him Robert de Gourgues is here to see him."

The man lowered his head and let them pass, then led them to the room on the left. The place felt familiar to Robert as they stepped into Tom Bennett's old library. The walls, wood paneling, warm and rich. The old varnish shined. The opposite wall was filled with shelves containing tomes that Tom Bennett probably never read. *Is this where the deed will be done, kind of ironic, yet appropriate? The pretend murder of his son, in the beast's old pretend office.*

"Man, Bennett has good taste," the blond man said. He picked up a few objects with a gloved hand.

"Yes, Tom loved to relax in this room."

"I keep forgetting you two were bosom buddies."

Jackson walked into the room and rushed over to Robert. They hugged warmly.

"Robert, my old friend. I'm so happy to see you." He tapped his back, then whispered in his ear, "Everything is all set."

Robert squeezed him back, relieved to know that Jackson was prepared.

"Jackson, my old friend. I hope things are going well. I've been concerned about you."

Jackson let go. He wasn't as tall as Robert, but built stronger, with wide shoulders. His sandy, blond hair waved back in a designer cut. Robert had always thought that Jackson's blue eyes matched the color of his sister Michelle's perfect. But no one would doubt the fact that she was Robert's sister. The French characteristics showed through, with dark hair and fine profiles, as if chiseled — prominent faces.

"I bet you have. No worries, friend. Things are fine since we last spoke, considering all that's happened. I've had a lot to deal with lately, what with my father disappearing and all. You've heard?"

Robert nodded. "Chelle told me."

"Yes, of course. So, I've been acting as a trustee this past month. The courts gave me power of attorney to keep things working smoothly. Mother, of course, wanted nothing to do with the business. Details, you know. She never was a very strong person."

Despite his sad news, Jackson still smiled while talking. No one would have been convinced that Jackson was anything but happy his father was missing. *Of course, we both know he's dead.*

"She still drinking?" Robert said.

Jackson nodded. A throat cleared.

"Robert, aren't you going to introduce me to your friend?" the blond man said.

"Sorry, yes of course. Jackson, this is Mr. Cool."

Jackson laughed. "I'm sorry. Really, your name is Mr. Cool?"

The man in the fedora nodded.

Jackson turned, walked to the doorway, and shouted out, "James, please bring us coffee."

The man with the fedora jerked his head at Robert, signaling to get things done.

"Do the deed," he whispered.

His heart raced and Robert felt perspiration swell to the surface of his skin and bead up. He wiped his forehead with his sleeve, then he pulled the gun out from the inside pocket of his pea-coat.

Robert raised the gun toward Jackson's back.

Jackson turned around, saw the gun, and let out a cry. "What the hell!"

Robert closed his eyes as he pulled the trigger. The bullet hit Jackson's midsection and pushed him back, then he fell to the floor. The gun slipped out of Robert's sweaty hands. The man grabbed the gun away and walked toward the still body on the floor. Robert watched him, as he stood for a moment, and stared down at Jackson.

An eternity passed. A garnet circle formed on the rug. The blood spilled out fast and Jackson's eyes didn't blink. He lay there, still on the floor, with open eyes. Blue glassy marbles stared back at Robert, calling out to him, traitor. Fear penetrated every nerve ending, jumping against his skin. Something must have gone wrong. Jackson bled so much. *Was he really dead?*

Someone was shaking his sleeve. Robert turned and saw the young man wearing the fedora. He handed the gun back to Robert, then said something, but Robert couldn't distinguish the words. The blast from the gun still rung in his ear. The metallic residue burned his nostrils, he could taste it in his mouth.

The blond man said again, "It's done, let's go now."

Robert took a few steps closer, stood over Jackson's body, and looked down. He wasn't moving a muscle, not breathing. Robert's chest tightened. *He shot his friend—shot him dead. This wasn't supposed to happen. Didn't they put a vest on him or something?* His vision zoomed in to the stained imported rug. The blood, now blending with the reds of the carpet design.

The man with the fedora yanked his arm, so hard that Robert almost stumbled to the floor. Robert followed him out of the house and hustled toward the car. His heart pounded and a frenzied cloud of panic tightened his throat. They shoved themselves into the back seat and the driver sped away.

Robert was frozen in shock, with the gun held tight in his hand. It felt warm, still glued in his grip. Paralyzed, he sat with a blank stare ahead, nothing penetrated his thoughts except one word, *traitor!*

CHAPTER 23

Hello Memphis

Robert endured the flight back to Memphis, ignoring the outlandish comments that the man named STRANGER expressed about life and death and his ten best ways to kill a person. Robert had no plans to raise a gun at another soul again. He gave the kid the cold shoulder and refused his request for a card game. Exhausted, Robert closed his eyes and pretended to doze off. The small plane landed, and he said a quick goodbye, then ran through the airport to the long-term parking lot. *Finally*, he looked over his shoulder as he unlocked his car door. *No one is nearby.* Robert slipped into the leather front seat.

He grabbed the steering wheel, held it tight, and pounded his head against it. Robert banged his head until it hurt, angry with himself and the situation. When he finally stopped, he let loose tears of regret. The unbearable frustration that had been pent up for days, finally released. With his eyes closed, Robert envisioned Jackson on the floor. *No, he couldn't be dead, that wasn't the plan.* He wiped his burning eyes, took a deep yoga breath, and calmed himself. A moment later, with regained focus, he turned the ignition key.

Robert arrived at the house just before the dinner hour. Parking his Jag next to Michelle's Porsche, he was slow to get out. Not in a hurry for the barrage of questions, which he reasoned would fly as soon as his sisters noticed that he was home. *They will ask about Brussels, then about Jackson.* To keep this charade going and his family safe, he had to play the part. He shrugged, reminding himself that he knew how to mask his true feelings after playing the game for years. But this time it was difficult because he was sliced up inside, conflicted. Worse, it was as if someone had mixed up all his pieces, and he'd never be put right again. *Lost.* He got out of the car and went inside to face the family.

"There you are, handsome." Rachael greeted him at the parlor entrance and kissed him on the cheek. "I'm so proud of you, Robert."

"I have no idea what I did to get your approval, but I'll take it." He warily smiled at his beautiful wife.

"Your sisters have been filling in the fine details that you neglected to tell me. You saved the day. Emilie could have been killed. You never mentioned it was the Black Wolf Society that took her."

"If they wanted to kill me, they would have," Emilie said. "I'm afraid they'd rather play with us all. What kind of group is this anyway? Bad enough they want to steal everyone's money, but now they're madmen toying with our heads." Emilie visibly shook, then wrapped her arms around herself.

Michelle went to her and put her arm in hers. "Don't worry. No one is getting by the extra security we have."

"Great, prisoners in our own home." Emilie went to sit on the sofa.

"Well, at least you'll be safe. And we aren't positive it was that group. We have no proof now, do we?"

Robert made his way to the bar. "Anyone need a drink along with me?"

His sisters darted a disparaging gaze. Robert took his time pouring his drink, took a gulp, then poured another. The warm, familiar barley felt soothing, and his nerves finally calmed down after a couple. *Maybe if I drink enough, the images in my head will disappear, too.* But he knew first hand it didn't work that way.

Nina walked into the parlor, spotted Robert, and pushed herself across the room until standing near him. She grabbed herself a hug, and Robert hugged her back without a fight. "I'm so glad to see you, Nina."

"I heard the news," she crooned. "You'll be all right, boy, I promise. Extra prayers are raised up for the lot of you. Now, come get some food, y'all. I'm not asking twice." She let out a slight laugh, kissed his head, then headed for the dining room.

"The dinner bell has rung," Michelle said.

They all followed Nina's lead into the dining room. They shuffled around the large table and found their seats in silence. The room was large with high ceilings, trimmed with carved molding gilded in gold. There was a fire blazing in the hearth to keep out the autumn night chill. On most nights, it would have made the ambiance romantic, but tonight the heat smothered Robert. He unbuttoned his shirt collar. The tinkling of dishes and activity in the room roused him from his reverie. Robert crossed himself and asked for a blessing. He looked up and saw Rachael, fixated on him wearing a peculiar expression, *bewilderment maybe?*

"Great. Salmon, again. Tell me, Nina, why do you always make Emilie's favorite?"

"Don't think I forgot you, little princess." Nina uncovered her favorite chicken.

"Thank you."

Small things go a long way in this house, Robert thought. The others picked at the food, troubled by the recent events, even Rachael didn't seem to have an appetite.

His internal thoughts began drowning him in negativity. He needed to get out of his head.

"What's up with everyone tonight?" he said. "Em, how's Jeremy doing? Is he upstairs?"

She nodded. "Yes, the flight took a lot out of him. He's resting soundly now, but he'll be up and about in no time. The Doc came by to check on him when we first arrived. He said that

Jeremy is recovering nicely."

"That's wonderful. So, what exactly was the nature of his injury?" Rachael said from concern.

"The bullet braised an artery on the way in, and so he lost a lot of blood. It's patched now and all sealed up nicely, thank God no organs were damaged. He'll be fine with some rest to get his blood count up and strength back. Good thing we got him to a hospital right away."

"Wasn't he in intensive care? Robert, didn't you say that?" Rachael said.

"Yes, he was at first. His vitals were off. Getting him to the hospital made all the difference. It was good fortune Mr. Sloan was there."

Robert choked, then took a sip of water and wiped his mouth with a napkin.

Rachael thumped his back. "Are you all right?"

"Fine, I'm fine." His face felt on fire. He wished that Emilie hadn't remembered Sloan's name, but no one here noticed the mention of it. He blasted himself for worrying about every little thing. *Who cares if the family knows the name Sloan, they have no idea he's FBI.*

"Oh Em, you must have been crazy with worry. I wish I had been there with you," Michelle said.

"Well, we're all together that's what's important." Emilie nodded, pulled her hair back behind her ears, and took a bite.

The conversation ended for a while. The heat had kicked on in the house. Robert heard the moans of the walls as the house expanded with the warmer air flowing into the room through the vents.

"It's been cold the past few days," Michelle said.

Robert noticed her bright blue eyes, sparkling as they had years ago when she was an excited child. Her dark, short hair spiked like a pixie. Despite all that's happened, he would always think of Michelle as his baby sister. He hoped that he could show her just how important she was to him.

"Looks like we might have snow soon. Thanksgiving is just days away. Maybe it will be a white Thanksgiving." Michelle said.

"That's right, Thanksgiving is next Thursday already. I can't keep up," Emilie said.

"Oh Em, you do as well as any of us at keeping up," Michelle said. "You need a holiday to rest and heal. Look at you girl! I never saw anyone so bruised up—except maybe that one housekeeper we had. You all remember. Nina tried to help her by giving her a job. Her husband beat her all the time."

"I remember," Robert said. "That poor woman, she always came here wearing black eyes. Finally, she said she'd leave him, but then they up and moved away. No one heard of them again. *Creepy*."

"Michelle, why remember such a horrible story?" Rachael said.

Her eyes didn't seem half as horrified as she claimed. Perhaps, Rachael was secretly entertained by the story. He shook his head. *Stop your cynicism.*

"We need to have a family dinner with all the trimmings this year," Emilie said. "After all, this has been a trying year, and a family holiday is exactly what we need to strengthen our bonds."

"Yes, that would be wonderful. I'll ask my father to join us." Rachael said.

They all turned their heads toward her place at the table. If she sought a response, it didn't show. Rachael carefully cut her meat, not seeking protest or approval. Robert wondered how well a fit her father would be at the dinner table.

"Of course, your father is welcome here any time."

They finished dinner, had a nightcap then went upstairs.

Robert switched off the light. There was a low fire in the grate, its reflective flames glowing across the white sheets. He looked down at Rachael, lying there so peaceful, like an angel. He tucked himself into bed beside her, holding her and pressing her back, spoon-shaped against his body.

"Rachael, I hope you know that I love you. I'm so sorry our trip to Brussels was ruined by everything that went on with my sister." He kissed the back of her head, wiped her hair away from his mouth, and felt its silky strands sliding through his fingers. The sensation awakened his desire. His groin ached for her hand to touch him in that wanton spot.

"Don't worry. It wasn't a complete loss of a trip. I did get to see my old friend, Marcie. And everything else . . . well, Emilie is safe and sound, thanks to your quick action." She sighed. "All is well." She turned around and kissed him.

Robert's blood rushed, and he returned her kiss. She moaned, and the sound of her sighs ignited an urgent want in him. He hungered to feel her love tonight, to connect with her and feel human inside.

Rachael responded to his advances and grabbed his hardened manhood. He touched her face, showered more kisses down her neck, and trailed her breasts. He cupped her full bosom under his groping hands and knew from her moans and returned stroking that she enjoyed his advances. The rhythm of her body rose slowly and aligned with his.

Robert lowered his head, kissing her farther down to her belly. She touched his hair, raked her fingers through his thick curls, then held his head at her hip level. He took the suggestion and began licking her body, delving his tongue in more deeply. Her voice grew louder with groans of elation.

The sex started out as a need for gentleness on Robert's

part. But soon, Rachael's carnal appetite turned into an urgent frenzy. She demanded more of him, pulling him up to see his face. She groped his ass, pulled him close until Robert entered her body, filling her with his hardened flesh. Her body rose with his as his blood rushed and pulsated until they both gave in to a final, gratifying moment. Frozen in euphoria, they lay in each other's arms, their sweat the proof of their drained tensions. He drew in a breath, smelled her exotic perfume, and wished he could do it again for her, somehow knowing she craved for more than he had to offer.

Tired, his mind began to drift off to sleep, peace at last. Suddenly, he remembered something. He opened his eyes, recalling the haunting words one of the members of the Black Wolf had said from behind the mask. It had seemed odd then, but there had been no time to contemplate what he had meant. But now, the words echoed in his thoughts . . . *maybe you share genes*. Was the robed stranger suggesting that Tom Bennett was more than a mentor, much more? That perhaps, Tom Bennett was his father. *No! Impossible.*

A sick feeling overwhelmed him. Did his mother get pregnant when that monster raped her? The thought drummed up such a strong revulsion that his stomach soured. He ran to the bathroom and vomited.

CHAPTER 24

Missed Message

Robert tapped the handrail as he went downstairs to the kitchen for coffee. It was early in the morning, and he hadn't been able to sleep, tossing and turning all night. He wiped his eyes and sat at the kitchen table with his sisters, fidgeting with a spoon, as he listened to them chatter away about things: the business, Jeremy's health, and plans for the holiday, *blah blah*.

"Rob, how was he?" Michelle's voice sounded frustrated. He hadn't been paying attention while she was speaking to him.

"What? I'm sorry, my thoughts drifted off."

"I asked you, how's Jackson coping? You never told us how your visit went."

Robert swallowed. "Jackson's fine and gives his best to you all."

"Really, that's it? Is he having a hard time dealing with things after his father's death?" Emilie asked.

"No, and why should he—the man was a monster for Christ's sake. Getting rid of his father was the best thing for him and for everyone else as well. He's managing his affairs just fine."

Robert was angry and needed to change the subject.

"You know, girls, if you need help with anything, I'm right here, an open ear or shoulder to cry on. And of course, if there's anything that concerns you with the business, just ask for my help. And before you protest, I'm not saying I want to go back to the office or anything like that. I understand my being there would be an issue, but if I can help with anything that arises, let me know."

Michelle smiled. "That's awfully big of you, Robert, but all is under control."

"We need more time," Emilie said.

Sure you do. Emilie, the diligent sister, always watching over Michelle. He wished that Emilie could protect him, too. But if she knew about his working for the Feds then she'd be at more risk. Already she'd been kidnapped. Perhaps he could help keep them safe by having Sloan add more security to patrol around the place. He felt uneasy about the old house. There were too many back entrances and big old windows easy enough to open from the outside. Worse yet, security-wise, was the drive from the house to the office. Why anything could happen in seconds waiting at a streetlight.

"Girls, maybe you should both work from home today."

"Robert, you worry too much," Michelle snapped.

"I don't think so. Just ask Emilie about what she went through. Not such a bad idea to worry a bit, Chelle. For some reason, they have their sights on all of us. It's as if they enjoy playing these games."

Emilie stood. "I'm going up to check on Jeremy before we leave, but Rob's right. That experience was horrifying, and they're definitely not finished with us yet. The man claiming to be a doctor suggested that they're interested in experimenting with my clairvoyant gift. Madmen." She cringed.

"Like the Nazis?" Michelle burst out. "So now we're being stalked by mad scientists. Why can't we just be a normal family, with average problems, like how we're going to pay the bills? No, we have to worry who's chasing us down streets and trying to kidnap us."

Robert got a chill. "I'm turning up the heat."

He stood and walked to the thermostat.

"Maybe you should reconsider driving into the office today."

Michelle nodded. "How about you stay with Jeremy today, Em? I'll drive to the office with a guard and will call as soon as I get there, okay?"

Emilie nodded. "If you're okay with that, then yes."

Robert felt some relief.

◻◈◈◈◻

Later in the day, Robert sat in his father's library, reading from his tablet. His thoughts wandered, uneasy not knowing the status with Jackson. He heard the alert announcing an incoming email. It was from STRANGER. He opened it right away. MEET ME AT ALCHEMY 3PM. The Black Wolf must have confirmed things and now wanted to set up his membership ceremony. Soon his espionage task would be completed, but not soon enough.

Robert thought this merited an update to Agent Sloan. He wanted to not only report the newest meet-up but also find out how Jackson Bennett was doing. Worried for the past twenty-four hours about him, he needed to know if his friend was safe. Good news might take away those nasty images that haunted the thoughts in his head.

He went to pull the old flip-style phone from his pocket. It was gone. His heart skipped a beat, his throat tightened. An awful feeling sank to the pit of his stomach. Robert ran upstairs to look for it. When he opened the bedroom door, he saw Rachael, she was dressing. He entered the room just as she was pulling up her stockings. She had the most beautiful long legs. Shapely and a distraction he couldn't leave unnoticed.

"You look like you've seen a ghost," she said.

"No, no ghosts. I'm trying to get a few things straight in my head, is all."

"Oh, by the way, a phone rang. I followed the sound until I found this. It rang three times." She tossed the flip phone onto the bed. "I answered too late. Whoever called hung up, sorry.

Is this your phone?"

Robert swallowed hard. *Be cool.* "Yes, it's an old phone. I'm surprised it even rang, I thought I disconnected that number."

"Well, not only does it work, but it's still charged up." She gave him a look as if she were saying, "You're full of shit."

"I found it in my desk the other day and plugged it in to see if it still worked. I was going to check my old contacts to make sure I had them all in my newest. Guess the battery is still good. Never thought the number was still live. I'll have Evans cancel it if I can even remember it."

"Yes, do that," she said. "I'm going shopping today with your Aunt Victoria. Need anything?"

Rachael looked great, dressed snazzy in a new slim-fitting dress.

"No, I'm good. Just need you to come home. You're dressed to kill, just to go shopping. Shopping for anything special?"

"Not really, but you never know what you'll find—or who you might bump into."

She grinned, and looked almost sinful, then reached up and kissed him on the cheek. He still felt the heat from her lips after she left the room. He wondered if she suspected anything off with him and if she knew about her father's secret room below his office. *If she knew, would she tell me?* It would be nice if he could just ask her, but they didn't talk like that. Rachael was a sweet daddy's girl and adored her father. He didn't want to cause any friction. Besides, when the two of them were together, they communicated more with sex than any other way.

All of a sudden, Robert felt a little lonely. He wondered if his marriage with Rachael would bloom into something based on more than sex—maybe a relationship like his sister and Jeremy had, based on trust. *Impossible because I don't trust anyone.* He wanted to work harder, and he would, as soon as these covert dealings were finished. "So, get on with it," he said aloud.

He flipped open the phone and called Agent Sloan.

"Good morning," the Agent said. "I tried calling, but you never answered."

"Yes, and unfortunately, when you rang, Rachael found the phone."

"Okay, you'll have to dump it after this call. I'll meet you somewhere and give you a new phone that's safe to use."

"Great, but let's meet before three. I'm scheduled to meet the man from the Black Wolf at three this afternoon, at the Alchemy."

"The what?"

"Alchemy. It's a bar, slash restaurant."

"Okay. Let's have a business luncheon there beforehand, say at one."

"I'll be there."

The line went dead. Robert became uneasy about meeting both contacts at the same place. He was being pulled like a Stretch Armstrong toy.

◻◈◈◈◻

Robert sat at a far-corner table, his back to the wall, in the Alchemy waiting for Agent Sloan. A boy approached and handed Robert a package, then nodded and left without a word. He turned the small box around in his hands and tore off the packaging paper. Inside the box was a new flip phone. Robert smiled. He pocketed the phone while looking around the room, but he saw no one unusual and no Agent Sloan. He turned toward the wall, his back to the room, and pulled out the cell. Flipping it open, he hit *2. The phone rang.

"Agent Sloan."

"Where are you?"

"Hello, Robert, I'm nearby. I thought maybe it is best to keep my distance."

"Great. But I have questions for you."

"Shoot."

"How did everything go up in Cambridge? How's Jackson?"

The line was silent a moment. "I told you not to worry. We took care of everything."

Sloan's voice sounded dismissive, and Robert felt he was being put off.

"So, just to clarify, you're saying Jackson is alright."

Again, the line was silent a moment. Robert felt uneasy, turned around, and stared at the table.

"Robert, I'm not going to lie to you. The bullet went through his vest protection. Jackson is in the hospital, but the doctors say he'll pull through. It's not life-threatening. The story hit the Boston paper this morning and says he was killed. Stick to it. If your family sees the article, stick to the story."

"That's not what I wanted to hear. You promised everything would be all right."

"Keep calm," the Agent ordered.

Robert closed his eyes a moment.

"Okay. I'm meeting the other side at three. I'll call you after that."

"Roger that. And Robert, stay calm. We're almost there."

The line went dead. A waiter approached and Robert looked up startled.

"Are you ready to order, sir?"

Robert ordered lunch. Just as he was being served, an old employee stopped at the table to say hello. It had been a while since he'd seen anyone from the office. He took advantage of the opportunity and caught up on things. Ned Banks was a young, ambitious man and also took any liberty available. Robert invited him to sit, and they had a few drinks and passed the time. While Ned babbled, sharing the social calendar of every person who worked for the de Gourgues, Robert kept checking his watch. It was two fifty-five.

"It was great seeing you, Ned, but do you mind? I have an appointment with someone. We're meeting here."

"No problem, I have to get going anyway. Nice talking with you, Robert."

The man nodded, awkwardly got up, and left the table, just as the man with the fedora walked into the bar. He spotted Robert at the table and joined him.

"Well, well. You know how to live it up." His eyes scanned the dishes and glasses on the table. "Enjoy your lunch?"

"Yes, thank you. I needed to get out of the house. Besides, I figured I'd get here early to ensure I didn't miss you."

"Not to worry. We can always get in touch with you. We're very good at surveillance. Speaking of such, how about we move to another table, just to be safe."

Robert was surprised. "Sure, no problem, whatever you wish."

They sat a few tables closer to the entrance.

"There, much better. Now I can look out of the window and watch the cars pulling in and out, and scan the people as they walk by. Are you a people watcher, Mr. de Gourgues?"

"No, actually, I'm not. I'd make the world's worst witness. I can never remember anything. I prefer to sit here and watch the screens over there above the bar." Robert pointed toward the array of sets tuned in to sports channels.

The man smiled. "Tsk, tsk. Well, I hope you remember your next instructions."

"What instructions? I thought I did my Benevolent Act?"

"I thought you understood how this worked. No one is ever finished with the Acts, and we call upon members whenever needed. As it turns out, there's one task that's especially suited for you. How do you say, you have immediate access." The man raised his brow, then slipped Robert an envelope.

Robert stared at it a moment, debating with himself if he wanted to play spy anymore. He didn't have a choice. He had already gone so far, and if he refused, then the Black Wolf would be putting a hit out on him. Robert slowly picked up the envelope and opened it. He read:

Kill Mr. La France

His face drained of blood, and a sick feeling grew in his stomach. How was he ever going to pull this off? If Mr. La France was a member himself, as he suspected him to be, then tipping him off to the undercover side of things could blow everything out of the water. For a brief second, Robert thought maybe he should follow along as if a real member and just kill his father-in-law. Revolted with himself and ashamed for the thought, no matter how brief, his stomach soured.

He got up. "You have one day. They want a quick turnaround on this. By this hour tomorrow, the old man should be exterminated." The man turned and walked away, leaving the bar.

Robert was shocked by his choice of words. *Exterminated*, of course, it was accurate. He got out of his seat and ran to the men's room where he got sick. When he returned to the table, he signed for his bill and called for a car to pick him up. He belted down one more quick scotch while waiting.

Robert hit *2 but no one answered. He hit redial, but again Sloan didn't answer. A sudden panic rushed through him, with little time and not knowing what to do next, he needed Sloan to be aware of the situation.

"Damned government," he grumbled.

CHAPTER 25

Missing Pieces

It was just past three in the afternoon. A bristling wind uplifted and swirled dried leaves across the pavement, making a clatter. Robert got into the car and instructed the driver to drop him off at Father Eddie's rectory. He didn't want to face an empty house and needed companionship.

Arriving in minutes, Robert stepped onto the porch and pushed the doorbell. He was invited into the front hall by the housekeeper, Mrs. Peterson. She wore her hair pulled back tight, away from her face, and immediately smiled at him. Her voice spoke in a soft Southern tone.

"You're in luck Mr. de Gourgues, the Reverend just finished with his last appointment for this afternoon."

"Fine. Thank you." Robert walked into the parlor and helped himself to a drink at the small bar set up in the far corner of the room despite already having a few at the Alchemy. Minutes later, Father Eddie entered the room. The air engulfed his large frame as he shuffled closer, drawing in Robert's attention. Eddie sat down in his armchair close to the hearth without saying a word. The sage waited for Robert to divulge his reasons for being there, he always was the patient man, though Robert felt his stare. He didn't look back but instead averted his eyes to the floor.

"Father Eddie, if I tell you something like a confession, then it's just between us, right?"

"Robert de Gourgues, you know that's the truth of it. It's a holy sacrament."

Robert raised his head, dared a glance back, and saw the priest's dark eyes blazing. He knew the rules, that was true, but he needed to be certain. He saw the honesty written in the priest's expression. Robert gulped back his angst and swallowed any pride he still had left at that moment.

"Just checking. I don't know how you keep all the secrets straight, Eddie. All the confessions you must hear. And what is truth—really?"

The big man wriggled in his chair until situated. "Robert, do you want to talk philosophy?"

"No, sir. You've got that subject all wrapped up, Father."

He finished his drink, then sat into a chair across from Eddie. He wore the dark purple sash around his neck and was mumbling a prayer. Robert crossed himself.

"Bless me, Father, for I have sinned, it's been too long since my last confession—"

"Let's keep this face-to-face confession simple. Tell me, Robert, what's troubling you?"

"Father, I'm stuck in the middle of a mess." He dropped his head, and felt his face heat up, sizzling as if he was burning in hell already.

"Rob, I know you feel embarrassed, but telling the truth is a way to relieve your burden."

"Thank you, Father. You see, I've been trying to get myself out of a predicament. The situation is one I totally blame myself for, but it feels things are out of hand."

Robert looked up and saw that the priest didn't intend to interrupt, but sat patiently, waiting for him to say whatever he needed to unload. So, Robert told him about his situation, working for the Feds undercover, while parading and pretending to do the Black Wolf's bidding. As he told his priest and friend all that was happening, the pressure released, a little.

"So you see, what I fear the most is that this situation is putting everyone in danger—my family in danger. Jeremy already took a bullet, Emilie was kidnapped, and I had to pretend to shoot my best friend. Now, they want me to kill Rachael's father. I can't do it. But I'm afraid of what will happen if I refuse to do it."

Father Eddie sat in silence, rolling his eyes in deep thought. Finally, he snapped his fingers. "Try contacting the Agent again. He'll have to take care of things as he promised. He put you in this dangerous situation."

Robert shook his head, "No, Father. It was because of my crimes that the FBI has this power over me. I did horrible things, to my own father."

"Robert, I know for a fact that Pierre forgave you. You must understand that your father hoped this day would come when you would realize the importance of family."

"So what do I do if I can't reach the agent in time?"

"You do nothing. You can't honestly believe that it would be good to kill your father-in-law for real, do you?"

"No. You're right, of course."

Father Eddie shifted in his chair and looked up toward the ceiling. Robert wondered if telling his priest a confession put his life in danger as well.

"I don't understand some of what you told me, Robert. For example, why did they kidnap Emilie?"

"For the money, I guess, although it wasn't all that much considering. Still, it was easy enough for us to come up with that amount in the limited time frame."

"Hmm. I wonder if there was another reason. Are you sure it was the Black Wolf who kidnapped her? It doesn't make sense that they'd kidnap a fellow member's sister, if they want you in the group, then why will they go after your family?"

Robert nodded. "Maybe it was a test, to show where my loyalties lie? Possibly, they want proof that I'm loyal to them over my family. That's how horrible these men are. I've seen what they're capable of firsthand. As I said, I need you to absolve me of the sins I've committed."

The priest rubbed his chin without a response. Robert leaned forward, anxious to get the last of his worries out in the open between them. If he was going to confess, then he might as well say everything that concerned him.

"Eddie, there's something else that has been bothering me lately."

"Like what you've said isn't enough," the priest attempted to get Robert to smile.

"Yes, for me it's even worse."

"Nothing can be worse."

Robert remained silent for a second, choosing his words wisely.

"I know you've kept secrets that belong to my parents, and that you haven't the liberty to tell."

Eddie nodded.

"Well, there's something that gnaws in my head. Tell me, honestly, when Tom Bennett raped my mother, did she get pregnant? With me?"

Father Eddie closed his eyes and mumbled prayers.

Robert's spirit dropped and a sickening fear slithered down his back.

"I knew my prayers wouldn't be answered. My natural parent was a monster." He swayed and thought he might faint.

"Don't assume things." Father Eddie's voice sounded bitter. "I never confirmed that thought! Your parents loved you dearly. When you were a baby your father showed you so much love. When he held you in his arms everyone saw the happiness and love there. Of course, Pierre's your father."

"That's not an answer, padre."

Robert jumped from his chair. Anger filled him, his hate for Tom Bennett surfaced, leaving his skin edgy and sharp. He twitched.

"Give me a straight answer, please, Father Eddie."

"I can't give you a different answer. I'm a priest. Everyone who speaks to me does so in the cloak of privacy. But know this Robert—your parents loved you completely. That's all you need to know, that's all that's relevant to this concern of yours. You must have faith in your parents' love. If this group of hellions tells you anything different . . . well, you need to choose which side to believe in for yourself. Have faith, Robert. Don't believe in the lies."

Robert walked over to the corner of the room and poured himself another drink.

"Stop right there." The priest shouted across the room.

He lifted himself out from the chair and made his way toward Robert.

Robert turned around and stood frozen.

"For your penance, you will say ten decades of the rosary." Father Eddie stood close to Robert, waved his arms in the air, and made the sign of the cross blessing over him.

"Thank you, Father," Robert said. "I feel much better."

The words sounded sarcastic to his own ears. I might be the spawn of the devil, how can I possibly wrap my head around that fact?

"Robert, remember that your family loves you. That is the truth. Anything you've done wrong can be forgiven if you first forgive yourself. Now, go back to your house and say your penance. Try not to sin again."

🔲◈◈◈🔲

Robert arrived home before anyone else. He tried the flip phone again, but still no answer. Frustrated, he moved his attentions to other things until his sisters' chatter from downstairs invited his curiosity. He joined them in the parlor, waiting for the others to return for the dinner hour. Rachael and

Aunt Victoria were the last to enter the room after a long day of shopping. Robert watched as his wife smiled at everyone in the room, made small talk, and laughed. He wondered if she were ever to become pregnant, would his offspring be a monster as well.

Rachael suddenly turned and stared at him, wearing a queer expression, as if she had read his thoughts. *Not another telepath*, he thought. He looked down, allowed his shoulders to slump, and then turned his gaze toward Emilie. She sat still, stared right back at Rachael, and looked horrified. *What in God's name is she sensing from Rachael?*

Robert waited for an avalanche to fall, but he had no idea why.

"What do you think, Rob?" Michelle must have been talking to him.

"Oh, I'm sorry Michelle. Zoning out for a second." He smiled but found it difficult to maintain.

"For a minute there," Michelle said, "I thought you stopped talking to me again. Hopefully, we're over that."

"Yes, of course, that's water under the bridge. It's just that I've got a lot on my mind, as we all do."

Michelle frowned and squinted as if she were peering into a window looking for something. Then, a spark twinkled in her blue peepers. She had made a major decision, it was written all over her expression.

"Robert, come with me. I want to show you something. You did say that you'd help with any question concerning the business."

He nodded. She grabbed his hand and led the way.

"Good. You're good with numbers and I know you'll spot it right off."

"Yes, of course. Excuse us, we'll be right back," he said as they left the room.

He sensed Rachael's glare burning his back as he left the parlor. He didn't understand why she was angry with him, obviously, he'd done something to upset her. Having felt that heat before, he understood that it meant that trouble was coming. He drew in and breathed out a few deep breaths as he followed Michelle into the library.

"What's this all about?" Robert marched behind her. He noticed the papers sitting on top of the blotter that covered and protected the old antique desk. A whiff of old tobacco still clung in the air near the desk, emanating from the small wood drawers, and the smell reminded Robert of boyhood days when he was still small enough to sit on his father's lap and played with the drawers...that was when his mother was still alive.

"Check out today's report. Look at the balances." Michelle's face was tense. She stood nearby and tapped her foot against the hardwood floor, her arms crossed and held tight.

"Relax, it can't be that bad." Robert moved his finger up and down the inked spreadsheet and scanned the familiar report, then ran his finger down to the end of the balance column.

"No, this must be a mistake." He flipped back a few pages and read the withdrawal log. He recognized the hundred thousand that had been transferred into the Sparbuch account. Then he scanned over some normal activity entries. On the last page, in one fatal swoop, all the balances were zeroed out.

"I don't understand." His throat tightened and he couldn't manage another audible sound. He looked up at Michelle, her expression beyond angry.

"Okay, now you tell me what happened." Her voice snapped like a whip. The sensitive sister asking for help had morphed into an accuser.

Robert sat down in the leather desk chair, leafed through the pages again, shaking his head, he moaned.

"No-o-o. This can't be," he managed to say.

"Well, it is. There's no clue of what happened. A security breach entered through that account, the one we used for the ransom. See!" Michelle pounded her finger on a column of the report. "It sent a virus of some kind through that account to all our other company accounts. I thought maybe you tricked me, but I can see you're as surprised and upset as I am."

"Upset hardly covers it. According to this, we're broke. The company's bankrupt. Everything, gone! How can that even happen? In one transaction, no it's not possible."

Suddenly the urge to vomit again had him running for the powder room. Robert made it just in time to spit up into the latrine. He washed his face and looked at himself in the mirror. He stared at his scar. It had grown brighter and wider than he thought. He looked into his eyes, bloodshot. *What the hell is happening to me?* Robert walked back into the library and hugged his sister. He rubbed her back and consoled her as she cried on his shoulder.

"It will be all right, Chelle. We'll figure things out."

"I've no idea what happened, Rob. The accountant can't trace where the money disappeared to. It vanished into some account originating from Austria. It appears that it had clearance to claim the money. No name holder info, no address, nothing! We can't find who's responsible."

"I didn't think something like that was possible," he mumbled. "Have you contacted the insurance company yet?"

"No," she shook her head against his chest. "I wanted your input first."

It was imperative to get in touch with Sloan. Maybe he could help them locate the money, it was after all the main reason behind the entire sting operation. He had said he wanted to find the headquarters by following the money.

"Michelle, I know someone from the government who

might be able to help. He works for a task force that handles international transactions, well really money laundering, but I have a strong suspicion that he can help. I'll call him right away, ask him to scrutinize our records and fix this problem. Who else knows and how long do you have before you have to say something to the board?"

"Only the two of us know so far, and the CFO of course. We have forty-eight hours before he goes to the core team, and he agreed we can wait until the next meeting before going to the board. It's pushed out to the week after the holiday. So, if we can fix the mistake, before the board's attention is focused on this, well then it will save our necks."

Robert shook his head. "Does Emilie know?"

"No, not yet. Let's wait. Jeremy is just getting up and around today. They both have enough pressure right now, and it's not like there's anything she can do. I hate keeping secrets, especially from her. When she uses her mojo she knows I'm holding back. But in this case, I think it's wise to hide the truth right now."

Robert nodded. "Agreed." He pulled out the flip phone and pushed *2, and still no answer. "Damn."

"What is it? You look as white as a ghost," Michelle said.

"I just might be one, very soon."

Michelle gathered the report and stuffed it under her arm, then they left the room together to join the others for dinner.

"After you." Robert opened the door. The man stood in the way and looked guilty as if he'd been spying on them. "Can we help you, Evans?"

"Dinner is ready, sir."

Robert rolled his eyes, and Michelle snickered.

CHAPTER 26

Another Killing

Robert had dialed Sloan's number all night, but no one answered. He began to worry that something might have happened to Agent Sloan, and Robert had no other contact name to even begin a search. He tried to remember the division Sloan said he worked for; he was assigned on a special task force with Fin CEN and the FATF. The man hadn't said much about the unit at all, only mentioned that they were working against some form of international financial terrorism. Baffled where to begin, Robert had no clue who else he could turn to and remain covert and safe.

He descended the stairs and headed for the kitchen for a needed cup of caffeine. Taking a cup off the counter, he poured, spilled, and wiped it up with a napkin. He sipped and burnt his mouth. "Ouch." He walked toward the breakfast room.

The day before, when he spoke with Father Eddie, Robert realized the priest was right. It wasn't feasible to just walk into the La France mansion and shoot Rachael's father. Besides, why should he even pretend to help this group while he had no idea of what happened to his family's money? They would think he was weak if he went along with the Black Wolf Society as they pulled strings.

The money was gone. They were broke. The idea was so abstract to him. How would his sisters survive, broke? All of them were accustomed to a certain lifestyle—worse, his wife would now have a reason to leave him since he had nothing left to offer her.

"Pull yourself together," he said aloud. There was no way he trusted the Society—and they obviously wanted his family hurt beyond repair. Stealing their money and now turning Robert into their assassin? No, he wanted no part of it. He needed another plan, and quick.

Reaching the breakfast room, he sat down with a cup of coffee.

"Rachael lazing in bed?" Michelle said.

Robert nodded. Emilie and Michelle munched on their breakfast while preparing for the office. They planned to travel in together, taking an extra security guard along. Michelle looked up at Robert, her gaze a conspiratorial insinuation, but neither of them mentioned the missing money.

"Em, since you're working today, want me to do anything for Jeremy?" Robert said.

"That's nice of you to ask. The past few days he's regained his strength remarkably. I'll leave it entirely up to him—Jeremy's a big boy."

"Leave what up to me?" Jeremy walked into the room.

"God bless you. You're looking better," Nina said. She had just walked into the room and placed a platter of breakfast meats on the table.

"Thank you. I'm feeling much better. All I needed was some sleep to get my blood count up. It was only a big scratch." He smiled, his dimples making his expression seem boyish and sincere.

"Things didn't look that simple when you were lying in the hospital bed," Emilie snapped.

Jeremy touched Emilie's arm and the tension in the room extinguished.

"How about if today we hang out together, Jeremy?"

"Brilliant. I welcome your company."

"I might need your help with a project around the house."

◻◈◇◈◻

Half an hour later, the house felt empty. Everyone left, including Rachael, who ran out the door without even coffee, late for a morning appointment. Robert wasn't entirely sure how involved Rachael was with her father's business, but he knew she did attend many meetings.

The two men sat alone in the parlor. There were a few minutes of quiet, and Robert tried to pull his thoughts together. He knew it was best if he remained calm and tried to methodically find a way to contact Sloan while figuring out his own failsafe plan, just in case he didn't reach the man in time for instructions.

"What's up? What do you need my help with, Robert?"

"You're straight to the point. To tell you the truth, I'm not sure you can help me, but I'm desperate. I'm in a situation and don't know which way to turn. I need to contact someone. They had given me a phone and the number to reach them is programmed into it, but the problem is they aren't picking up when I call. Is there some way you can check the device to see if that's the problem?"

Jeremy nodded, and Robert handed him the flip phone. Jeremy wrote the phone number retrieved and handed it to Robert. "Here, try calling it on another phone."

"No, I can't. He said to use only secure lines."

"Robert, what is this all about? It doesn't sound above board."

"You have no idea. Listen, thanks for retrieving the number. But I think instead of taking chances on a possible insecure line, I'll get a new phone and then call the number."

"Okay, but if this mystery person is so keen on security, they may not answer when you call from an unknown number."

"You're right, but I have to take a chance. It's imperative

that I reach them."

"Here, use mine."

Robert took the phone offered and thought a moment. *Would Jeremy's line be secure?* He punched in the numbers and waited. It rang but still no pick up.

"That's strange," Jeremy said. "Wait, let me try calling Emilie."

He took the phone back and called her number with the same results.

"There's something odd here. I think something is jamming the phone signals. Look around the house for a jamming device. They're usually black boxes, about so big. Its size would fit in a big hand and it would have a prong or two sticking out of it."

"I'm checking upstairs in my room," Robert said.

"What the hell is going on, Robert?"

"If someone is jamming the signal, it would be aimed at me, so my room gets searched first."

They went up together. Opening closets, searching under the bed, but they found nothing out of the ordinary. Robert raked his fingers through his hair, yanking at the roots, anxious. Only a few hours remained before he was forced to perform his next Beneficial Act. How could he pull it off without help?

"Thanks for the help Jeremy, but I'm off to buy a new phone."

◻◈◈◈◻

Thirty minutes later, Robert was at a mall store, standing in line by a cash register. He purchased an untraceable prepaid phone, then stepped into the mall corridor and unwrapped it. He had a signal in seconds. He took out the note from his pocket and dialed. Someone answered, but it wasn't Sloan.

"Hello, can I help you?"

"I need to speak with Agent Sloan. This is Mr. de Gourgues. It's an emergency."

"Sorry, sir, but no one is here by that name."

"Listen, I know I'm supposed to use a special phone, but it didn't work any longer. The signal was jammed somehow. I have an urgent message to give him. It's time-sensitive."

"Sir, why don't you give me the message, and I can pass it on to someone here, to help you."

"You don't understand. I was dealing only with Agent Sloan."

"Sir, please tell me, what is the nature of your situation."

"Nature of the situation! It's a matter of life or death. In just a couple hours from now, they want me to enact again, like back in Boston. Only this time with my father-in-law."

"Look, Mr. de Gourgues, you're not making a lot of sense. Slow down, tell me everything from the beginning."

A strange feeling welled up in Robert, terrified he might have jeopardized the covert operation already. He hung up the call. He hastened to the nearest trash barrel and threw away the new phone.

Upstream without a paddle . . . without Agent Sloan.

Half an hour later, Robert pulled into the driveway. He noticed an unfamiliar silver sedan parked in front of the house. He got out of his Jag, the stranger with the fedora stepped out as well.

"Hello, Robert. Nice day, don't you think? Ready to go?"

"I need to freshen up a moment. Please come in."

Robert escorted him into the house and pondered how to slow down this train wreck.

"Please, seat yourself comfortably in the parlor," Robert said. "Nina, bring coffee for my guest," he called out down the hall. "I'll just be a moment."

Robert bowed his head and excused himself, then darted to

the library. He bolted to the window and looked out, hoping someone was there watching the house as they had spied in Brussels. This was his last-ditch effort to seek out help before it was too late.

To his surprise and delight, a lone man walked across the lawn. Stepping onto the back porch, he moved along the length, staying close to the side, hidden from view through the glass panels of the door. The man was dark-haired, tall, and slender. He wore a cheap suit just like Agent Sloan and exposed perfect pearly whites.

"Yes, do you need something?" He asked without any expression on his face, all business.

"Where's Agent Sloan?"

"Unavailable. What's up?"

"They want me to kill Mr. La France. Soon, like within minutes from now, literally."

The man nodded, touched his ear with his finger, and jogged away. Once again, the man concealed himself in the tree line. Robert wondered if this meant all was well and that they would take care of the details. He returned to the parlor and drank a cup of coffee with the man. He tried to delay the inevitable as long as possible.

"Here. Use this weapon this time. Catch."

The man with the fedora heaved a gun, which landed heavily in Robert's lap. Startled by the abrupt toss, Robert relaxed once he saw the Korth combat .357 magnum, the Rolls Royce of revolvers, sitting in his lap.

Robert enjoyed guns and often went shooting for sport. The action of the trigger—the recoil—all helped him to relax, that was until recently. He hesitantly picked the revolver up and turned the gun around in his hands, appreciating the fine craftsmanship. It felt comfortable.

It was a German gun. A work of art...produced with only

hardened tool steel that took on a bluish sheen when the light hit its barrel just right. He turned the piece in his hands, admired the exposed chrome pins, and fittings—all the shiny details pleasing to his eye. The walnut wood grain was polished to perfection. Gun collectors appreciated this kind of craftsmanship. He owned one himself. A Korth was legendary and so well made that it often endured generations of use, yet remained like new. The gun for the pretentious buyer, who believed no expense was too great for true quality.

"You should be more careful," Robert said. "Where did you get this piece? It looks like expensive customization."

"It belongs to some rich person we want to frame for the murder." The stranger smiled but sounded nonchalant as if framing someone was a common occurrence for him. Considering what he witnessed the past few days, the man probably witnessed illegal activities on the bequest of the Black Wolf daily.

"Really," Robert said. "So who's the unfortunate soul? I bet the Society wants to take all his money, too." Robert hoped to keep the conversation going, but the man fidgeted as if tired of the stalling.

"It doesn't matter who. Let's go, it's getting late. We'll take your car if you don't mind."

He smirked. A suspicious evil grin slid across his mouth.

"You know, for a man who wants to be a full-fledged Black Wolf member, you ask a lot of questions. Word of advice, friend, keep your trap shut. You must be excited about the chance to kill your father-in-law, non? After all, he's loaded, and you happen to be married to his only heiress. Cha-Ching. Non?"

"Well, on the last point, you're right. But I'm not relishing the idea of explaining things to my wife. She'll no doubt be upset over her father's death. I'll be stuck dealing with the regret for the rest of my life."

"I wouldn't worry about that if I were you. *Le mari fou.*" The man with the fedora laughed aloud.

Robert pulled his head back a tick, confused about what the man thought so comical. His babysitter demanded to drive, so Robert tossed the man the keys to his Jag. They sped off, the quickest trip to Rachael's father's house, ever. Robert kept glancing at the side door's rearview, waiting for a cop to pull them over. Unfortunately, no one noticed them zipping around the other cars, racing through Mid-town. The man behaved like a kid, driving in his first sports car, joyriding, and trying to impress his groupies.

They arrived at the mansion in one piece. Robert got out of the car and held out his hand until the man wearing the fedora handed back the keys. *They took all the money, no way in hell he's going to take my car, too.* Suddenly the reality of that thought hit, and Robert never felt more horrified. *I lost my family's money, and now I'm about to kill my father-in-law.* How had he gone down this steep spiral, and so fast?

In a matter of days, his life had changed drastically—from a rich businessman, only looking out for himself—to a sorrowful brother who behaved desperately, trying to do penance. Then it hit, the full realization of what was happening to him. The Black Wolf Society intended to frame him. *I'm the patsy!*

A sick feeling swelled from his gut. *They want it to look like I killed him for my wife's inheritance because I lost all of my family's money. Oh God.* He inspected the gun's details again, turned it over in his sweaty hands, trying not to lose his grip. Years ago, he had purchased a Korth magnum similar to this one, but he had his name engraved. It was the same size, just over six inches. He recalled that it never concealed well, but the gun had performed with accuracy. *This could be the same six-shot chamber from my gun.* It was a definite possibility.

The outside handle could have been customized to look different, easy enough. He opened it to expose the cylinder, which was loaded with bullets, then he spun the tumbler and locked it into position. He heard the fine-tuned click and felt all the springs locking in place. Hope for an acceptable ending was fading.

Robert would be branded a murderer for the sake of money, and he knew in his heart that wasn't such a long leap for anyone to believe. After all, making money had been his life's ambition. Anyone who knew him would easily swallow that pill. The cover story would be printed in the papers no doubt because Sloan was all about having the scenario play out. Any chance for Robert to turn his life into something good vanished before him.

Maybe his life and dreams had always been an illusion. A brief thought passed. He pictured himself raising the Magnum to his head, waiting for relief to come. Then her face surfaced in his mind's eye—only the image of Rachael stopped him cold.

They entered through the back door of the mansion. Turning right, they walked down the hallway and stopped at Mr. La France's office door.

"Ready, Robert?" The man wore a smirk again.

"Not really."

The stranger took off his fedora and opened the door anyway, then stepped inside. Robert followed.

The space looked different in the daylight than he remembered from the other night. Light flooded into the span from the bank of windows on the far wall. The bookshelves looked brighter with the colorful spines filling the spaces. Robert stared at the section in the corner. His sister had told him about the hidden secret passage behind the panel, and he wondered why Mr. La France had it constructed.

Maybe it started out as a harmless tornado shelter. Some

new homes in the area made a point of building shelter below ground as a safety precaution against tornados. It made for a great sales pitch when trying to stand out from other contractors. No matter, the room below was decked out as a secret meeting place, according to Emilie. *And why the mysterious disappearance in the middle of the reception?* It didn't make sense. A man of his means had no need to join a group full of moneymongers that would only want to suck him dry. Robert's face flushed. He felt foolish because that's exactly what happened to him.

"Robert," Mr. La France said, "I'm surprised to see you. Rachael's not here if you were looking for her."

Robert jumped and turned around. Mr. La France stood behind him. His eyes were too blue and stared through him like sharp icicles.

"Good afternoon, sir." Robert cleared his throat. "No, I'm not looking for Rachael. We're here to see you."

The old man looked at the stranger standing next to Robert. He couldn't make proper introductions since he didn't know the man's real name and introducing him as STRANGER just didn't seem wise.

"No one's here. Let's get it done fast," the man holding the fedora said.

Robert plucked his hand from his jacket pocket, raised the Magnum, pointing it at his father-in-law. He witnessed Mr. La France's eyes as they popped open, wide with surprise. His expression verified that he wasn't in the know. A message from Agent Sloan's people had never arrived. Either that or Mr. La France was a damn good actor. Maybe the message never got passed on and was lost in the shuffle of red tape. Obviously, the stage wasn't set up like back in Boston. Robert's conscience felt unsettled, unsure of whether he could go through with the plan. What would happen when he refused to pull the trigger?

Mr. La France's eyes watered, tears rolled down the side of his face. The old geezer was petrified. Robert couldn't do it. He knew that the probability of Sloan being aware of the situation was slim or null. He understood that if he went through with this—fired a shot at his father-in-law, then he would lose his soul for good. Robert lowered the revolver.

"Hell, I knew you didn't have the balls." The man with the fedora sneered. He put on his hat, grabbed the gun from Robert's hand, and aimed it at the old man.

"No, please." Mr. La France begged his voice a mere whimper.

Then things happened fast and simultaneously. Robert made a split-second decision to grab back the gun. A section of bookshelves pushed open, leaving a dark space behind them. A shadow appeared in the corner of Robert's vision. He twisted his body during his attempt to grab the gun. He saw Rachael, as she leaped out, in front of her father. She yelled aloud. "No!" Her voice rang in Robert's ears while his eyes spotted that weird painting on the wall behind her. It was the Goya knockoff, the one with the dark horned figure addressing the distorted faces. The man with the fedora pulled the trigger just as Robert's hand touched the gun's slide. The shot rang out. His hand burned from the heat of the firing pin that had gone off. Robert was gripping onto the gun then let it drop to the floor.

Rachael was hit, her blood squirted in mid-air. Her body fell hard to the floor. Robert looked down at her in disbelief. Her green eyes winced as if in extreme pain, then she closed them. Robert was numb and heard Mr. La France call out, "Holy God." In a rage, Robert stormed at the kid with the fedora. He stood with the gun in hand and squeezed out another shot before Robert could stop him. To Robert's horror, Mr. La France dropped dead to the floor and landed next to Rachael.

Robert fled to their side and knelt on the floor. A flood of

blood gushed from Mr. La France's middle. Picking up his father-in-law's arm first, he touched his wrist for a pulse. He confirmed his worst fear, Mr. La France was dead. Robert rolled
him aside and scooped Rachael up into his arms. He held her
close to his chest and cried like a wanton baby denied his needs.
Afraid to check her for a pulse, fearing she was dead as well, he
refused to confirm her status. He rocked her body while warm
tears dripped down his face and salted his dry lips.

"Oh, Rachael, I'm so sorry." Robert droned in between
sobs. "What have I done? Lord, what have I done?"

"What are you doing? Come on, let's get out of here," the
man with a fedora said.

Robert looked up. He hated the man standing there.

After placing Rachael back on the floor, Robert rose and
faced the man. Robert pulled out his Glock that was hidden in
a holster resting on the small of his back. Ever since he had returned from Brussels, he carried it as a precaution. Although he
deplored the violence, he had been coerced to undertake as
Beneficial Acts, and Robert had felt more secure carrying a
weapon, especially since they had kidnapped Emilie.

He pointed the gun at the man with a fedora, aimed at his
midsection, and pulled the trigger. Again and again, shots rang
out, but the intolerable man didn't flinch. He stood, uninjured,
his face red from anger. Robert slid out the clip—it was empty.
The man with a fedora laughed.

"I knew you wouldn't do the Act, coward. Looks like I won
the bet that some of us had going."

Enraged, Robert lunged forward and smacked the man in
the jaw, then wrestled him to the floor. He threw another
punch, but he dodged it, and the blow landed on the floor instead. His hand ached, but he fought on anyway, throwing
crazy lunges one after another. Some hit the target, but Robert
received as many hits as he delivered. With the taste of blood

in his mouth, Robert scrambled on the floor. He tried to reach for the Magnum, but it slid further across the floor with every attempt. The man with the fedora jumped to his feet, picked up his hat and the gun, then headed for the door.

"We don't have time for this shit. Let's go before it's too late," he called over his shoulder. He left the room.

Robert sprung to his feet and followed him out to the drive-way. A car pulled up, and the man with a fedora got into the small compact. Robert leaned his head inside of the vehicle and could only stare. He recognized the driver. It was the tall, slender man in the cheap suit. He must have been working with this guy all along. The driver winked at Robert as he shifted into gear. The car rolled forward. Robert felt his face boil, enraged, he started after the car. He beat his fists on the trunk as they drove away. Dirt ripped from the ground as the tires spun dust all over his clothes.

Angry and grief-stricken, Robert stomped down the drive-way, pounding his feet against the pavement. He wanted to punch someone, he wanted to hurt someone, and then he saw Agent Sloan. He walked across the lawn as if nothing was of consequence, not a care in the world. *Was he whistling?* Robert ran toward him with fists clenched and ready to be raised.

Agent Sloan stopped. A wary expression glazed over his face, and he raised his hand in protest, bowing his head slightly, indicating he wasn't about to partake in any banter with Robert.

"Really!" Robert said. "Now you're here." His tone purposefully demonstrated his anger and disgust, as he spat the words between short breaths. He dropped his arms. "Now that my wife is already shot—no, murdered. My life is over. You promised that you'd protect us. My family—they've suffered because of you, and the deal that we made. It wasn't supposed to hurt anyone."

The Agent snapped his head back as if confused. "Take me to the scene."

Robert lunged forward, in an attempt to strangle Sloan. But the Agent was quicker and was already heading toward the house. Robert followed. They jogged back to the house, but when they entered the office, there were no bodies.

"Oh my God. Where's Rachael? She was lying right here, next to her father. There was blood everywhere." Robert bent down, on hands and knees, and touched the carpet. In a panicked motion, he swept his hands across the floor, feeling for traces of wet blood. Nothing was there, it was dry as a bone.

"I don't understand. I'm going crazy." He gasped. "Rachael fell, right here. She was shot right in front of me." Robert pounded his fist against the floor.

Agent Sloan remained silent, stood in the center of the room, and leaned against the table. Robert looked up and watched as the agent combed the room with his inspection, section by section. Methodically. Then Sloan walked to where Robert knelt and held out his hand to help him up.

"Tell me exactly, what happened here."

Robert explained as best he could in his agitated state of mind. His recollection of the incident was interrupted every few minutes when he broke down and shook with tears. Whenever he thought about Rachael and envisioned her mischievous green eyes, her smell, and all the little things he loved about her, then he collapsed. He couldn't imagine living without her touch against his skin. He was addicted to her—a shudder coursed through his body. A flash image of her face with that last worn expression of pain. Wiping his eyes, Robert stood and said, "Please, help me find her body."

CHAPTER 27

Death Follows Me

Robert walked over to the bookcase and pushed against the shelves, no give. Tugging at the spines that were lined up straight and orderly, he searched for anything that could be a trigger.

"What are you doing?" Agent Sloan asked.

"My sister and her fiancé said there was a hidden panel that led to a secret room below. I'm looking for it. Maybe that's how they took Rachael's body away."

"Hold on, let me get my tech guys here. We need to protect the scene and you're getting fingerprints all over everything and making a mess."

Robert rolled his eyes and shook his head. He continued his search while listening to Agent Sloan as he called his team to send forensics to the scene right away.

"While you're at it," Robert called over his shoulder, "have them bring Jeremy Laughton here. He's been down there once before. I know for a fact that he's at the house right now with nothing to do."

Agent Sloan nodded and conveyed his orders, then hung up the call.

"Robert, stop. While we wait, let's talk. You can catch me up on everything that happened."

"Really?" Robert smirked sarcastically. "You want to talk now. Why didn't you pick up the phone when I called before? I was completely in the dark. This entire disaster could have been prevented. It's on your head, Agent Sloan. You're as much a murderer as I."

Robert stopped himself cold, closed his eyes, and held back

his screams. Inside he was on fire, his nerves burning against his skin. The image of Rachael lying on the floor, dead, made him ill. And now her body missing—nowhere to be found. This was his worst nightmare, her being shot. He wanted to kill someone and make someone accountable for her death. His only love, Rachael, was gone.

"As you may have already assessed, the operation has been compromised. The phone I gave you was no longer safe to use. Quick thinking on your part, to get a new device and call. I received the message but we had so little time. None of this going sideways is your fault."

Agent Sloan reached his hand up to touch Robert's shoulder, but it was abruptly shrugged off.

"Yes, well, what about the man who came to the door at my house? Wasn't he with you? I told him about the next Beneficial Act, all the time thinking he worked for you, and then, I see him drive away with my Black Wolf contact. Man-o-man, I blew it. Rachael, please forgive me, sweetheart. Sloan, I have to find her."

Robert slumped to the floor and cried. Agent Sloan patted Robert's shoulder.

"You didn't mess anything up. Robert, he is one of us, he's working undercover."

"So, does this mean that Rachael is all right?" Robert was hopeful for a moment. "I'm impressed, you arranged things in time and she's all right," he sighed. "Then where is she?"

"Well don't be impressed." Sloan walked toward the window. "I have no idea where she is, nor a clue of where to look. There's still something we're missing—a missing piece to this puzzle." His voice trailed off as he thought. "Even though we instructed everyone, and put in security measures around the mansion, something went wrong. The disappearance of the bodies had nothing to do with our plan. Plus, it looks like a professional clean-up job, but how? How did they do it with the surveillance we had around the perimeter of the house? Strange."

Other agents entered the room, along with Jeremy.

"Thank God. Jeremy, I'm so glad you're here," Robert said.

Jeremy squinted, questioning. His glance went to Sloan, who stood beside Robert. Jeremy held out his hand. "Well, hello again. It's Jeffrey Sloan, right? The last time I saw you, Emilie and I were being shot at, and you were saving our ass. Here you are again with my soon-to-be brother-in-law. Tell me something, I'm curious. After everything settled down in Brussels, I realized that you must have taken the book I had with me that night for safekeeping. Where is it now?"

Agent Sloan smiled. "Mr. Laughton," he reached out his hand and shook Jeremy's. "Yes, indeed, I have your book."

Robert was confused by this added information.

"So, are you two going to share? What book?"

"Robert, when Emilie and I followed you down to the basement levels of the chamber room, we stayed after you were taken away. They brought in another person, and I use that term loosely. It was actually a creature with some human features, but more like a body that had been pieced together. It was Doctor Frankenstein's lab experiment gone bad."

"You're kidding me," Robert said, repulsed. "How evil does this group go?" He grabbed his gut.

"Are you okay?" Jeremy's concern was genuine.

"I'm fine. Just getting ulcers. Continue, please. I want to hear everything."

"Myself as well," Agent Sloan said.

"Here's the weird part," Jeremy continued. "They were electrocuting the thing, or something similar to that, with a contraption. Your sister connected with the feelings of the creature somehow. When they shocked it, Emilie felt zapped as well and she jumped out from our hiding spot. She instinctively flung her power on them."

Robert knew what Jeremy meant. Emilie's strange gift, the flowing of energy from her hands. "My God. What happened next?"

"She held her arms out, and they disintegrated, Robert. I mean, gone completely. We unbound the creature, but it was too late. We knew we had to get out of there quick before someone else returned to the room. But I happened a glance down on the makeshift altar and spotted my uncle's book. I'd recognize it anywhere. It was opened to a page, but we didn't have time to check it out, so in a hurry, Emilie bent some of the old pages to mark the spot, even though it pained me to have her do so. The pages are fragile, and we took a chance of harming the parchment. Still, we did it against our better judgment. I grabbed hold of the book, and then we ran out of there as fast as we could. We thought we were safe once we exited the door, but then the shooting started. Mr. Sloan saved us, for which I am very thankful."

"Jeremy, meet *Agent* Sloan."

Jeremy twisted his head sideways. "Hmm. Figures. Thank you for saving us, Agent Sloan."

"All in a day's work. You look much better; you heal fast."

"Thanks. And my uncle's journal . . ."

"I do have your book and intend on returning it to you, but we've been studying it first. Thanks to you for marking the pages, we knew where to begin. The open page had some kind of old incantation written. All those years ago, when the journal was written, European sailors took port in the towns of the West Indies. Back then, there were rumors of evil sorcery that could raise the dead.

"Stories of the living dead and the fountain of youth were

common folklore back then. Some sailors were willing to pay for talismans, potions, amulets, hex bags, spells, the list goes on with things of that nature. They procured these things from the local voodoo priests and witches. The conjuration written on that particular page is supposedly the words of an evil priestess, who claimed to know how to make the cursed dead come alive once again."

Robert laughed aloud. "Give me a break. More curses again. This time, raising the dead! Zombies? Really?"

"People were superstitious back then, so I understand it exists. But why would anyone give merit to the idea today?" Jeremy said.

"As if you don't give superstitious beliefs a moment's notice?" Robert blurted. "Please. Not too long ago you traipsed around France with my sister, to break a curse."

Bitter, Robert was ready to explode. This was too much for him to handle right now. The real world was hard enough to navigate these past few weeks. *Curses, skinwalkers, monsters from the other side of the veil, and a murderous secret society.* All bad enough, but now they want to bring dead creatures to life. The world had gone mad, and Robert tipped over the edge as well. *Why can't we just concentrate on finding Rachael?*

"The open page referenced a secret code used to disguise ingredients and a procedure. We deciphered the cryptogram and discovered the details of an experiment, which we named project Frankenstein for a lack of better words. Its intentions were purely to animate life back from the dead. Virtually creating the living dead."

Agent Sloan walked over to the bookcase. "Jeremy, can you show us how to get in? We're looking for two bodies that were shot, presumably left here dead on this floor, but have tragically disappeared."

"It's not a joke, Sloan. My wife's safety is important."

"Rachael's shot? Dead?"

"Missing, we hope that's all," Robert said. "We need to find her quick to get her to the hospital."

"Sorry, Robert," Sloan said. "I didn't mean to make light of things. Of course, it's not a joke."

"Thanks. And by the way, you'll need to talk with my sister about this experiment business. I just remembered. Emilie told me that she saw some experiments when they held her captive."

Sloan stopped and turned to face Robert.

"Really. Interesting. I'll speak with her, but first, let's find your wife. I promised you I'd keep everyone safe, and I failed. The least I can do is find her. Until we know different, assume she is alive, Robert."

Those words gave him the added boost he needed. Robert looked toward Jeremy, who had already released the hinge, and pushed the panel open. Agent Sloan led the way, and Robert was right behind him.

They walked down to where Jeremy had seen the altar, but it was gone. The space was empty, but they discovered a door at the far wall with a backway out. Climbing the stairs, the door at the top opened into the side garden of the estate.

"Be careful where you step, gentlemen." Agent Sloan raised his arm to stop Robert from going into the yard. "Let me call forensics here to check footprint patterns."

"Now what?" Robert said. "I can't even search for my wife."

Jeremy was behind him and put a hand on his shoulder.

"Let's go home and let the agents do their job. There's nothing else for us here."

"Sounds like a good plan. You all need some rest. I'll stop at the house later this evening with a briefing of what we learn. Then we can decide how to proceed." Agent Sloan looked at

Robert as he spoke, but he was unable to connect all the words.

Everything Robert felt inside tumbled into one big mess. He was angry, hurt, depressed, and confused. Without any energy left, he complied with Agent Sloan's wishes and followed Jeremy to his car. He let Jeremy drive his Jag home. Jeremy pulled the car up next to Michelle's and parked. *Great, everyone is here.* Everyone except my wife. Robert got out and aimlessly walked toward the house.

"Robert, let me pour you a drink," Jeremy called out.

They went into the parlor, and Robert poured his own drink, gulped it down, then poured a second and a third. Emilie and Michelle stared at him. He dared them to say something. After a few moments alone in his glow, he turned and sank into the armchair.

"Well, doesn't anyone have anything to say?" He heard himself speak, his voice sounded harsh. "Sorry. Please forgive me." He blathered on, "I'm in a mood and not fit to socialize right now."

Emilie sat on the sofa with Jeremy by her side. He gently stroked his hand on her arm, as if caressing her, calming her down. Robert knew his sister felt his pain. He shook his head. "Emilie, you don't want to feel this, please get out of my emotions."

"Robert, this emotion you're feeling is nothing new to me. It's exactly how father felt."

Her words didn't help. Instead, it made him feel worse, knowing that his actions had added to the grief Father had already felt after Mother died. "Death seems to follow me around."

"Don't be ridiculous. Any of us could say the same thing," Michelle said. She was standing behind his chair. She reached down and placed her hand on his shoulder.

"Why in God's name are you two so good to me?" Robert

started to cry. Inside he was even angrier at himself. The past couple of days he had let his heart pour out, the wall crumbled around him. He had become a blubbering idiot. Though he vowed to stay strong, that mental state was only an illusion. Michelle came around the chair to face him, hunched down, reached out, and hugged him. He breathed in her hair and touched her cheek with his. She felt soft like she did when she was nothing more than his little baby sister. His tears were dried on her blouse's shoulder.

After a few quiet moments, Jeremy started the conversation. "You two must wonder what's happened. Robert, do you want to tell them?"

"You explain it to them, old sport, will you?" Robert closed his eyes and listened. He hoped that maybe the words would make sense now, that somehow what he understood was wrong, and that Jeremy would somehow tell a different truth. It didn't happen that way. The words flowing from Jeremy's mouth were the unfortunate reality that Robert knew and had to find a way to deal with, somehow.

"Remember Jeffrey Sloan?" Jeremy asked Emilie.

"Of course."

"The guy who drove you two to the hospital?" Michelle asked.

"Yes. Well, it turns out he is Agent Sloan, a Federal Agent. He had recruited Robert's assistance, which apparently he gave, in hopes to keep everyone in this family safe. Unfortunately, something happened today—Rachael was shot by a man who was Robert's contact in the Black Wolf Society."

Emilie stood up, fists balled. "You promised me that you weren't going to join them."

Her voice sounded accusing. Part of Robert wanted to fight back, but he was too weary to care.

"Emilie, he's not. He was trying to help the government."

Jeremy clarified for him.

"Wow, that's cool. My brother's a secret agent. I love stuff like that," Michelle added.

"Don't try to make this sound like fun, Chelle. It's not." Robert turned to address her directly. "I wasn't asked—exactly—to do this. It was more like I had to—to atone for my previous unlawful sins. I had an *in* with the Black Wolves that the FBI needed; a peek into one of the worst groups ever in history, and only because I was going down that road. It's all my fault. If I hadn't been so foolish . . . then Rachael would still be alive."

"Robert, we don't know she's dead for sure. There's nobody. Maybe she was taken to the hospital." Jeremy pulled out his phone. "Let's call Doc, see if he can make inquiries at the hospital."

Emilie stood, took the phone from him, and walked away to make the call. They could hear her talking, asking to speak with Doc Hannigan, their family physician, and confidant.

"We won't give up hope, Rob, and neither should you until we know for sure. If she's alive she's going to need you to be strong," Michelle said.

There's that word again, strong. Robert closed his eyes and prayed for some kind of inner strength to carry him through this ordeal. He knew who he was. A spoiled brat, an eccentric playboy who desperately wanted to be legitimate, like his father. A man who feared he was more like the wolf, Tom Bennett. His nightmare that he might be Bennett's biological son, drilled open a deep pit filled with self-loathing. *If he was the son of a psychopath, what would that mean?*

"Emilie and Michelle, I need to level with you both, just in case."

"What do you mean by that?" Michelle said.

"Just listen to me, without interrupting. I want you to hear it all, while I still have time to tell you from my heart."

Robert exposed every secret he had, each thought of his supremacy that had been knocked down by cold reality. He confessed everything he did to their father and explained the ache he still had when he thought of their mother. Robert admitted he murdered Mr. Pierce and red-faced, he told Michelle about his involvement to get her out of the way. He had gone down a dark path of a killer, a follower of evil. Then he told them of his worse fears—that he had suspicions that he was the son of a monster, and he worried whether he deserved to live.

"Rob, no matter what, we are blood. We're your family. I forgive you and hope someday you'll forgive yourself," Emilie said. "I'm happy that you've come to terms with the things you've done but they are in the past, and now you see the error of your ways. That's the pathway to true redemption."

"Michelle, I see you're not as forgiving, and I don't blame you. I was horrible to you," Robert said. He lowered his head and closed his eyes.

"I never dreamed that my big brother did all that—I think I draw the line with murder, Rob. Maybe the Feds gave you a break, but I'm not so sure I can. By the way, you forgot. One more thing you should mention with all this confessing."

"What?"

"Tell Em about the missing money."

Robert shook his head. "I'm drained of energy. I'm going to my room. You tell her, Chelle. You can use any foul language you want. I deserve it." He walked away and went upstairs. He lay on the bed, closed his eyes, and went to sleep. He couldn't face one more thought.

CHAPTER 28

A Dead Body

It was seven in the evening when Robert was woken by a phone's ring. It was the flip phone.

"I'll be there in fifteen minutes," Agent Sloan said then hung up.

Robert wiped his hands over his face, opened his eyes, and got out of bed. Making his way to the bathroom, he drew in a deep breath. He smelled her perfume, a whisper remembrance that Rachael had been there. He hoped he would see her soon, but feared she might already be dead. *Remain hopeful,* he scolded himself.

He had fallen asleep in his clothes. Undressing from his rumpled shirt, Robert looked at himself in the mirror. His focus went straight to the scar on his face. Rachael had never asked him about it. Not once had she mentioned the lines of thick pink flesh, shiny in the light, while still healing. Tom Bennett had scratched his face, swiping it with his claws, after he had turned. *How could she not have noticed this thick scar on my face? She did of course, but she chose not to ask anything about it, curious.* A burning sensation churned in his stomach and traveled up to his chest. He rubbed his body and tried to quell the pain. Furious that she was missing and horrified that she was most probably dead, but even more—he was angry. He realized for the first time that Rachael didn't care about him at all. She had never been concerned enough to even ask about the scar.

Rachael played the part of the lover, willingly eloped, and she wanted a big party to celebrate. But had Rachael ever said that she loved him? No, it had always been him. She played along, they had great sex, but that wasn't what his soul needed.

He wanted her to love him, the way his sister loved Jeremy. *Who am I to complain—I'm a louse and don't deserve her love. It doesn't matter if she only pretended; I'll take whatever she offers. I love her enough for both of us.*

Robert splashed water on his face and rubbed himself dry with the towel a little too hard. He changed into a fresh shirt and hurried downstairs. His sisters were gabbing away in the parlor but quieted down as soon as he walked into the room.

"Where's Jeremy?" he asked.

"He went to rest, but he'll be back before dinner."

"Is he alright?"

Emilie nodded, and Robert sensed her sending out her feelers, felt her presence in his thoughts.

"Em, stop it! Get out of my head."

"Come here, sit with us," Michelle said. She patted the sofa cushion beside her. Robert reluctantly sat between his sisters.

"You sure you want me here Michelle? You hate me, remember."

"No, I don't. Don't put words in my mouth—I do a great job sticking my foot in it all by myself." Michelle faked a smile. "You disappointed me, but you're trying to make up for the things you did, so relax. Isn't this cozy? Just the three of us together, like when we were kids."

Her voice soothed Robert a bit, his chest expanding more easily with his breathing.

"Do you remember when we dressed up for the Halloween party that mother's friend hosted? We were pirates that year, remember?" She giggled.

"I remember that party. Robert, you had your sword out, swinging it about, and organized a contest for best technique." Emilie added to the story, smiling.

"Yes, as I recall, I was the best swordsman," he said.

They smiled, but tender memories weren't enough to take

away the pain Robert felt inside.

"Agent Sloan will be here any minute. I hope he has some good news, Lord knows we need it. I have to find Rachael. I assume Jeremy told you about Sloan?"

His sisters nodded. The doorbell rang. The three siblings remained seated on the gold velvet sofa, waiting for Evans, who escorted the agent into the parlor and introduced him. "Mr. Sloan is here to see you, sir."

"Yes, thank you, Evans." He stood and watched as Evans left.

"Good evening," Agent Sloan said. "I have some news."

"Have you found Rachael? Is she all right?"

"No, I'm afraid she's still missing. My update has more to do with the Black Wolf Society."

"Oh," Robert said. He hung his head and sat back down. "Well, I don't know if that even matters anymore."

Michelle jumped up. "Hell yes, it matters. Agent Sloan, please will you explain things to Emilie and me. I don't understand why we were left out, to begin with, I mean this affects us as well."

The agent ticked his head toward the chair and Michelle nodded. He sat in the wing chair and Michelle went over and stood behind him, her hands resting on the top. He looked up, his expression stern, but she kept it in place. As he opened a file on his lap, she looked over his shoulder. He sighed, loud enough for Robert to hear his exasperation ten feet away.

"First, I want to thank you, Robert. When we followed you to Brussels, we were able to locate one of their meeting places. We found another when we followed up on your sister's abduction. Although we hadn't followed her right off, we did discover things by backtracking the person who had returned her to the Square. We used the public cameras, captured the plate ID, and traced that back to a hidden corporation. The car they used had a GPS tracker, which pinpointed the location."

Agent Sloan closed the files and grinned up at Michelle. Then he turned his gaze toward Emilie. His dark brown eyes poured out compassion, and his words sounded sincere and from the heart. "My God, that place was a mess. The experience you endured must have been horrible for you, Emilie. I'm sorry you went through that escapade."

"What escapade?" Jeremy heard the last line of the conversation.

"You're welcome to join us, Jeremy," Robert said. "Agent Sloan was just explaining everything they've been able to unfold because of our romp in Belgium. The place they held Em was obviously a dump."

"No. It was worse than that, tell them, Agent Sloan. I may have been blindfolded most of the time, but I didn't have to see to know what a horrible a place it was—best I figured, it must have been the lost crypts."

The Agent slapped his hand on his thigh. "Correct. It was the underground crypts—in the oldest section. We found the room they must have used. It was originally a workmen's space for tools and the like, but we found gurneys and electrical equipment in the small space. Our team will inspect all of it, look for DNA, and see if we can trace anything back to a living, breathing person."

"Ew, Em! You were held up in a crypt, with dead bodies. How awful." Michelle pinched her nose.

"When I first came to, the space I was in was nothing more than a closet with a low ceiling. I couldn't stand upright, and my hands were chained to the wall."

"Oh, Emilie." Michelle took hold of her sister's hands.

"Then they flung a hood over my head and pushed me down, along a corridor of some type; it smelled horrid." She quivered. "One of them pushed me to the floor on purpose, and

I felt the hard cement. I knew it was someplace neglected, because the pavement crumbled under my fingers, and there was muddy dirt in the cracks like it had been leaking. I remembered what I read about the lost crypts in Brussels, so figured maybe, that's where I was."

"You are so creepy, Em. Reading about lost crypts." Michelle sat back, clearly upset by the conversation's topic.

"Then I was brought to another room and they took off the hood. I saw the place. They had experiments going on behind a glass partition. And well, let's just say they had bodies lying around. I'm not sure if they were human or creatures, but they looked dead. The doctor said he liked to experiment with the paranormal, and I would make an interesting subject." Emilie abruptly stopped.

"So, Sloan, will this information help you take them down for good?" Robert asked. "No one should get away with the stuff they pulled." He turned to face his sister. "I'm so sorry, Emilie."

Agent Sloan shrugged his shoulders. "We hope so, of course. Remember the nature of this group. They've been around for ages, morphing into new entities to survive. They have a long history of tormenting, controlling, and surviving. Their agenda is one of gaining control of money and power. They create wars, to control the masses. But this information is giving us headway."

He stood and paced between the chair and sofa, glancing at Robert, then his sisters and back, as he spoke. "The fuel that feeds this beast is money and power. The most important information we've been able to trace in a long time was thanks to the ransom payment. Although they used an old Sparbuch account, which doesn't have to have a name or address attached to it, still when they went back the second time and dipped into your other accounts—it was then, we were able to plant a virus into the bank code that tracks the movement of the money." He smiled from ear to ear.

"Second time?" Robert said.

"Yes, they double dipped you. We discovered the Black Wolf Society had corrupted someone on the inside of the Austrian bank. Maybe that person was a member of the group themselves, anyway whoever it was held onto your account information. Later, while you, Robert, were busy performing the Beneficial Act, they went back into the account and wormed into other connecting accounts as well, transferred funds, and drained all of your accounts. We let them do it and watched, planted the virus that tracks, to see how they maneuverer money. It worked. Now we have a good insight into their procedures."

"Damned right it worked." Michelle fumed. "They took all of our money. Stop smiling, Agent Sloan. There's nothing funny about this situation."

"Yes, well just for the record, may I say, that for three wealthy people who just supposedly lost it all, you don't seem overly upset by the theft."

"Maybe it hasn't sunk in yet," Robert said. "Besides, we do have other issues more pressing, like the whereabouts of my wife. What are you doing to find her?"

"Well, since you let them take the funds—you can reverse it all, right?" She stared at Agent Sloan, her gaze burning. Michelle wasn't about to let the agent off the hook.

"We'll do our best."

"What kind of answer is that?" Michelle stood and began pacing the floor. Sloan sat back down.

"My mistake. You're not all cool and collected."

"Okay, let's assume you can get our money back, for now at least," Emilie said. "How about finding Rachael? I hate to think of what they might possibly do to her. My God, they're probably after the money from her father's estate. They might be torturing her, or worse experimenting."

"Em, don't say such things," Michelle scolded. She darted her eyes toward Robert. He knew Michelle was more concerned about Rachael than she let on.

"We have a team of detectives looking for her. We did some digging on her father, too." The agent said.

"Is he a member of the Society?" Michelle stood still a moment.

Robert was relieved she had stopped her pacing because he couldn't take much more of the fidgeting. His nerves were frazzled enough without the extra tension she added to the room.

"We have to find her body, even if Rachael's dead already, to ensure no one can experiment on her. If her father is a Black Wolf, how could he let them hurt her?" He shuddered at the revolting idea.

"As a matter of fact, no. Mr. La France wasn't a member of the Black Wolf. It seems the only group he had joined was a local businessman's club. They fancy themselves a group similar to the Masons. They meet in secret, work their way up the social ladder, and donate funds to good causes, that sort of thing."

"Again, like the Elks club. Unbelievable." Michelle said. "Why do these groups always need secret rooms?"

"Agent Sloan," Emilie's voice sounded irritated. "You mean to tell me there was nothing sinister going on down there?"

"To be honest, I have no clue what they did in their ceremonies or meetings, but I do know for fact, he is not a member of the Black Wolf Society."

"It doesn't sound like we've learned much," Robert said. "I need to find my wife. Now."

Agent Sloan's phone buzzed. He listened and nodded, then said, "I'll be right there."

"What is it?" Robert stood.

"They found a body."

"I'm going with you," Robert started for the door.

"Me too," the others all said simultaneously.

Robert went with Agent Sloan in his bureau car and the other three followed in Jeremy's truck. They drove north going toward Millington, then veered off the main highway, and drove down Shake Rag Road until they ended up on a lonely dirt road that worked better as a path. It led them to a place where two very old and large smokestacks stood alone in a vast emptiness. For as far as the eye could see, there were no other buildings in sight.

"This is the location of the old guncotton plant that had been knocked down back in 1946 after the war." Agent Sloan slowed the car. Scrap woods surrounded the now barren fields. "An ammunitions plant once stood here. It had over a hundred buildings, and there was a system of railway tracks and tunnels to transport explosive materials."

Robert remembered something. His father had mentioned this property once before. Pierre de Gourgues had turned down an opportunity to buy some of the land here. He passed the deal up, even though it had been thousands of acres priced well. When Robert questioned him about it, his father said that he feared the soil was contaminated from all the chemicals used years ago when they manufactured smokeless powder for the war effort. Other prominent local businessmen bought the land, and as far as Robert knew, it remained owned by private entities. They drove a short distance and stopped when they saw the flashing lights of the Sheriff's car.

Robert closed his car door and followed Sloan along a path until they reached the edge of a small stream that ran through the area. They scampered down a low embankment. A Sheriff spoke to Sloan and pointed, and the two men continued along the stream. Robert followed them until they spotted a body. The coroner was already there, leaning across the corpse, adjusting his angle to allow the turning over of the body.

"On the count of three," the coroner said. "One, two, three . . ."

The corpse was dressed in men's clothing, the head was swollen, most probably because it had been facing down in the cold running water. Rocks on the shoreline had dark red blotches, smeared with blood.

"Robert, do you recognize the body? Is this Mr. La France?" Sloan's voice sounded all business.

Robert leaned closer, stared, and tried to make out details. The clothes were stained with blood and had holes where bullets must have entered. "It's him. I recognize the suit. It was his favorite deal-making outfit. Some people have lucky hats, he had his lucky Zegna threads." *Poor man.* No deal mattered now—the man was dead.

The sight of his dead father-in-law and the realization that the man was indeed shot dead earlier that afternoon right in front of him, nauseated Robert. He feared the worst for his beloved Rachael. He gagged, cupped his hand over his mouth afraid he was about to lose it all, but with an empty stomach, he was only able to dry heave. The reflux burned against the back of his throat.

His sisters and Jeremy ran to his side.

"Oh my God!" Michelle said aloud, then covered her mouth, truly horrified.

Jeremy reached down the embankment and grabbed Robert's arm, and pulled him up. "Come on, let's go home. There's nothing we can do here."

No one disagreed with Jeremy. They trampled through the dry weeds, back toward the vehicles in silence. A minute later, Agent Sloan joined them and they left the crime scene.

"Sorry we haven't found Rachael's body," he said to Robert as they drove to the house.

Robert shook his head, with eyes closed. "No news is good news. Maybe she's not dead." *A man can dream,* he thought to himself.

CHAPTER 29

Abducted

By the time they returned to the house, the dinner hour had passed. Famished, the family decided to eat together in the kitchen. Aunt Victoria had waited for their return and joined them. She listened to the news and gave her laments. All the while, Nina whizzed about in the room, serving food that no one ate despite their claims of hunger. All the soothing talk and comfort food couldn't console Robert.

Rachael's chair remained empty. He glanced to his left as if searching to see her shadow. Not able to bear the torment of her absence, Robert excused himself and stumbled upstairs with a drink in his hand, a full bottle in the other. His intentions were to drink until he passed out.

He opened the French doors that led out to the upper porch and let in the night air. Coldness blew into the room, the drapes flapped, and papers that were stacked on a table flew up, swirled, and landed on the other side of the room. Without notice or care, Robert slumped into the armchair and stared out into the night. Not moving a muscle, he watched the pitch autumn sky twinkle with bright stars. They blurred as tears clouded his vision.

Sniffing back his sorrow, he poured another drink and swigged it down. The bottle was half gone already, so he downed it as well. Then Robert threw the glass across the room. It collided with the wall, shattered, and pieces of glass rained down to the floor. Robert closed his eyes and passed out, still hanging on to the empty bottle.

When he came to, it was complete darkness. Robert wondered where he was and felt the chair underneath him. The lush cloth cushion had disappeared—he wasn't in his room any longer. He was seated on a chair made of hardwood. He opened his eyes but couldn't see a thing except for pitch black. He drew in a breath and sensed the room's stuffiness as if an oven or fireplace blazed nearby, but there was no evidence of such. He reached his hands out in front of him, trying to touch anything about, as he called aloud. "Hello." He heard his voice echo. "Hello," he said again, and again his voice carried as if in a hollow chamber. Then he heard a noise, a thud. Footfall, someone wore boots, heading toward him.

At a distance, maybe about twenty feet away, he heard the jingling of keys, then the clunk sound of a bolt being relieved of its position and slid sideways, scraping metal to metal. A door groaned as it opened, and a sliver of light spread into the room.

"Are you awake yet, Mr. de Gourgues?"

"Where am I? Who are you? How did I get here?"

"All in due time." The door widened to its fullest. Robert noticed a large room just beyond, glowing with amber light. The person drew closer to the area. He wore a black robe, and a mask covered his face. When he stood beside Robert, the man yanked him up from the chair.

"Over there, on the table. Put on the robe and mask."

Robert stumbled in the dark until he bumped into the leg of the table. His fingers searched the top, groping until he found the robe and mask. The man struck a match and lit a candle. Finally, a warm glow illuminated the room. Robert recognized the standard Black Wolf garment in his hands.

"There, now put it on like a good newbie. You have one minute. I'll be back to take you into the big hall to join the others."

"What others? How did I get here?"

"Stop asking questions," the masked man said. He turned his back to Robert without another word.

Robert slipped on the robe.

"Again with the pig face," he mumbled to himself.

He snapped the rubber mask into place, snug over his face. The air behind the facemask quickly heated up from his heavy panicked breathing. *Yoga breaths, slow and easy, use Yoga breaths.* He tried his best to control his breathing and keep his perspiring to a minimum.

"Okay then, let's get on with the show." The white-masked man waved his arm for Robert to follow.

Robert turned quickly and bumped into a whiteboard, causing it to roll back a few feet. It was the kind of board he had seen before on manufacturing floors when he did business tours to evaluate companies' production processes. Often the boards would be littered with lists of the goals, targets, and tasks that needed to be executed in a work area. He squinted to see what was scribbled on this whiteboard in black marker.

He read the names listed on the board—Emilie de Gourgues, Michelle de Gourgues, Bethany de Gourgues his mother, Nina Parks their cook and homemaker, and of course their father's name Pierre de Gourgues listed on the top. They were all scratched through, except his own name, which was written underneath his father's. Scribed on the top in red marker like a heading in large letters was written: *"Kill them all."*

Robert stepped back in shock, horror gnawed inside his gut. He dreaded the implications and whatever this board's message meant. Just like Tom Bennett had wanted them all dead, obviously, someone here, wherever this place was, felt the same sentiment.

"Now," the man yelled out.

Robert rolled the board away and followed the masked

man in the black robe. They walked down a wide hallway and entered into another grand space. The walls in the great room were made of stone blocks. Jerking his head left then right, Robert scoped out the place. Coat of arms flags with varying designs hung sporadically. He counted over a dozen different emblems hanging, some with animal faces, and others with swords, helmets, and the like, but none of the designs looked familiar.

A shove from behind encouraged Robert to trudge forward into the middle of the room. He spotted the opposite wall approximately twenty yards away, and a structure resembling an altar of a church. The robed man shoved him from behind again, coaxing Robert forward.

The space around him was filled with a mass of robed people, gathered together as if waiting for a show. They stood in rows facing the altar ahead. Space was reserved for a center aisle, wide enough for Robert to pass through.

Making his way down the aisle, Robert turned his head to glimpse at the others in the room. They willfully turned their masked faces toward Robert as he progressed down the aisle and passed them. They leered at him with eyeballs peeping through the holes of the masks. It was a sea of white masks, complete blank faces with only small slits for the eyes.

Robert only saw black shiny circles staring at him. He peered back. He wanted to recognize one of them and hoped something would be uncovered by their pupils. He noticed blue eyes, brown eyes, some with obvious menace intent in those eyes. Still, none that he recognized.

The wall of unknown white faces made his skin crawl. Row after row, he must have passed twenty, thirty, or more, he couldn't count, too distracted by the eyes staring at him. He began to feel squeezed between them as if the mob was using up all the oxygen in the room. He panted, his sweat dripped down his face. The air heated and thinned, he needed to get out of this place, and as far away from the situation as possible.

All his hope fell to earth. Robert realized the gravity of the situation. He had no clue where he was, but he understood all too well, that this was a ceremony of the Black Wolf Society and he, smack in the middle of it all. Swallowing his fear, he knew this was a moment of truth. Something was about to happen that was going to change his life forever.

CHAPTER 30

Hideaway

Another shove to the middle of his back almost knocked Robert over. Convinced, he stepped up the pace. When Robert drew closer to the altar, he observed a body tied down with dark leather straps embellished with silver studs. They shined like glitter from the candlelight reflection. The candles were placed in the elaborate candelabras that stood five feet high.

He caught a slight movement in the corner of his eye, then nothing. He tried to catch another glimpse, but nothing. He wondered if they expected him to make some kind of gesture or sacrifice at this fraudulent altar, or was he the lamb? *No matter, I'll refuse. No matter what they might do to me, I won't partake in any human sacrifice or torture of any living creature.* He shivered from the thought, and goosebumps rose on his arms, his arm hair stood up straight.

Robert and his masked escort reached the altar platform. Looking down, he realized that instead of a person lying there tied to the altar's top as he assumed, it was an atrocity—a creature bound with straps, tied snug to the brass handles on the sides. It was an odd-looking being, exactly as Emilie had described. Part human in appearance, with a body containing the normal extremities like arms, legs, and topped with a head. But not completely, human.

A thin silky cloth was draped over the being and revealed the contours of its body. Its legs appeared thick muscled like an animals' limbs, enabling it to roam free and run about in deep forests, loose somewhere. The joints were bulky and bent differently than in a human body, backward at the arms. Where our elbows point out, this body's joint pointed inward. Its hands were placed outside the covering. They were folded and appeared webbed, a thin, almost translucent skin folded between each phalange.

The creature's hair was downy and thick knitted, resembling the double fur coat of a Great Pyrenees but dark in color. The hair covered its head, shoulders, and arms. Except on its face—there was no hair on its face. Robert assumed its legs were covered with fur as well. Patches of hair were missing on its head and exposed a pinkish skin underneath.

The facial features looked all too human, soft pale skin, fragile even, and badly bruised. Blue and yellow marks splotched the face as if it had been beaten. Stitches marred the temple and upper cheekbone area, and thin metal probes were sticking out of the top of its head and the sides of its neck. *A Frankenstein.*

A strange smell accosted Robert's nose—a sulphuric rotten smell, like scorched oil, or perhaps chemicals. He turned his head back and forth, searching his surroundings for the source. Instead, his attention was drawn to the walls in front of him. Upon closer inspection, he observed they were cement blocks. The entire space surrounding him was comprised of thick decorative cinder block walls, some cement, and stone. It was a basement foundation. The walls gave away clues. White calcium leached out from the crevasses, showing the underground wall's old age.

This place must have been an underground bunker of some sort, dug deep into the ground. There had been rumors of underground tunnels in the area, but the lore said they were flooded and dangerous. *Another elaborate cover story.* Trapped like a rat in a cage, he broke out in a cold sweat.

The creature twitched, Robert noticed it from the corner of his eyes. He stepped back in alarm, only to be pushed forward again. The creature went limp as if it had used up all its power, and there was no fuel remaining to run the engine any longer, it just stopped. He sympathized with the thing lying there but was more concerned for himself. Robert thought that maybe he should just about-face and run out of this place.

He turned around ready to bolt. Looking ahead, he saw the mob—members standing at attention, looking back at him. A sea of white faces. The crowd of white masks and black robes started to chant. Eerie overtone singing reverberated from the walls. Robert noticed some of their throats, then gawked higher at their masks, hoping to find someone familiar. He thought he saw Rachael's eyes, green eyes—no such luck, the iris was blue. He must be hallucinating in his panic.

Suffocating in this crowded space, he counted in his head, to get ready to run. One, two . . . at three, the cloaked mob pushed forward, swallowing up the aisle, leaving no room to flee.

Robert stepped back toward the altar and stopped when his back touched the cold stone marble top. Freaked out, he turned around again, his back to the others. He wished they'd stop massing forward and stop the chanting. The sound made him feel dizzy like he was being hypnotized. The crowd stopped in place when a lone person on the other side of the platform stepped forward from the shadows.

The mysterious figure moved forward then stopped. Whoever it was, they remained on the other side of the altar. Also wearing a black robe, the lone person carried a bishop's staff, the same one that Robert had seen before in Brussels. He recognized the etched cross designs, glaringly apparent when the candle's light flickered across the gold. *This is blasphemy, using a holy artifact for a secret society's meet-up.* He remembered that during the previous meeting, when they gave him the initial instructions, they had promised him a ceremony after his Beneficial Act was completed. *Was this it? A ceremony?*

"Welcome, little piggy."

The metallic voice came from the lone-robed figure holding the staff, from across the altar. The crowd behind Robert laughed.

"We are gathered here with you for your initiation ceremony."

The synthesized voice sounded scratched and irritated Robert. A cold shiver ran down his back, and the walls were caving in on him. Chimes rattled from another direction. The high tones annoyed him even more. The chorus resumed, the people hummed for what stretched on like ages, then they turned the sound into a mesmerizing chant.

"Take this and drink."

High-pitched bells rattled. Robert was handed a golden chalice filled with a dark liquid, like wine, by another member who was standing to his right side.

"All of it," the other member instructed.

He reluctantly took hold of it and sipped, then handed the goblet back. The aftertaste lingered in his mouth; it proved to be bitter yet salty. Then Robert realized it was red wine ruined with the addition of blood. He gagged and held his hand to his throat.

Robert wasn't sure if he could handle much more of this experience—it was more than anyone could handle. The room spun. Dizzy, he grew ill. He closed his eyes and felt himself swaying and getting light-headed. *Drugged? I'm fucking tripping!*

"Time to pledge your life."

The harsh voice cut through his weariness. Robert attempted to be alert. He focused on each movement and noise. Everything moved slowly, and voices sounded distorted.

"You have done your duties as required, little piggy."

The crowd behind him laughed. The metallic voice continued.

"Because of your successful Beneficial Acts, we no longer have the threat of young Bennett stirring things up by digging into his father's work, and we no longer have Mr. La France poking his nose into our affairs, either. You have completed your missions and ready to be pledged in as an official member. You answered the call and have earned the privilege to be one of the Black Wolf."

The person standing to Robert's right took hold of his arm and raised it in the air. The mysterious figure continued talking. Distorted reality deepened.

"Do you, little piggy, pledge to be faithful to the brotherhood of the Black Wolf Society, above all others? Are you prepared to uphold all credo of the Black Wolf Society, and work in collaboration for the common goals with other members, like it has been carried out for centuries?"

Robert remained quiet, not knowing what he should do. Play along, and lie? What about the money they stole from his family, should he mention that? No. Or should he make a stand now, declare his true feelings and save his soul? There was only one answer if he wanted to live, though he dreaded spitting it out.

"I so pledge." He almost choked on those three words that he just uttered. Robert held back his vomit and felt the burn in the back of his throat.

More noise clamored from the crowd behind him, voices mingled with each other until it sounded like a hum. The golden staff stomped up and down, against the floor three times, and obtained instant silence.

"You have been bestowed membership, and now you are a brother of the most powerful group in the world. We are the relevant force behind all society—influencer of world affairs, the living dominance for a millennium. We welcome the new Black Wolf member. Once you sign these papers, the deed will be done."

The words sounded wrong to Robert. He looked up at the leader who held the staff, Robert's vision drawn to the mask, searching for a face . . . he needed to match the mysterious leader to something other than the synthesized voice. The man to his side had papers in hand. He laid the pages on the altar, unfolded them, and extended a pen to Robert. He jerked forward a bit and motioned for Robert to sign. He seized the pen then bent down to examine the papers, but the words blurred. Afraid to sign, he hesitated a moment.

Robert raised his head, one more glance at the leader. Zooming in on the eyes, he focused on two green jewels. *Rachael's eyes? No, impossible.* The drugs still disoriented his senses, so he shook his head and took a second look, surely he was mistaken. He would rather believe that she was dead than to know that it was her standing across from him, the leader of this group. His wife would never be a part of this horrendous group. *She loved her father, she would never order him to be killed.*

Sudden pain interrupted Robert's thoughts. The brute standing to his left side twisted his left arm, then gripped and applied pressure to his forearm, forcing him to sign. Robert cringed and signed the page.

"Good! The deed is done. Signed, sealed, and delivered." The synthesized voice bellowed.

Robert glanced back across the altar, stared at the eyes behind the mask of the mysterious figure again. They no longer looked green, they were just two dark eyeballs with no life at all. Relieved, he wondered how he could have thought such a thing. Applause broke out behind him.

The leader continued with the agenda as if nothing of relevance just happened. "Let's celebrate an even more spectacular feat." The synthesized voice was giving a speech, like a true crooked politician.

Robert felt robbed of everything, including his soul. The effects of the drugs kicked in. Swaying while standing, Robert tried to make sense of the words being said, but everything sounded muffled. He looked across at the mysterious figure's face again, but everything was blurry.

"My fellow members, tonight we celebrate the success of phase one. We are very close to finding a way to achieve immortal life. Never-ending life—imagine. The specimen upon this altar was declared dead. The body sat in a morgue with no brain activity for two days. Yet using the secrets revealed to us in ancient documents—books found completely by accident by none other than the newest member standing with us today—our scientists will bring life back into the corpse."

Robert sucked in a gulp of air. Is the speaker referring to the ancient book that belonged to Jeremy's uncle? The journal I had arranged to be stolen? No, it can't be.

The leader continued to rant.

"Our scientists continue the search for answers, and like previous generations, they experiment with life and the wonders of the paranormal. This formula to everlasting life originated in the West Indies. For years our South American friends, former Reich scientists, tried to uncover the exact secret. Finally, after acquiring many ancient documents, we found the one formula that works. Corrections were made to the specimen's body as well, and now phase one is completed. You will witness what we've created—the walking dead."

There were gasps and mumbles. Then a lone person started to clap, loudly. Soon every other robed idiot in the room joined in and clapped in unison. Clap—clap—clap. The sound rose, filling the heights of the space with a freakish intonation, louder with each round. Robert's fear rose with the mood.

Again the staff thumped to the floor three times. Silence. A ghostly man wearing a white lab coat rolled out a machine. He connected thin colored wires to the probes on the creature.

Afraid of what the next step might be, Robert pushed to the side, trying to get as far away from the altar as he could manage. He hoped to slip into the crowd unnoticed. After all, now that his part was over, he was no longer the center of attention. His internal voice feared that he was to blame for this demented use of life science, and was doomed to hell with the lot of them.

"I'm ready," the man in the lab coat said. He turned the machine on and some type of current flowed into the creature.

Robert heard an electrical hum and watched as the creature twitched. He wanted to turn away but his eyes were glued, riveted to the horror in front of him. The creature oozed blood from its nose and ears. Even the webbed hands dripped with blood from under its nails. The man finally stopped the machine. Another person unfastened the leather ties from the brass side handles.

The creature sat up and faced the crowd. Everyone clapped. The creature stood and took a step forward. Gasps of surprise spread around the great hall. Then a moment of silence, until a storm of applause erupted.

Voices with various expressions of praise floated above the applause—*bravo, perfecta, magnificent.*

Robert stared at the crowd, a sea of white masks. He was more afraid of these lunatics than anything else imagined. They truly believed they had conquered death.

CHAPTER 31

Powers

It was ten o'clock and everyone had turned in. Emilie and Jeremy were the last to climb the stairs.

"I'm worried about Robert. Let's check in on him," she said.

Jeremy followed her and opened Robert's bedroom door. The room was frigid. The French doors leading to the porch were opened wide, the wind blowing across the dark room. Emilie snapped on the light. Her brother was gone, only his bottle of scotch lay empty on the floor. Emilie rushed to the porch.

"Look, is that Robert driving away?"

Jeremy rushed to her side. "Don't worry, Em, I'll go after him."

"We'll go after him," she corrected him.

Jeremy flashed a smirk. "Of course, we'll go together."

They hurried downstairs, ran outside, and slipped into her Z4. The car zipped down the driveway, chasing after Robert's Jag.

"Slow down. We're not in a race to die," he said.

"I'm not letting him get away. Look, is that his car ahead?"

"Yes, keep on the tail. I'm dialing Agent Sloan."

They continued to follow the Jaguar north toward Millington. His small car took a turn off the main road and went down a lonely street. The houses continued to be spaced farther apart as they proceeded until all that was left around them were flat open fields. Emilie followed far enough behind not to be spotted, but close enough to see the Jag's car lights.

"Jeremy, don't freak. I'm turning off the headlights."

After her eyes adjusted to the darkness, Emilie sped up and

drew closer to Robert's car. They saw it turn down an even more private road with sapling trees growing on the sides. Ahead of them, yet still far off, they saw the outline of a large building of some sort, unlit; a dark shadow standing alone against the night sky.

The Jag stopped, but the engine remained humming. A man got out of the driver's side, standing a good foot taller than her brother and sporting broad shoulders. It wasn't Robert driving. He walked up to the entrance gate's post and punched in a code to unlock the barrier.

Emilie heard the metallic clang of a gate opening. The driver got back into the Jag's driver seat and drove through the entry. In split seconds, Emilie accelerated her little Z4, propelled through the gateway, and just missed being hit by the metal bar that dropped behind them. Once through, she braked and waited to ensure they were undetected. Everything around them was quiet.

"That was a close call," Jeremy said.

"What time is it?" she asked.

"Eleven thirty. Why?"

"In the movies, bad things usually happen at midnight. That means we have half an hour to prevent something bad from happening."

"Emilie, you watch way too many horror flicks. You'd think with a life like yours, you'd have had enough drama."

"I totally agree." She accelerated at a steady pace. The road was barely visible without lights but she managed to follow the tread marks in the dirt. The road led them to the front of a dilapidated building, an abandoned manufacturing plant of some sort, with crumbling smokestacks similar to those they had seen earlier near the crime scene of Mr. La France. She let the car idle as they took in the scene.

"When I was a child, I dreamed of a place like this—no, not

a dream, more like a nightmare," she said.

"Is the eeriness of this place giving you second thoughts about storming in without police backup?" Jeremy's voice sounded hopeful.

"I'm wary, yes. But, it's not as if it's my brother we're following. The man who took him has to be from the Black Wolf Society. The police would never be able to handle a group like this, and besides, you already called Sloan. Agent Sloan will be here any moment now. Look over there. They went to the back." She pointed.

"I'll call Sloan back with our exact location so he can get here quick. He's our only hope against the Black Wolves." Jeremy called and listened more than spoke, nodding to instructions.

"Emilie, Agent Sloan said to sit and wait for his task force. They're fifteen minutes out. If there are other members like the guy we just followed, then we're way over our heads. Sloan believes they abducted Robert, because last he knew, your brother wanted nothing more to do with them."

"You think I can sit here and wait, doing nothing, while they take my brother—and do, who knows what to him."

"No, of course, you can't. But please, do me one favor. Drive around back and a little closer, so we can evaluate the situation before we storm into a lion's den."

"You mean wolf den."

"Yes, that's exactly what I mean."

Emilie had never seen Jeremy so intent. His gentlemanly charms were replaced with an intent scowl that could scare off the nastiest of brutes. She put the car in gear, headlights still off, and drove the small sports car around the building. In the back, dozens of other vehicles were parked on the wild grass field. She pulled up her Z4 between two compacts parked furthest away from the ram-shambled building. They got out to sneak a closer look, stealing between parked cars as they threaded their way toward the only building standing for miles.

"This has to be one of the old ammunitions plant buildings from the forties. I thought they were torn down, but look." She pointed to a broken down conveyor system clinging to the side of the metal frame, hanging from the tracks. "I can't imagine anyone is safe inside this shambles."

"Look, over there." Jeremy jerked his head toward a door that was just closing. "He went in that way, dragging Robert in."

She nodded while scoping the area. "I don't see anyone else around. We have to follow so we don't lose the trail."

"Maybe we should have brought a gun," he said.

"Oh, I'm pretty sure there's plenty of guns here already."

"Yes, exactly my point," Jeremy said. "We need something to defend ourselves. Maybe we'll get lucky, and this is nothing more than a friendly meeting. There may not be any violence whatsoever."

"Sure. And maybe the Black Wolf Society is akin to the Masons, and want to be our best friends."

"You're so sarcastic lately, Emilie. You can't give in to these guys. We won't let them destroy your family, promise. I know I hate killing anyone, but I'll always protect you, no matter what."

"Sorry, Jeremy. I know how difficult this situation has been for you. Killing Bennett tore you up inside. I hate that you had to do it, but I'll always be grateful because you saved our lives. I guess I'm just tired of all this heinous conspiracy. I want a happy life for you and me, without all this shit going on. It's too much sometimes, you know?"

Jeremy reached over and wrapped his arms around her, and hugged her tight. She smiled, soaked up his good vibes that calmed her anxiety like magic. "You have no idea how wonderful your touch feels." She drew in a breath. His cologne drifted under her nose, an earthy, manly fragrance. "Thank you, Jeremy. You ready?"

He released her and gave the thumbs up. They crept closer to the building and scrutinized some platforms that were situated on the upper levels, but they didn't notice any guards standing above. The building was constructed of iron beams. At either end, old holding towers with metal shoots jutting out, the kind used years ago to slide warehoused materials from silos into the plant, stood in the darkness. Discolored and rusted, the metal siding was bent up or torn off in places from years of wind and harsh weather.

A shiver ran down Emilie's spine. This place in real life was creepier than her dreams ever were. She realized that her nightmares years ago had never ended well and hoped they weren't some kind of foretelling sign. *No, they were just dreams,* she thought.

Taking a moment, she envisioned what life must have been like when this place was still alive with people working for the war effort. The workers suffered through the macabre, the shadow of war, and some of their latent emotions lingered, trapped here in the physical world. Her clairvoyant gift filtered the heart-breaking loss that had remained. Sometimes people's spirits stay in the shadows of the past, especially when they can't see beyond the pain and don't cross over into the other realm. Misgivings had become a spiritual blockade, as it would for any dweller on the threshold of transcendental consciousness. This time thankfully, Emilie only felt leftover emotions filling the space around her, and nothing more. Her power could deal with this encounter.

The night air stung her cheeks when the wind blew. The building creaked and moaned around her. Pieces of rusted metal siding flapped in the wind, fighting against each other. Scrapping and grinding noises, high-pitched squeaks, prickled against her skin. Goosebumps rose on her arms, and she rubbed them to warm herself. The sounds did well to camouflage their advance toward the entrance, and they made it to the door without incident.

"Here goes nothing," she said.

The door opened with ease and led them through a maze of hallways, with many other entries on each side. Jeremy opened and closed a few, but they only revealed empty darkness. They continued, following the lighted hallway, which eventually led to a staircase spiraling down.

Emilie whispered a lament. "Why does every secret place we encounter end up underground?"

Jeremy shrugged. A sound echoed up the stairwell from below. "Shhhhhhhh. Something is going on. Hear that? "After a second, "Are you ready?"

Emilie nodded and followed Jeremy's lead down the stairs. The sound grew louder as they drew closer. Slowly they descended deep underground, at least two stories before they reached a landing. Another lighted hallway led them down to a larger room, which glowed with amber lighting.

"I think we found the place," Jeremy said. "Let's sit tight a bit and give Agent Sloan time to catch up to us."

Suddenly Emilie doubled over in pain. He reached for her, and gently rubbed her back. "Are you all right? What happened?"

"I'll be fine in a moment," she said. Her eyes were wet, tears of pain stung the corners. "I feel those emotions again. Not human, but those primitive feelings, like back in Brussels from the creature."

"Do you think it's here? Can't be," he said.

"No, probably not. Maybe it's another creature. Could they

be experimenting in this place as well? Oh no, Jeremy, my brother. I have to go in there and find him before it's too late. What if they experiment on him? You saw him earlier, he's drugged or shit-faced. Either way, he can't defend himself."

"Okay, but let's not go charging in this time. We'll advance cautiously, and try to stay undetected."

Emilie nodded, and they walked toward the light until they reached the great hall. Both were surprised the space was filled with people. Everyone wore black robes. Noticing a folded pile of robes resting on a table pushed up against the wall, they each grabbed one and slipped it on over their clothes, and pulled up the hoods. Jeremy pointed to the stack of white masks at the end of the table, and they each put one on as well.

Mingling with the others, they squeezed their way toward the front of the hall. When they reached a vantage point where they could see the altar, they spotted Robert standing off to the side. Suddenly, everyone in the room applauded.

Emilie covered her ears and continued moving forward. Once she reached the front and was close to the altar, she sighted a creature. It sent out emotions similar to the creature in Brussels. This person or creature-like thing standing in front of them like a zombie god, however, wasn't dead.

A blast of pain emanated from the creature. It wasn't an emotion, but rather more like a beckoning. The creature desired to die, it was suffering. Pain—pain—pain, that's all Emilie could feel when she focused on the creature. If she unleashed her power now to release the creature from its hell, then every other body in the place would be on her in no time. Emilie wanted to help but knew she had to wait. Her energy fizzled, drained by the pull of the creature's pain. She faltered with no resolve left, so she grabbed Jeremy's arm to regain some balance. Nothing. She looked to her side and realized it wasn't him.

Panicked, she wondered what happened to Jeremy. She closed her eyes and tried to get a sense of which direction to find him. She couldn't feel his good vibe anywhere and guessed that he probably didn't have any positive thoughts left right about now. Without his touch, Emilie wouldn't be able to pull herself together. All the robed people surrounding her pushed toward the front. She sensed their hate and dark places, and Emilie's empath sensibility was being pushed over the edge.

Tension built up inside her and she was losing control. To save herself from the throe, and to release the creature from agony, she opened herself up. A telepathic convulsion detonated.

Using the technique that Chief Flying Crow had taught her, Emilie sucked in every emotion from the room. Hostility, conceit, and psychopathic malice filled her soul until the energy was bursting from her. Stepping forward, she opened out her arms and flung the force of energy outward. The release was cathartic.

Everyone shielded their eyes, surprised by her sudden appearance. Then screams sounded.

Emilie felt people push and toss her about in a rush of panic. She drew in the energy from the room once more, as if drawing in a deep perfect yoga breath. She held the explosive emotions in herself for a second, then exploded the energy again. Beams of light extended from her hands. She aimed the power at the creature, and it looked back at her with an expression of relief. The creature collapsed to the floor.

"No!" One of the robed figures who stood on the other side suddenly leaped over the altar, stooped down to the floor, and held the creature. "What have you done?"

The synthesized voice sounded cold, jarring Emilie. Yet the words sounded personal, and she sensed an unsettling danger behind them.

"You ruined it." The robed person held the creature to their chest and cradled it for a moment. Emilie felt a loss, no it was more like a longing that spilled from this robed person.

"This was the miracle of life—our creation—our dream to live forever is ruined because of you." The robed figure stood up, turned, and a white mask faced Emilie.

Emilie couldn't see a face but she certainly felt the hate emerging from this Black Wolf member, and the dark emotions she felt were familiar.

"What have you done? You bitch." The figure lunged out at Emilie, grabbed a hold of her shoulders, and shook her in a rage.

Emilie bobbed about as if she were a rag doll or a chew toy for a dog. She tried to block the emotions that were spilling into her psyche, to protect herself, but the rage was so raw, so edgy, it was difficult to screen. She began to lose her sense of time and closed her eyes.

Emilie suddenly sensed Robert's appearance, recognizing his emotional thread. Emilie opened her eyes and watched as Robert took hold of the crazed figure from behind, knocking the person down to the floor.

"Thank you." Panting, Emilie leaned forward holding her hand to her chest, then reached out and hugged her brother.

Just then, Jeremy broke through the crowd. He had struggled against the horde of Black Wolf members who were running for the exit in a mob of madness. He rushed to Emilie's side and took hold of her arm.

She immediately felt his goodness and smiled behind her mask. "I guess my power freaked out most of these folks."

CHAPTER 32

Raid

Robert stood back and watched the surreal scene unfold. His attention quickly returned to the robed member with the synthesized voice, struggling up from the floor. He took hold of the leader's arms and held them back in a firm grip, allowing no chance of his sister being attacked again.

Mesmerized, he watched the panic—the room was utter chaos. The sea of white-masked faces that had scared him before, retreated into a wall of black robes pushing into each other during their exodus. Robert felt shoves as some of them bumped into him as they fled past. Black robes rushed for the nearest exit, terrified by his sister's powers, they scrambled away from the altar peering over their shoulders to make sure they weren't in her crossfire.

The light that had beamed from her hands was beyond the scope most people could comprehend, he knew that first hand. If he hadn't seen it for himself, he never would have believed. Agent Sloan's words echoed in his head, *"you don't believe in much, except yourself. This might be your chance to prove me wrong."* Things had changed. He witnessed, he believed, and cared now, more than ever before in his entire life. He wanted to keep his family not only safe but sane as well.

A few loyal members remained nearby, brave enough to stay behind to protect the leader. Robert felt their preying eyes on him, waiting for him to let down his guard, ready to act. He wasn't psychic like his sister, but he knew they wanted him dead.

Robert pulled the masked leader's arms back tighter in a grip-hold. He had learned the restraining maneuver years ago during one of his martial arts defense classes, and now Robert used it for the first time in five years. Proud of himself for remembering how to engage the move, he also cursed himself at the same time, unsure of how long he could keep the upper hand of the situation.

Screams flooded the hall, echoing off the walls. Noise blared from a bullhorn, "Please remain calm."

The second wave of mayhem erupted as uniformed SWAT team members and officers wearing vests marked FBI, swarmed into the space to apprehend and arrest. Many fled, resorting to frantic measures. Literally, they climbed the rock walls to escape the police's reach. Black robes hung and flapped in the air, as the people scaled the height like professional climbers mountaineering a cliff or an acrobat in a circus act. Those who made it to a balcony area might have escaped.

BANG, shots were fired. Robert saw Jeremy pull Emilie to the floor and he covered her body with his.

Robert pulled the robed leader closer to his chest and held tight. If anything, the ploy proved to beget a protective shield, when seconds later three G-men pointed guns at them. Robert couldn't see the officers' faces through the dark visors attached to the helmets they wore, but he trusted they recognized him as a good guy. *Was he a good guy?* The thought inspired a chuckle and smile, and he wished he had ripped off his piggy mask.

"Hold your fire," Robert said. "Innocent man here, holding this one for the police to arrest."

A shot blasted, then Robert heard a whizzing sound. He felt a sting by his ear. A second shot roared out, and something nudged him backward. Unsure of what was happening, Robert felt a force push against him. A bullet hit the robed leader in the left shoulder. A mist of blood splattered up to his face. The person he held was hit again with a third and fourth bullet, each time another force pushing Robert back. The body in his arm-hold went limp. Robert sensed the abandon of the muscles and eased up on his grip, then let go and allowed the body to fall to the floor.

"Hold your fire!"

Robert ripped off his mask when he heard Agent Sloan above all the other frantic voices in the room.

"Hold your fire!" Agent Sloan repeated.

The guns that had been pointed at Robert lowered. A few stray bullets rang out from another section of the hall, and then things quieted.

"Up there," Agent Sloan screamed.

Robert looked up in the direction the agent pointed. Officers rushed to overcome the shooters above.

"The shots came from one of them. Place them first in line for questioning at headquarters." He barked the order, then turned his attention back toward the altar.

"Are you all right, Robert?" After a second, he said, "Well, well, well...who do we have here? This must be the ringleader. All dressed up and nowhere to go?"

"Sloan, can you help me," Robert said. "The leader was shot. We need an ambulance, that is if you want them alive for questioning."

"No worries, we have one on the way now."

An officer wearing protective gear jogged up to the altar. "Sir, we have most of them rounded up, and we're in the process of loading them into the buses which just arrived. Should we de-mask them or wait for interrogation?"

"Let's wait. We may be able to use their desire for anonymity as leverage against each other when we dig for intelligence."

"Yes, sir. Understood." He nodded and left the area.

"Gentlemen, and ladies," Agent Sloan acknowledged Emilie, "We've hit the jackpot. With this many Black Wolf Society members arrested, surely we'll learn some solid intelligence. Thank you, Robert, for your help."

Two men from the SWAT team picked up the wounded leader from the floor and carried the body to meet a gurney halfway into the hall.

"Wait. Who is that masked leader? I think I have the right to know after all the trouble they've caused me," Robert said.

"All in good time," Agent Sloan answered him. "First, Emilie, tell me about the show we all witnessed a few minutes ago. Quite the miraculous spectacle."

Jeremy hugged her close and whispered something into her ear. She nodded.

"Agent Sloan, I'd be happy to tell you everything, but I would prefer to do so at the house. We need to get out of here. As you might imagine, I'm a bit exhausted from the entire ordeal."

"Yes. Yes, fine. I understand." Agent Sloan stopped a moment in thought, then said, "Robert, you and your sister go home and rest up. After the team gets this bust organized, I'll meet you there. Promise me that you'll be ready for questioning, and without lawyers would be best. If that's okay with you?"

Robert nodded his agreement.

"Good, okay then." Agent Sloan called out. "Officer, please escort these fine people to their cars. I'll see you all by tomorrow evening is my best guess." He looked at his watch. "Make that later on this evening. It's past midnight, folks."

"Come on Em, let's get you back to the house," Jeremy said.

Agent Sloan smiled at them and waved as they walked away. His grin made him look like a little boy who just won a game. Robert looked back over his shoulder. Sloan stood there like any normal man, except something about him glowed. It was as if he were some kind of angel sent to save them all. Robert admired the odd man, who entered his life only days ago, and brought with him more trouble than he ever conceived possible. Still, there was something about the FBI Agent that made Robert feel safe.

They left the hall and climbed up the metal staircase. Their heavy footfall echoed in the stairwell. Robert smelled the lingering odor of blood; it leaked from the walls. He could taste the sour smell, which triggered memories. *The warehouse in Massachusetts, filled with blood, another murder.*

Not even a month ago, he had stood face to face with a different leader of the Black Wolf Society, Tom Bennett. Robert recalled the madness he had seen in Bennett's eyes, just seconds before he had morphed into a blood lust monster. That look, those dangerous eyes, had shaken Robert to his core. The Black Wolf Society still existed, and in fact, thrived. Many more members were out there throughout the world; that knowledge scared him even more.

This group had more than political and financial agendas on their radar. They were experimenting like the Nazis had in Germany during WWII and afterward in hideaways throughout the world. Mad scientists were creating freaks, playing with DNA to create life apart from God's holy order of things. A crazed group like this knew no limits to the atrocities they'd commit—but a boundary had to be drawn to stop them before it was too late.

Understanding the cost, Robert hoped that his family's sacrifice would help the effort to stop the group before they spread their evil further still. Agent Sloan had said they've been around for centuries. *Could they find them all, and wipe them out completely?* With politicians, financiers, lawmen, and prominent businesspeople amid the group, it proved an almost impossible feat. But then again, he thought, with talented people like his sister—who possessed powers—maybe there was hope for the world to overcome the Black Wolf Society yet.

They exited the building. The autumn night was cold, fresh, and invigorated him. Robert swallowed a breath of fresh air, his lungs hurt a moment from the frigid temperature, but he was happy to feel it and know that he was alive.

"Emilie, are you all right to drive?" he asked.

"No, not really. I mean, yes. Jeremy will drive us home. I'm tired and struggling with all of this knowledge about what this group is doing—and has done. I'm not sure I can fight these people off. There was so much hatred in that hall, deep dark secrets, and power lust."

"Was that creature human?" Jeremy asked.

"Part human, as far as I can tell. I could feel emotions more so than the first time. Mostly fear, the strongest sender of course. But even animals have those feelings, especially when cornered and bound. This creature didn't feel completely human, though. Who knows, maybe it was a human, but in leftover pieces after being stripped to the core with some kind of torture and fear tactics. I wouldn't put anything past these people."

"Fear. Hmm. Do you think Bennett had experiments done on people like that, just to feel their fear? Remember how he thrived and grew in power from our fear?" Robert's thoughts went dark.

"Robert, he didn't need to torture anyone to feel fear. Hell, everyone around Bennett feared him, all of the time. He had an endless supply to feed on." Emilie hung her head. "I'm glad Mother is dead so she didn't have to deal with any of this absurdity."

They walked across the open field until they reached the

cars. The southern night air irritated Robert's nose, laden heavy with the foul moldy stink of the dead grass that was wet from the dew.

"We really don't know the extent of what our parents knew or suffered, do we," Robert said. He rubbed his nose.

"Maybe we should concentrate on the future from now on, Robert." Jeremy put a hand on Robert's shoulder. "You have your sisters back in your good graces. Michelle and Emilie are both safe and sound. You have a home to go to. And don't worry, we'll find Rachael as well, you'll see her again any day now. Have hope."

Robert shook his head and said, "I just don't know. I hope everything is all right, truly. But I feel in my gut that something is very wrong. I wonder where she could be. I saw Rachael fall to the floor after being shot, but still, no body was found and she didn't show up in the hospital. I'm confused about so many things. Like if the Black Wolf had taken her, wouldn't they have given her back to me at the ceremony back there? And the same goes with the money. Why did they take it when all they had to do was ask? No one said anything about what they wanted it for or about giving anything back to us. Why not?"

Quiet for a moment, Robert tried to recollect the night's activities. His memory was in a fog, he had been so plastered when he first woke up. Still, nothing sobers a man better than the fear of dying, and that's exactly what Robert had considered.

"Oh my God."

"What is it?" Emilie said.

"I just remembered something that happened . . . tonight I signed something. They forced me to sign some papers, but I have no idea what they said or what happened to them. Wait! Those papers." Robert turned and started heading back, panic struck.

Jeremy grabbed his arm and stopped him.

"Please, let me go. I have to go back and find those papers and tear them up. I was so wasted, everything was blurred, and I couldn't read a word. What have I done? I have a bad feeling about it all."

"Let's not worry about that now," Emilie said. "We'll ask Agent Sloan about them later on. Hopefully, as they round up the evidence, the papers will show up, too."

Emilie opened the door of her Z4. "Robert, are you okay to drive? Maybe you should come with us."

"A gunfight helps sober a man up, Em." He smiled. "I'll be all right. Let's go directly to the house. I'll follow you."

CHAPTER 33

Short Temper

Robert watched as Emilie and Jeremy drove away.

In the distance, he could hear the shouts of protest as the members were arrested. He witnessed from a distance that the FBI task force herded the suspects into buses. The angry voices overshot the usual night sounds. The task force was prepared, and despite the resistance, they were not likely to let any member escape their net tonight.

Robert slid behind the steering wheel of his silver Jag. He turned the key that had been left in the ignition. The engine roared, and for a moment, Robert felt in control again, comfortable sitting in the familiar driver's seat. He squeezed the steering wheel and allowed his fingers to experience the leather grip. He reached his hand down to turn on the music. Suddenly, the passenger door opened, and someone slipped into the seat. Robert turned to face a white-masked man.

"Drive," the stranger ordered.

Shifting his glance downward, Robert noticed a gun pointed at his midsection. He pressed his foot down on the accelerator and inched the car forward. Robert headed toward the worn road around the dilapidated building, remaining cautious as he navigated over the bumps in the field. Then he circled around the metal structure to exit the area by a lone dirt road.

The flashing lights of the law enforcement vehicles, red and then white, glared. Robert squinted his eyes, his head already pounding with a migraine. Officers were coming and going, a complete hive of activity. He thought of pulling the car over and chance a run to get someone's attention for help. But then he thought of all things that could go wrong. The creep might shoot him, or take off with his car, or both. If Robert tried to get an officer's attention, with all the confusion of the night, they might misunderstand his message and go after Robert instead of the passenger. Exhausted, he decided that he couldn't take any more drama tonight. Robert had reached his limit.

"So, what do you want from me? More money. Sorry, too late. The society took it all," he said.

"All I need is a lift out of here," the masked man said. "And in return for your kindness, I'll let you in on a little secret. The likelihood of any Black Wolf member ever speaking to the likes of you again, is null. As a matter of fact, they'll want to kill you after tonight. I'm sure there'll be a price on your head. There's something about a traitor that just doesn't sit right, you know. Even if you are royalty and destined to be part of the group's leadership, it doesn't matter anymore. *Capeesh?*"

The voice sounded familiar, but he couldn't place it. He drew in a breath and realized he didn't care who this guy was—Robert wanted the creep out of his car.

"No worries—I won't be losing any sleep over it."

His response sounded sarcastic, and why not, he thought. Robert's spirit was broken, and his body, sore. The muscles in his neck were wound tight, his anger mounted, and his head pounded.

All he could think of was stopping the car to kick this guy out, maybe grab the gun and shoot his head off. This prick, who had the nerve to jump into his car, deserved it and much worse. And he would have done exactly that, except for the fact that Robert was curious about what the man had said, about him being royalty.

Robert wanted to hear what the man meant, then maybe then Robert could figure out what the hell was going on. He remained silent and waited for a chance to provoke a response.

"Man, you really blew it. You had the world at your feet. You were royalty in the group's eyes, what with being married to Rachael and your father..."

Robert laughed aloud, trying to bait the scoundrel for more info. "Okay, whatever," he said. He shook his head with a wise-ass grin across his face.

"I'm serious, man," the intruder said. "You were hand-picked by the boss. Tonight the leader wanted you up there on the front line—most of the privileged few had to prove themselves with years of Benevolent Acts. But you—handpicked. Gossip says that you're the son of the most powerful of all Black Wolves. Like a descendant of royalty, an heir. Your father is feared in our circles, and it's good to have people fear you. It's power, man. Don't you get it? You blew it. You had the world by its balls. Now, you're a disgrace. No one from the Black Wolf Society will ever follow you, no matter who your father is." The man grunted with disgust.

Alarms went off in Robert's head. "And just who is my supposedly powerful ancestor? No person from the de Gourgues family ever belonged to this society. Not ever."

The man laughed aloud. "Of course not. I meant your natural father, Tom Bennett."

Revolted, Robert stomped on the brakes. The car came to an abrupt halt. The masked man in the passenger's seat jerked forward and hit his head on the dash.

"What the hell, man. Don't do that shit again." He raised the gun and pointed it at Robert's face.

Robert didn't care; he was blinded with rage. "Listen to me, you asshole. I don't know who told you this lie, but I'm not his son. The idea is absurd. My mother hated the monster. My father is Pierre de Gourgues, the greatest businessman in the world."

"Not what I heard. Rumor has it your mother was impregnated by the Great Wolf, himself, back in the day. I heard that she liked things rough." The man laughed.

Robert's brain dived into primitive mode. Reaching over, he knocked the gun from the man's hand in one rash movement. Then, Robert grabbed the man's neck and squeezed. His mask got pushed aside and tangled up in his hoodie, as Robert's chokehold covered the man's neck as if in a vice. Robert recognized the face; he was a man he had done business with before. A man whom his father had trusted. Robert felt betrayed and squeezed tighter.

Frenzied pangs of hate channeled down to his hands. Robert imagined Tom Bennett was in his hold, in his hands. Reveling the sight of the man's eyes, as they turned blood red and popped wide opened, Robert heard the man's gargled sounds from his throat. The noise lasted until the gasps became more of a silent call for mercy, whispered screams. Wet drool dripped from his mouth and slipped across Robert's hand. The man's weight went limp, and his body no longer fought against him.

Horrified with himself, that he allowed his rage to blaze so intensely, and that his hands had done such harm, Robert realized that his actions were just as repugnant as those Benevolent Acts carried out by the society. He heard the man gasp for air, he wasn't dead. Robert stopped himself. He let go of the man, dropped his hands, and reached over to open the passenger door. He unceremoniously kicked the man out of his car.

Robert slammed the car door shut and sped away, fearing he might lose control still, turn around and finish the man off. His hands gripped the wheel, his knuckles pressed until ghost white. He shook inside like a ragged jigsaw slicing back and forth.

He was a madman behind the wheel. Robert raced down

the dirt road, and for a brief moment, he contemplated smashing his Jag into a tree and end it all. This plan quickly evaporated because there were only saplings lining the makeshift road. Robert's mind sank to a dark place. *I have no right to live. I'm as bad as the monster.*

A sudden bright light blinded his eyes. He slowed the car, then pulled to the side and unrolled his window. An officer's face smiled at him.

"Mr. de Gourgues, are you all right, Sir? You were clipping a bit too fast around that there corner. It's dark in these fields, what with no street lights. Maybe with all the trouble you've had tonight, someone should drive you home, Sir."

It wasn't a question. The officer opened the door, and Robert got out. Another officer slid into the driver's seat, his expression all business.

"Have a cruiser pick me up at the residence," the other officer said.

Robert was escorted to the passenger side.

"Wait," Robert said. "Back there, there's another one of them. He jumped me, trying to escape, but I pushed him out of my car. He may be hurt and need medical help."

"No worries, Mr. de Gourgues. We'll do a sweep and find him. You're a real sport even giving a shit about any of them," the officer replied.

"Whatever," Robert mumbled under his breath.

The officer drove Robert back to the house. The outside lights beamed all around the perimeter. The family's security detail was on high alert.

Robert got out of the car without uttering a word to the officer and dragged himself inside. Everything around him muddied, his vision tunneled to a small point ahead, which made him nauseous. He glanced sideways and noted that Emilie and Jeremy were sitting in the parlor.

Then Robert became dizzy and weak.

Everything went black.

Robert woke up alone. Confused, he opened his eyes and wondered what time it was. *Did I have a drink in the parlor?* He couldn't remember, so checked his hand to see if he had a glass. Instead, Robert noticed that he was in his room, lying across his bed. He wasn't in control and had lost any recent recollections.

What was real, what was the truth? Robert wondered. Am I losing my mind? Am I the son of a monster? Did I murder someone tonight, or did I spare them? He wasn't sure of the answers, but he knew that in fact, he had wanted to kill that man. His mind was cluttered with all kinds of crazy thoughts, and he struggled through them all until his only concern was Rachael.

He heard the sound of his chattering teeth. His entire body was shivering. His room felt cold, and Emilie apparently covered him with only a sheet. Robert groped his hand about the bed, grabbed the quilt, and pulled the comforter up from the end of the bed. Closing his eyes, he tried to sleep. *Please keep me sane, Lord, please save my soul. Keep my family safe, even if it's from me.*

He dreamed of crazy thoughts and images wavered in and then left. Not a single idea stuck with him, except for the vivid phantasm of Tom Bennett's head, placed on the floor, at his feet. His own body was covered in Tom's blood. Robert thought that he smelled the blood, felt the warmth, and was horrified beyond belief. He woke in a sweat. That imprint would never leave him, it was his lifetime personal curse.

CHAPTER 34

Depression

Robert awoke, terrified. His dream had been so vivid that he swore someone's hands groped around his neck, choking him to death. Sweating from the fear of it all, he opened his eyes and recognized the ceiling fan above. He was in his own bedroom. He rubbed his hands up and down his face, fast and hard, drew in a breath, and exhaled slow. *Get a grip.* His guilty conscience troubled his dreams. He could try to forget his past, but the truth remained that he had done it again, his scruples were compromised, and there was no escaping the facts. Robert wanted to kill a man as surely as he wanted to see his wife again.

He tried to be kindhearted, worked hard to stay positive, and yearned for a better future—after all his effort, it had taken only a split second last night for him to revert back into a bully. No, not a bully, a murderer. *Maybe I'm the monster's son after all.* Was the man who raped his mother his blood father? No, he refused to believe it.

He shook his head. Robert's stomach soured, he sprung up and ran to the bathroom. The raunchy taste burned the back of his throat. He figured the agony was well deserved. He rinsed his mouth and looked up into the mirror. Sickened by his own reflection, he stared at the side of his face that bore the scar inflicted by the claws of a monster. Robert shook his head. *No, it has to be a mistake!* Were his features like Bennett's, he wondered. No, everyone had always said he looked like his father, Pierre.

"Why is this happening to me?" he said aloud.

All his life, there was never any doubt that Pierre was his

father. Surely, his father wouldn't have tolerated the bad behavior Robert displayed, had he not been his real son.

His world lay shattered around him. Robert had lost everything dear to him, everything that made him Robert de Gourgues: his place in the family business, the family fortune, his mentor, his wife. And still, things would get worse if it were true that Tom Bennett was his natural father. *No!* His sisters would loathe him once they discovered the truth. *What was the truth? What's worse, that he might be Bennett's son, or that he wanted to murder a man last night?*

He returned to his room, opened the nightstand drawer, and found the mahogany case that held his handgun. He kept a Smith & Wesson for protection, a model 640 Revolver. It was always kept loaded with five rounds. He picked it up and felt the weight of it in his hand, the same hand that had choked a man last night, and almost killed him. How easily his hand gripped the revolver. Its stainless barrel and dark-wood handle were engraved, a beautiful piece.

Robert sat on his bed, pulled the trigger back, and heard the click. He lifted the gun to his head. Tears ran down his cheeks, his breathing sounded shallow. Robert closed his eyes and thought about all of the evil things he had done in his life. He hated himself for causing so much pain to others. Hated that he had wanted to take a life—the one thing God asks of all people—to cherish—life. He wasn't worthy of life.

He questioned his existence and felt undeserving of his dear sisters' faith in him. Both loved him no matter what he had done to them, but *if they could see my ugly heart, the darkness inside of me, then they would give up on me. I can't have a happy life.* He had killed, but was he a killer at heart? Why was he torn apart inside?

Sickened by his actions, knowing they were wrong, he no

longer wanted to be that person—to be evil—but he didn't understand how to stop it from happening inside of him.

An unexpected wake of peace passed through him, and for a split second, he saw it—a way to find relief from the guilt. He could end it all now, just by pulling the trigger. He could leave his farce of a life behind him and follow an unknown road—leave it all. One split second, that's all it would take. The last bravado act, to end his pain, free him from the truth of himself. *Do it*, the voice inside his head said. *Pull the damn trigger.*

Robert fell over, landed on the wood floor, and hit his head hard. The weight of a man crushed him. Stretching his neck around, he looked up and saw Jeremy's tanned forearm extending out, reaching for the gun Robert still held tightly in his hand.

"Bloody hell, man." Jeremy grabbed the gun away from him. "I won't let you do this. The last thing we need is another dead body." Jeremy pulled himself up. "It doesn't matter why or what you've done. Get a grip. We'll deal with this mess together. Talk to me. Let it out, Robert."

Robert pulled his body into a fetal position and cried like a damn baby. He sobbed until his body trembled with uncontrollable shakes. Jeremy sat beside him on the floor and waited for Robert to finish. After a bit of time passed, Jeremy pulled Robert upright to sit on the floor near him. He wrapped his arm around Robert's shoulder and allowed him to finish his tears and calm his trembles.

"Robert, tell me what happened. Why resort to this?"

"I can't tell you. Even the words are too disgusting." Robert broke away and leaned his head on his knees with eyes closed.

"Nothing is so horrible that you have to resort to committing suicide. I need you to say the words, Robert. Get them out, man."

"The thought of my mother, of her being raped by Tom Bennett, rips me up inside." Robert pressed his lips together as if holding back, waiting to explode again. "But worse yet . . . he gulped back a breath. "I think he's my father. I think that she got pregnant from the rape. Me—I'm the son of a killer. My God, I'm the spawn of that monster." Robert burst out with more tears and hugged his own legs.

"No, that's rubbish," Jeremy spoke with a raised voice.

Robert turned to look at him.

"Why do you even think this? Who told you this nonsense?" Jeremy said.

"It was one of the Black Wolves, last night. He said I was Bennett's offspring. And there was another time, someone made the same suggestion. Eluding that I might share genes with Bennett. And well, just look at the horrendous things I do. I'm bad."

Jeremy shook his head. "No, sorry, I don't buy it."

"Why not?" Robert scrutinized Jeremy's face. *What did he know?* Any hope was worth hanging onto.

"It's not logical. First off, you've never turned into an animal." He smiled. "Sorry, couldn't resist. Okay, sure, you're no choir boy, nor an evil monster."

Jeremy nudged Robert's shoulder, but his words weren't a comfort. Robert sneered and hung his head.

"Second, and the more relevant fact, is something Emilie confirmed when she researched your family history. She discovered your parents tried to get pregnant for a bit before anything worked. Your parents visited a fertility clinic. Robert, your mother wasn't pregnant when they married. That means you can't possibly be Bennett's son. You were conceived much later, after the crime against her."

"Are you sure?" Robert asked.

"The Black Wolf Society plays head games, you should

know this by now. They wanted you twisted up inside so they could manipulate you. Don't you see—you're not bad. If evil was truly your disposition, then you wouldn't be so shaken up every time things go wrong. You wouldn't feel guilty over things if you were a monster."

He grabbed Robert by his shoulders and shook him.

"See, you're human. You made mistakes, and now you're living with the guilt like a good Catholic boy. But those who repent can be forgiven. You only have to ask to be forgiven. Seek redemption, Robert. If not for your own self, then maybe for your family's sake. Your sisters believe in you, Robert."

Robert sat quietly and thought about Jeremy's words. He remembered something Father Eddie had said. Maybe he was right, there was hope for them all.

"I need to see Father Eddie."

"Brilliant. Let me call him while you get dressed. We'll wait for him downstairs in the kitchen, together. Nina has breakfast on the table for us all."

"You came up here to get me for breakfast?" Robert smiled. "Sorry to give you such a scare, old sport. I'll be fine after a cup of coffee, promise."

Jeremy waited while Robert dressed. He'd be okay now, the moment of insanity had left him. But Robert knew that Jeremy would still, most likely, stick to him like glue. The man took responsibility to a new level. Deep down, Robert was glad for the company. He had scared himself as well and didn't want to end up in the same low place again.

They stomped downstairs together. Everyone was in the room off of the kitchen, sitting around the morning room table. *Everyone except...Rachael.* It didn't matter if Robert received forgiveness or not, nor did it matter that he was given a pass by the FBI.

Nothing in his life would mean the same without his Rachael.

"Nina, please bring another pot," Michelle called out.

Emilie didn't ask but instead took the liberty to fill Robert's plate with food.

"Eat, you need your strength," she said.

She placed his plate in front of him. Robert looked up, their gaze met. She knew. Emilie always knew his feelings. He was an open channel for her to probe with her gift, then wear his feelings as her own. He saw his pain reflect back at him from her eyes.

"We're a sad bunch, aren't we?" he said.

"Things will get better, I promise. It's always darkest before the true light." Emilie smiled.

"I'm afraid of the truth, Em."

Nina carried in a pot of coffee, the smell alone comforted him.

"Watch up, cumin through with hot stuff," Nina said.

"You sure are damn hot, Nina." Robert joked. It felt good to tease, he felt like himself if only for a moment.

She slapped his head. "You watch yourself, young man." She smiled wide and handed a cup to Robert.

He accepted the cup filled with hot coffee and closed his eyes as he sipped. The smell filled his nostrils, and for a second, he felt safe and warm.

Nina stood behind him and placed her hand on him. "God be with you, child. That's a message from your momma."

"So, you're clairvoyant now, Nina?"

She slapped his head again. "You stop sassing about that. No poking fun today." She wagged her finger at them. "The lot of you look like the cat dragged you in. That FBI man is coming over today, you know. Let's pray he has news about poor Miss Rachael."

"Yes, Ma'am." Robert was grateful for Nina's caring way.

When he smiled at her, he saw light reflected back in her eyes, giving notice of her love.

"I'm sorry folks, but I have to go to the office. Please, when Agent Sloan gets here, call me right away. I'll zip back."

"Yes, of course, Michelle," Emilie said. "Want me to go to the office with you?"

"No, but I need to know when our money will magically return to our accounts. I'll hold off the board members, as best I can. But the accountant said that he can't hold his tongue for long. Rob, please stress to your Agent Sloan that we need our money back. We have suppliers and employees that have to be paid."

"Michelle, we all know how important that is. We'll get to the bottom of things. If we can't get the funds back, we'll go through our lawyers to pursue other avenues. The Black Wolf Society has a ton of money somewhere. We'll sue the pants off them all." Emilie kept her voice even.

"And what good will that do? Their money is hidden, re-member. And we can't sue the government, I checked. None of this would have happened if not for them, but we're the ones who initiated the transfer." Michelle escaped into a dark mood herself.

"I'm so sorry this is happening, Chelle. I'll make it up to everyone, somehow. I won't let any of us end up in the streets. We'll always have this house and each other. My apologies for dragging the family down and getting involved in all of this, to begin with." Robert felt depressed again.

Aunt Victoria had been quiet for days, but this morning she spoke her mind. "If any of you think Robert or anyone else in this family is to blame, well then you need your head examined. That group has been a thorn in your parents' side since the '70s. Tom Bennett had his agenda and I'm sorry that this family ended up the casualty of his trap, but believe me, it wasn't your doing. It's been a ploy all along, a well-executed plan, conceived long ago. He got what he wanted and so did the group. They're both evil. I say, help that Agent find the money and bring them all to justice."

"I agree, Auntie. No worries, Robert." Emilie said. "We're a family and we'll get through this together. Have faith, I do."

She smiled, and Robert knew she meant every word. Everyone else in the family was moving ahead, dealing with the horrors that happened this past year without losing faith that they'd prevail. But Robert just couldn't, as much as he wanted to, his burden held on tight. He knew all too well, what had grown in his heart, and nothing discharged him from answering for his deeds. Maybe, if only, he found Rachael and had her by his side again . . . maybe then he'd be a good man.

CHAPTER 35

Seeking

Later in the afternoon, Robert sat in the parlor with Jeremy, who patiently stayed by his side looking busy doing a crossword, pretending he wasn't keeping an eye on him. Robert knew he would rather be doing other things. Finally, Jeremy was relieved of his duty when Father Eddie arrived at the house. After pleasantries were exchanged, Eddie and Robert went into the library to talk.

"Please, take a seat, Eddie."

The priest situated his large frame into a chair near the fireplace.

"This feels nice, cozy," Father Eddie said.

"Yes, it still looks chilly out there. We traipsed about outside last night, in the cold air. I hope we don't come down with a cough or anything." Robert bent toward the hearth and jabbed the fire, then returned the wrought iron poker to the stand. He settled into the complimentary armchair.

"There was a frost last night. What were you doing out there in the cold?"

"Well, I had a bit too much to drink, so I can't remember the details very well." Robert tapped his head. "A bit fuzzy. I was taken to someplace, up in Millington."

"Taken, what in heaven do you mean?"

"Like I said, I was plastered, even unconscious for a while. Anyway, I came to and was in this strange place—well hell, I guess I had been abducted. Of course, my responsible sister chose to follow the guy who snatched me, to keep me safe and all. Which I sorely needed, by the way, and I'm eternally grateful to her and Jeremy. They saved my life last night."

Father Eddie was quiet a moment, then spoke gently, as if Robert was a fragile child. "Tell me what happened. How did they save your life?"

"Father, what I really need is to tell you my confession. I feel so bad inside and need my sins absolved before . . ." He breathed out a heavy sigh. "You see, they might have saved my life last night, but I experienced something else. I wanted to take a life, Father. I am evil."

Father Eddie nodded.

"Did you hear me, padre? I have the desires of a killer. I need a confession."

Wasting no time, Father Eddie pulled out a deep violet stole from his black jacket's inside pocket and unrolled the length. He draped it around his neck so it fell down from his shoulders to his front. The damask purple material had embroidered gold crosses on each end. He leaned forward and waved his arms in the air and made the sign of the cross in front of Robert's face.

"Begin," the priest said.

"Bless me, Father, for I have sinned . . . "

Robert said his confession, and Father Eddie listened. When Robert finished unburdening his soul, Father Eddie asked some pointed questions, which ripped straight to the heart of the matter.

"Do you want to be good?" the priest said.

"Of course I do, "Robert replied.

"Do you love the Lord?"

Instantly Robert blurted, "Yes."

"Do you seek God's redemption?"

"Yes. Father, please tell me how. Tell me what I need to do."

"Those who ask and seek with an open heart shall find it."

"Father Eddie, I guess I'm more of a hands-on kind of guy. I need instructions because I've messed up so badly on my own."

The priest smiled. "There's no denying, you've messed up. But you've asked for forgiveness and we have a loving God who will forgive you as long as you sin no more."

"Then I'm doomed because I'm no saint, Father. I know I'll do something wrong again." Robert lowered his head and stared at his hands.

"Of course. No one is perfect. What I mean is, don't repeat the same mistakes. You have acknowledged that what you've done was wrong. Don't do those things again. Instead, I suggest you do the opposite. Every time you get frustrated with your family, instead of hiding away or scheming something behind their backs, confront them with your feelings. Talk with them and work things out. That's what family love is all about. Being there for each other during a disaster is the natural reaction, but being there when you'd rather not, well that's courage. Robert, you can do this. Be honest with your feelings and open yourself up to others. Share. Be part of other people's lives and take care in all that you do and say. Your family loves you and will always listen."

"Yes. That much I know is true. I can see the disgust on Michelle's face sometimes when I've done something that hurts her. But she still comes around and asks how I am. It amazes me every time. And Emilie, well she's a bit scary at times, her power and all, but I see so much love in her eyes. When she's around I feel cared for and loved."

"Yes. You are very fortunate to have their love. I think it's about time you thank God for your blessings. The money and power your family holds can do so much good. Your parents were generous, not only with money but with themselves and their time. And so should you be."

Robert laughed.

"What's so funny?"

"You haven't heard, padre. We lost our money. Michelle insists that the FBI will somehow find it all and return it to our accounts, but I don't have any faith in the government giving a shit about our finances."

Father Eddie tossed his head back a tick. "If you don't get your fortune back, will you still believe in the Lord? Will you still try to be good?"

"Yes. That's not negotiable. I want to change. I want redemption."

"Then, I will absolve all of your sins. You will be forgiven by the Lord, everything. But you must keep true to your commitment to try to be good every day, everywhere, and with everyone. I'll be there whenever you need me for guidance."

"Thank you, Father."

Robert was given his penance, prayers he must say on his own to be fully cleansed. Then with his eyes closed, the priest mumbled some prayers to absolve the sins. The Sacrament of Confession, one of the seven holy held by the Catholic Church, brought Robert's soul back to a path where he could walk in faith again. When Father Eddie raised his arm and made the final blessing with the sign of the cross over Robert's head, he imagined himself cleansed. Hope returned to his heart.

Thankful that Father Eddie hadn't been judgmental, but instead had given wise counsel and hope, Robert wondered how the priest dealt with all the bad things he was told. He knew that priests kept everything said between them secret because of the holy bond, but how did he carry the burden of knowledge without his faith in humanity collapsing? Each time they met and talked, Eddie grew more human in Robert's opinion, and yet more saintly at the same time.

"Thank you, Father Eddie, for everything."

The priest nodded and kissed Robert's forehead.

"I wish you the best and I'll pray for you to receive good

news from that Agent. I pray he finds Rachael safe."

"Yes, please, pray for her safety. I am afraid for Rachael—it's been days. I hope they trace the stolen money, too. But I have to admit, no matter what happens—whether we get our money back or not, I admire the man. He remains calm under pressure. He commands, does his job, and helps others without expecting anything in return. And believe me, I've pushed him, but I also understand there's only so much a man can do."

"Miracles happen, Robert. The agent sounds like a priest," Eddie said.

They both laughed until interrupted by the doorbell.

"That's my cue. I'll let myself out. Good luck." Father Eddie left the back way, down the hall then through the kitchen.

Robert walked toward the front door anticipating it was Agent Sloan with his update, as promised.

CHAPTER 36

Status Report

Robert glanced up at the grandfather clock as he headed down the hall toward the front door. Seven in the evening. It occurred to him that it was the dinner hour, but there would be no family meal tonight. The house manager, Evans, answered the door.

"Agent Sloan, please come in." Robert met him in the foyer, and they went into the parlor together. "I'm anxious to hear what you've uncovered. Let me call my sisters down."

"Can we put that off for a minute? I want to speak to you alone." The Agent's face matched his serious tone.

"Rachael. Is she all right?" Robert's stomach flipped. Then he had another thought . . . maybe Sloan knows that he almost strangled a man to death last night. *Maybe he's here to arrest me?* He rubbed his hands together to stop them from shaking, trying hard not to appear guilty. *He wasn't guilty—he was absolved. Right?* Despite his rationalization, he sweated like a guilty man. Robert looked away. That's when he noticed Evans standing near the doorway, lurking within earshot.

"Wait a moment." Robert put his finger up.

Evans noticed that Robert had spotted him and immediately left the area. When Robert was assured that Evans was out of earshot, he turned to speak with Sloan.

"Okay, I'll bite. What's up, Agent Sloan? Tell me about Rachael."

"You nervous, Robert?"

Robert wiped his forehead with the back of his hand. "Of course I'm nervous. Did you find my wife?"

"Yes, we've found her," Sloan spoke the words softly, as if in mourning.

Robert's heartbeat throbbed against his rib cage, his throat tightened. He thought the flooding emotions would overpower him and land him flat on the floor. Relieved—yet Robert was still wary—sensing something was wrong. He jerked his head back and whispered, "Alive?"

"Yes, however, there's a complication. Something we couldn't have foreseen. I'm not sure how to put this."

"Put what?" she said. Emilie and Jeremy entered the room, both wearing expressions of concern.

"It's okay, Agent Sloan. You can tell us all," Robert said. "No more secrets in this family."

Emilie slipped her arm in Robert's. "That's good to hear, Rob. "She waved to the sofa and chairs. "Please, have a seat, Agent Sloan. From the urgency in your voice, you apparently have much to reveal."

Agent Sloan sat down in the armchair his eyes cringed with worry, the others sat on the sofa across from him.

"First off, we located the money."

"Forget about the money right now, tell us about that later. Where's Rachael? Can I see her? Is she okay? Did you see her?" Robert's voice edged near to panic.

Silence hung in the air, a moment too long. Robert couldn't stand the waiting.

"You can't see her just yet," Agent Sloan said.

"Why not? You said she's alive . . . "

Agent Sloan inhaled deeply and let it out. "Robert . . . she was there."

"What do you mean she was there? Where?" Robert's voice grew louder. "You mean they held her captive in that horrid dungeon? Oh my God, poor Rachael. I must see her. She needs me by her side."

"No," Sloan said. "Not just yet. She's not allowed to have

visitors. She wasn't held captive, Robert. It's a bit more complicated than that."

"Oh, for God's sake, tell us already. You're killing me here with the suspense. What's going on?"

Robert's stomach twisted with a pain he never thought possible. He stood and paced the floor, unable to stop from moving. Even though now convinced that he wasn't Bennett's son after all, and relieved from the burden of his sins, still, Robert knew karma had a way of coming back at him. That was a boomerang that we all faced sooner or later. Deep down he understood that there was no such thing as a free pass, things didn't work quite that way.

The priest had said to repent and go forward to do good. Easier said than done when there's so much evil and deception surrounding him. Deadly sins fringed just outside of his control, provoking his primal responses to kick back in. Frustrated, Robert felt so angry. He wanted to punch Sloan just for stringing him along.

But he had vowed to be good, so he said a brief prayer for patience, and searched his own mind, trying to understand what was happening even if it meant that he might get hurt in the process. *At least Rachael is alive,* he thought. Honesty often caused pain. Hearing the truth and being empathetic to it hurt. Hell, he saw it every day with his sister; Emilie suffered. When he opened up his heart more, would it get broken? *Is my heart about to break, to get so twisted, that I'll never recover?*

Robert stopped, turned around, and watched. He tried to detach himself for the moment and let things happen as they needed to unfold.

"Agent Sloan, please tell us straight," Emilie said.

Robert stared at Sloan's face. His brow was furrowed with beads of sweat, and his eyes revealed his struggle with telling the truth.

"It's okay, Sloan. I'll behave, promise. We need to hear the truth," Robert said.

Agent Sloan cleared his throat. "Rachael was at the ceremony. She was at the altar, actually," he said.

Emilie gasped. "You're not saying that she was the creature lying there under the sheet!"

"No, No. Absolutely not," Agent Sloan said. He waved his hands in the air in protest. "She most definitely was not experimented on."

"So if not, and she was there," Jeremy recanted the facts, "that means she was one of the robed members of the Black Wolf Society."

Sloan nodded.

"N-n-no. That can't b-b-e-e." Robert stammered. "She'd never be mixed up with that lot. I'd have known. No, it can't be."

"Robert, I'm so sorry. We have her under our custody. However, it's a bit complicated right now."

"Agent Sloan, you said that before. Please, what exactly is so complicated?" Emilie asked.

"Remember at the scene? Some members, presumably leaders, stood at the altar. Well, she was one of them. I'm sorry, Robert."

Robert felt his muscles weaken and give way, his weight dropped to the floor. He felt a knock to his head, a bright light flashed in his sight, right before he passed out.

🔲◈◈◈🔲

When Robert came to, his sister Emilie was slapping his face.

"What are you doing?" he said.

She handed him a glass of water. "Are you okay, Robert?"

He took a sip and handed it back. Then he pulled himself up from the floor and brushed off his clothes. "I'm fine, just startled. I guess I'm reaching my limit for surprises."

"You mean disappointments," Michelle called out. "I can't believe that she was one of them. I mean, she was family. How could she have done this to us?"

"When did you get here, Michelle? And do what to us?" he said.

"I arrived just in time to see you pass out on the floor. And you know exactly what she's done — she stole our money."

"We don't know that she had anything to do with that. Besides, just because she was standing there with a robe on, doesn't mean she was a member. I was standing there, for Christ's sake, but it was all against my will. I wasn't hurting anyone except myself. Let's give Rachael the benefit of the doubt."

Robert glanced over and saw Agent Sloan's face turn red, his head bent, and eyes stared down at the floor. Robert went back to the sofa and sat down again.

"Tell us everything, Sloan. I promise to handle the truth."

The agent drew in a deep breath, and with resignation, he revealed what he knew.

"Once we realized it was her, we dug into things. It seems Rachael has been at this game for a while now. She's been accumulating wealth, for many years, using her father as the money holder. He was her figurehead. But all along it's been her financial enterprise," Agent Sloan said.

"No, that means that she was complicit in her own father's murder. She loved him, we all knew that. It can't be," Emilie said.

Sloan walked across the room then stood near Robert's end of the couch and looked down at him while he spoke.

"Believe me, she had many men fooled, Robert. Remember what I said to you weeks ago. I said it would be someone close to you."

Robert remembered the agent's words. All this time he thought he was protecting Rachael, but she was actually behind all the ploys of the Black Wolf Society. *Or perhaps . . . maybe she was being played just like him.*

"Sloan, how sure are you that she was involved—what do you know? I mean, maybe they were forcing her to participate, just like they did to me. Maybe she was coerced to believe in the Black Wolf Society, just like I was."

The Agent shook his head. "Unfortunately, things get worse. We've been sifting through all the Intel discovered at the underground scene. The old ammunitions plant's underground maze was more than a meeting spot, it was one of the many headquarters here in the United States. From what we've been able to decipher, not only was Rachael in the know of all the events going on, she was one of the main leaders. The task force from DC is now involved and they ran traces on her father's money. Turns out, she had filtered funds into her father's business interests with a very elaborate scheme, almost undetectable. Professional money laundering. We finally got to the truth. Of course, it helps when you have a team of digital forensic agents under your wing for help to untangle the web."

"You mean, all the family money was a scam? Wow." Michelle marched across the room and faced Agent Sloan. "Tell me, Mr. Agent-man, by any chance did they run a trace to find our family's company money?"

He nodded.

Michelle leaned into his arms, hugging the agent, then just as quick she stepped back.

"What a relief!" she said.

"It will all be returned exactly as it was. In a few—"

A loud thud sounded from the other room, a voice screamed, and a sudden noise of dishes smashing to the floor. They all ran to the kitchen and found Evans on the floor, pinned down by Nina. She sat on his chest, her left hand gripped his collar, and she held a marble rolling pin in her right hand, threatening to hit the man. "You no good—"

"What in God's name is going on? Nina, get off the man." Robert called out.

"I caught him, Agent Sloan. Just like you said I would. You said he might go after that phone of yours, and sure enough, he did. I caught him red-handed."

"Thank you, Nina. Good work." Agent Sloan tapped his phone and ordered another agent to come in and properly apprehend Evans.

"Good heavens. What did Evans do wrong?" Emilie asked. Her face paled as a look of recognition washed across her face. "Oh my, it was him. Him all along. That's the voice I thought I recognized when I was kidnapped. Evans, how could you?"

Agent Sloan pulled the man up off the floor by his collar.

"Your house manager has been spying on all of you. He's a planted snitch and has been reporting back reconnaissance about the household. The Black Wolf Society knew about our initial meeting, Robert. That's why I couldn't use the flip phone I gave to you after it went dead. It caused some communication issues, I know, but we couldn't chance using it any longer. Evans had tapped the line. Later he blocked all transmissions from the house."

"My goodness," Nina said. "I knew he was trouble. Always lurking around this place ever since your father died." Nina's face beamed with justification.

Ten minutes or so after the commotion, they calmed down and went back into the parlor. Questions swarmed in Robert's head, but he wanted, more than answers or anything else, to see Rachael.

"Sloan, I understand why you're holding Rachael, but I still want to see her. She is my wife, after all."

"You're a good man, Robert." He patted him on the back.

"Harrumph. I don't know about that. Why do I feel like you're hiding something else from us? I mean, what else could she possibly have done? She betrayed the family, schemed against us, robbed us . . . Is there anything left she can do to hurt this family?"

"It's not that simple," the Agent said.

"Did you fly her to DC?" Jeremy asked.

There was an awkward pause. "No, she's in the hospital."

Silence. The fireplace sparked, the pop awoke them from the daze.

"Hospital? No, don't tell me, she was the one shot." Robert covered his eyes and tried to recall exactly what happened the night before.

He played the scene, in slow motion. He pictured where each person was standing. He remembered that he had grabbed the robed member who appeared to be the leader of the group. He shivered, hearing in his head the mechanical sound of the voice synthesizer. *That had to have been Rachael.* Repulsed with the thought, Robert broke out into a cold sweat. He wiped away the perspiration on his brow and asked the obvious question, needing to be certain of the truth.

"Agent Sloan, the person I held against my chest—the person who was shot while in my arms—was that Rachael?"

Emilie groaned. "Oh no. I am so sorry, Rob."

Jeremy put his arms around Emilie. Robert once again was amazed at how they zeroed in on each other when they needed support. He envied them and wished he could have had that kind of relationship with Rachael. Now there will be nothing left for them, except a divorce if she managed to survive.

"Sloan, I still want to see her. I feel incredibly guilty about everything that happened to her."

"Guilty. Why? Robert, believe me. You've done nothing wrong."

Agent Sloan sat down and motioned for them to as well.

"Listen, the agent who stood guard in the balcony above reported that she was shot for a very good reason. First off, I know you think that you had the upper hand in the situation, but believe me, you did not. When we took her to Emergency, we discovered that she had many hidden weapons on her person. The SWAT agent said he witnessed her pulling out a knife and was about to stab you, Robert. She almost killed you. But it turns out that it wasn't the officer who shot her, it was one of her own. Another member of the Black Wolf took aim and fired off five shots before he was apprehended."

Agent Sloan waited for a response to his update. Robert sat still, thinking the events over in his head.

"I guess, deep down, it doesn't surprise me. I mean, how could anyone love me," Robert said.

"Rob, no. Don't say things like that. She loved you. It's just that she's a bad girl. You always seem to attract the type."

"Thanks for that, Chelle."

"Sorry."

"Seriously," Robert said. "I loved her. I always knew it was one-sided, but I guess I just didn't realize the extent of the imbalance. I had no clue. What does that say about me?"

"Robert, we'll go with you to the hospital," Jeremy said.

"No, that's all right. All of you stay home tonight. You've been through so much already. I want to go alone, with Agent Sloan. If that's okay?"

Agent Sloan nodded.

Robert had been wrong about so many things, all along. But this was where it would stop. He didn't have the stamina to keep living with secrets, or hopes that things would magically work themselves out. He knew now that he had to take charge of his own life, make decisions for himself, and face the consequences.

"Let's get this done."

Agent Sloan and Robert stood and left the parlor together. Robert felt his sister's stare on his back and hoped that Emilie could sense that he was okay. Yes, heartbroken, drained, but he would find his way out of this somehow. He was a changed man—he was hopeful.

Seeing Rachael would be the last step needed for him to make his peace with the chaos that he had called his life. Then he would accept the consequences and start building a future for his family, better than the life he had stolen. He was hopeful that they could be happy.

CHAPTER 37

Unexpected Blessings

Thirty minutes later, Robert and Agent Sloan walked into the hospital. They stepped into an elevator that stunk of body odor, and Robert was relieved when the doors finally opened on the fourth floor. He and Agent Sloan walked toward the room together.

"This is where we're keeping Rachael alive," Sloan said.

Robert looked through the glass panel on the door. The room was white with blinds that were partially closed and let in only the barest of the daylight that remained. His attention went to the tube that was plunged down her throat; the apparatus was breathing for her. It pushed air in, pulled it back out, and pumped her body with the vital oxygen. She lay still in that raised bed, with wires connected to her arm and hooked up to machines that read off her vital signs. There was an intravenous feed connected to bags of glucose that dripped into the thin tube.

Sloan opened the door. A rush of medical smells assaulted Robert's senses. He pinched his nostrils together, then followed the agent inside. Robert walked closer and took her hand in his. Her hair was draped across the white pillowcase, her bright red highlights were now the only thing vibrant about her. Her skin, pale and sickly looking, revealed her true status. The pigment reminded Robert of sour milk, and a memory from years ago popped in his head of being forced to drink the putrid stuff while at school—the smell of it made him ill. His teacher had said, "*Drink all your milk.*" He blindly had obeyed despite his discomfort, unaware that he was lactose intolerant. He wanted the holy nuns—the Sisters of The Holy Trinity—to think of him as a good boy. *Still, he wanted to be good.* He smiled to himself, but it quickly slipped into a grim frown.

After a few minutes of silence, Doctor Hannigan stepped into the room. His gray-white hair was messy, nothing new. He wore his glasses at the end of his nose while reading his tablet.

"You've been working too hard again, Doc. Won't they let you out of here? Some spare time to go home and groom yourself?" Robert said. The hint never registered with the man.

"Tsk tsk. The poor girl," the Doc said. "She didn't have a chance, Robert. One of the bullets damaged her heart. She's only being kept alive by that machine pumping for her heart muscle and the respirator flowing air into her lungs. I'm afraid Rachael is brain dead."

"Doc, if you're suggesting that I should take her off life support, well, I can't do that right now. I won't sign anything just yet."

Doc shook his head. "No, Robert. You don't understand. You see, we can't do that, not until we determine the probability of survival."

"I don't understand." Robert had heard about cases when a person became brain dead, and the plug pulled. *Maybe they want to harvest her organs?*

"Doc, they said there's no hope of recovery. Why keep her alive like this? I'm grateful because I'm not ready to sign off on things, but I guess I'm a bit confused."

"Here," he slid a chair across the floor. "Grab a chair and sit down. We need to talk."

The doctor and Robert sat in the hospital's plastic chairs, now pulled up close to Rachael's bed. The room felt cold, and Robert wished he could leave and pretend none of this was happening.

"Rachael had three bullets inside her. She held on long enough for us to discover her condition. Then she flat-lined.

She died, Robert. We immediately put her on life support. It was the only way to keep the baby alive."

"Baby?"

"Yes. You didn't know?"

Robert felt his heart drop to the floor. Adrenaline kicked in, rushed through his veins, and pumped him up with a euphoria he had never known before. *A Baby—his child.* He had forgotten about his suspicions that Rachael might be pregnant. Now, with all this heartache, a baby, a ray of hope shining through the darkness. He had never felt so happy in his life. He saw that Doc was rambling on, but Robert hadn't registered a word of it.

"Excuse me, sorry. What did you say?"

"The hospital might want to unplug her anyway. The baby is in the early stage of pregnancy."

"No, they can't do that, not now."

"Well then, as an option, I strongly suggest, Robert, that since you have the means, you should bring her back to the house. You could hire a nurse to monitor Rachael and move her body for therapeutic purposes. Ensure all the body fluids are moving properly for the baby's sake. It's important, as well, for you and your sisters to talk to the baby. He'll be able to hear you if you speak close to the womb."

Robert felt a warm rush. "I've heard of things like that. Play music, read to the baby."

Doc Hannigan nodded. "I am very sorry for your loss, Robert. You loved Rachael. But this baby, well, think of him or her as the silver lining."

"This baby is more than that, Doc. He's my miracle. Or she is, I don't care which. This baby is the second chance—the one I don't deserve—but I'm taking it anyway, with an open heart."

Doc patted his shoulder.

"Your father would be proud of you, Robert. You've come a long way."

Robert sped up the driveway, parked, and leaped from the Jag. He couldn't find his sisters fast enough, as he rushed into the house, hollering.

"Emilie, Michelle."

"We're out here," Michelle yelled back.

Robert ran through the downstairs of the house to the back porch.

"Holy cow, why are you two out here when it's cold again tonight."

Robert was shivering and rubbing his arms to keep warm. It didn't matter though, he was too excited. He blathered on.

"I've got the best news. I mean the most incredible thing, you won't believe it. I've been blessed."

"Have you been drinking, Rob? Haven't you had enough to last the rest of your life?" Michelle said.

"No. I'm as sober as a monk. Just listen a minute. We're going to have the best Thanksgiving Day."

"Rob, how can you say that with Rachael in the hospital?" Emilie said.

"No, not that. Rachael won't be with us any longer—not really."

"She died?" Emilie's eyes teared up.

"Well, yes. They have her on life support but said she's brain dead."

"Rob, how the hell can you be so happy when she's dead? I mean, we know she betrayed us all, but you loved her," Michelle said. "Are you that cold-hearted?"

Nothing they said stopped Robert from smiling.

"This year we have something special to be thankful for, a

blessing that I never expected."

"Like what? Do we have our money back?"

"Better than money, Michelle."

"Okay, enough cryptic speak—what gives?"

"It's Rachael—she's coming home tomorrow. She'll be here for Thanksgiving."

"Oh, you poor delusional soul," Emilie said. "Honey, Rachael isn't making it. You just said so yourself. She died."

"No. I mean, I know, it's not like that. Rachael is already declared brain dead, but we're keeping her alive—"

"You're sick," Michelle said.

"No, you don't understand. It's for the baby. We can keep Rachael's body on life support to allow the baby to come to full term."

"Oh, Robert. For real? Rachael has a baby inside? That's wonderful news." Emilie said.

"I know." He beamed and couldn't remember a time when he had smiled so much that his cheeks hurt.

"You're going to be a daddy?" Michelle clapped then hugged him jubilantly. "I'm so happy for you, Rob."

He smiled wider than the Mississippi.

"Thanks for your support. Now I'm off for some rest, I feel dead tired."

He kissed his sisters' foreheads goodnight and left the porch.

◻◈◈◈◻

Emilie and Michelle stood looking out over the backyard.

"You're awfully quiet, Michelle."

Michelle had her arms wrapped around herself fighting off the night's chill.

"Yes, well there's a problem, I think."

"Hmm, what does that mean? Haven't we had enough for a day, and then some?"

292

Michelle inspected the area.

"Listen, I'm not sure who needs to know about this, but . . ."

She didn't finish but instead looked again making sure no one was standing nearby in the shadows.

"Okay, you're killing me. What is it already?"

"After Rob and the agent left, well, I did some snooping in their room."

"Michelle, no."

"Well, I wanted to see if Rachael had anything in the room to help the case. Anyway, the problem is, I found some letters between Rachel and another man."

Emilie knew this was bad news, one didn't have to be clairvoyant to see where this was leading. "Do you have them?"

Michelle nodded.

"Here, you read them for yourself."

Emilie reached for the handed letters, opened the one on top, carefully unfolding it as if it were about to bite her.

"Oh my goodness. This can't be," Emilie said.

Michelle sat down on a chair and stared at the floor.

"What are we going to do, Em? What should we tell Robert?"

"Are you kidding me—we tell him nothing. There is no way he can process this right now. We have no idea if it's true or not, anyway."

"Yes, we do. It plainly says she was in love with Tom Bennett. They were having an affair. Oh my God, the thought of it makes me sick. And to think, Robert is so happy about this baby. But it's not his."

Emilie pulled Michelle up from the chair and kept her hands around her forearms.

"We don't know that. It very well could be Rob's."

"Ouch, Em. You're hurting me."

Emilie looked down at her hands and let go of her sister. "Sorry."

"It's okay. I understand exactly how you feel." She rubbed her arm.

"Michelle, we can't tell him. He'll sink into depression again. We can't have that on our conscience. Besides, no matter who the father is of Rachael's baby, it will need love and care."

Michelle made noises through her nose.

"Michelle, we have to keep this a secret between only you and me."

"I thought we weren't supposed to keep secrets from each other anymore."

"And we aren't," Emilie snipped. "At least not between you and me. We wouldn't from Rob either, except that he's too fragile right now."

"I hope to God this doesn't bite us in the ass someday."

Emilie shook her head. "I'm sure it will, but right now there's no other choice. Agreed?"

Michelle closed her eyes and nodded. After a moment she opened them and said, "Agreed."

The sisters hooked arms and walked back into the house together.

CHAPTER 38

Family Bonds

The late morning sun slipped through the bedroom window on a cold Thanksgiving Day. The temperature was unusually low, for the Mid-south, and the local weather forecast had predicted that snow would arrive later in the evening.

Robert stood looking out over the lawn. The grass was dried up and looked like tawny brownish hay. The trees were nearly bare, only oak leaves hung on, colored with burnished browns. Reflecting over what transpired the past year, Robert was amazed at the major changes that occurred—life changes for them all.

He married the woman of his dreams, only to discover he'd been duped. It happens to most people sooner or later, but he deserved it. He received what he had dished out, after all. They lost their father, a man he had barely tolerated. Now he wished for more time to make up for his failure as a son.

Robert knew his parents would be proud of their children now. They survived the monster that had haunted their parents an entire lifetime together. His sister, Emilie, succeeded in bringing the family together again. She deserved all of the credit. No one could match her power, persistence, and loyalty. Robert understood that without her, Michelle and himself would be floundering lost souls.

He left the window and walked away from his reverie to stand close to the bed. A team of medical personal had brought Rachael's body to the house yesterday. They transported her up to the blue room, the front room of the house with the morning light. He remembered how she had enjoyed the room once before, with its cerulean blue satin drapes hanging from the

French doors, the toile wallpaper with ancient maidens garnished in flowers that matched the Wedgwood lamps and vases adorning the bedside tables.

The equipment had been set up ahead of time and now used to keep her vitals going. Robert even took the precaution of having a backup generator in place, in case a nasty storm sailed its way through the area and cut off the electricity for a spell. It was a costly endeavor, but worth every cent.

Nothing was going to get in the way of his baby's growth and health.

He tried not to think of Rachael and how she betrayed them all, though it was difficult with her body lying there. Her hair still shone brightly as the sunlight filtered from the window and touched her golden highlights accentuating her auburn hair. He loved her still. Insane as it seemed to the others, he couldn't help himself, so he decided to forgive her, though she probably never wanted him to do so. That didn't matter to Robert. He was a changed man. He refused to carry hate in his heart any longer.

"There you are." Michelle walked into the room and came to his side. "She was beautiful. No doubt the baby will be good-looking."

Robert smiled. His sister was right. The baby was going to be a looker, divine, and so very much loved. He leaned his head down to Rachael's stomach. "Hello, baby. Did you hear your auntie? She said you're good-looking."

He stroked the belly gently.

"Let's go downstairs. It's time for dinner. Emilie and Jeremy cooked a feast. Wait until Nina returns and discovers her kitchen was taken over. She'll never leave us alone to visit with her family again."

Michelle giggled, took Robert's hand, and led him out of the room.

"Pans and bowls cover every inch of counter space," she said.

"After dinner, we'll have a cleaning-up party. Something new that we can do together, as a family. Worth a try at least once," he said.

"I'll dry," Michelle said.

"Hey Chelle, what do you think Nina will say? About keeping Rachael here, I mean. It's not something most people would do."

"It doesn't matter what people think. We have to protect that baby."

Robert nodded and tightened his sister's hand.

They walked down the staircase, smelling the lingering aroma. The redolence of spices, herbs, and sausage stuffing drifted from the dining room. A feast was spread out before them, covering the table and every other flat surface available in the room. Colorful platters were filled with antipasti, green and orange salads, red sauces, spicy relishes, raisin bread, crisp, bright veggies, and a beautifully carved turkey.

"Goodness. You don't mess around in the kitchen," Michelle said.

"Since this is Jeremy's first Thanksgiving in the U.S., I wanted to include every possible holiday favorite. I dug up every special recipe we ever served. Even cooked a turducky."

"No way. Wonderful, assuming that's a turkey stuffed with duck?" This amused Robert.

"Absolutely. We're going to eat until oblivion. Gotta love the leftovers, too." Emilie and Jeremy took their seats.

"I'm looking forward to sampling every dish," Jeremy said. "It's too bad your Aunt Victoria isn't here for this feast."

"Yes, but she had other commitments," Emilie said. "Besides, she'll be back when it gets closer to the birth. We'll need her help then when the baby is here screaming and kicking."

"Em, you made enough food to eat all week long." Robert pulled out a chair for Michelle. "Madame."

"Merci," she said.

Emilie cleared her throat. "Before we dig into some major munching, I think it's only fitting that we share what we're all thankful for," she said.

"Is this part of the holiday tradition?" Jeremy asked.

"Yes," they all replied together, then laughed.

Robert stood and clanged his fork against the crystal water glass.

"Since I am the oldest, and the only son so far as we know —
"

"Robert," Michelle remanded.

"Well, since I am the oldest, I'd like to be the host of this fine tradition. Emilie, will you please be the first to share with us?"

He sat and Emilie stood.

"I am thankful for my family, and especially my fiancé. Jeremy, you were there when I needed someone the most. You knew when to give me space when to listen, and you were never afraid to walk into the unknown with me. I raise my glass to Jeremy, and to the future of the family."

"To the future," Jeremy repeated her toast.

"Here here," the others said.

She sat and Robert stood.

"Next, can we hear from the other lady in the room?"

"Where's the other lady? Rob, you make us sound so old," she said then laughed.

Robert sat and Michelle stood.

"Sorry. Seriously, folks, I'm thankful for my family's faith in me. My judgment was tested, but in the end, you all came to my rescue and supported me. In the past few months, I've been frightened out of my wits, learned of horrors I never dreamed existed in this world, and wound up with more self-esteem and faith in my family than I thought possible. So here's to the de Gourgues family. And that includes you now, too, Jeremy."

"To the family," Emilie said.

"Here here."

Michelle sat and Robert stood. "Jeremy, I would be honored if you added your thanks on this day."

Jeremy stood. "It's been a crazy ride since I met this family. This bloke from Surrey never expected so much drama, life, and love. So on this day, my first Thanksgiving with my new family, I share with you all a thankful heart filled with love. May we all keep and cherish each other forever."

"To love," Emilie said.

"Here here," they all said at once.

"Come on, Rob. Get on with it, the food's getting cold." Michelle said.

Robert stood and cleared his throat.

"Very well, I won't take center stage long." He adjusted his shirt sleeve and ceremoniously turned to face his family. Robert smiled freely, feeling compassionate for the first time since he was a child.

"There is so much I want to say—too much for one toast. But for Michelle's sake, I'll try to keep things brief.

"This past year has been arduous but has also proved to us all that we are indeed a family. We love each other, unconditionally. I promise to you today, that I will embrace my second chance and the blessing bestowed on me. I am thankful to God for His unexpected gift, my child. It's the miracle of life. So please, hold up your glasses, and let's drink a toast together."

He raised his glass and waited for the others to stand and join him.

"To the future. To family. To love. To second chances."

He wiped tears from the corner of his eyes then downed his glass of wine. The spirits and the burning hearth behind him were nothing compared to the warmth in his heart.

Robert was a transformed man and embraced whole-heartily his newfound freedom from hate. He received atonement. Robert had found what he sought, redemption.

From the Author

I'm fortunate and humbled to have had the eyes of Richard Thomas, the Editor-In-Chief of The Dark House Press, on this novel Seeking Redemption. I'm thankful for his insights and for pointing me in the right direction to make this a strong story with developed characters and plot. Richard Thomas is a recognized author himself, please check out his work and website.

Your support for all authors is appreciated.

The third story of the Curses & Secrets serial was written in response to my sister's request. After she had read book one, Breaking Cursed Bonds, she wanted my antagonist character, Robert, to have a chance to redeem himself. This third book, Seeking Redemption, was written because of her heartfelt theory that everyone deserves a second chance. Thanks, Barbara, because I had fun creating the story.

Thank you, my family, siblings, children, and cousins, for your continued support of my late-career choice of writer. I am grateful for my ever faithful yet reluctant Alpha reader, Jerry, my husband. Thank goodness he likes to correct me.

Encouragement from other Independent Authors is also appreciated. Approachable at tough moments when inspiration is hard to grasp, as a group Indie Authors are supportive, honest, and share great learning moments. They voice opinions, give advice, and share experiences. The publishing world is changing because of the Indie explosion. Voices will never be censored again.

Writing is a long process of research and re-writing. Lines are written only to be tossed aside, then the writer begins again. It's the part I enjoy most about writing, the never-ending process of refreshing itself, like a blooming flower that dies only to be reborn the following spring. Each of our stories has a life cycle of its own.

A writer develops characters, gives them their unique history, needs, and goals, then allows them to grow into the story, weaving their voice into the pages. It's an amazing process and gets more involved with each new page. Characters become part of a writer's life, we speak with them, and hear their voice as we develop scenes.

When the last page is written, we say goodbye to our heroes and villains. Ending this serial is bittersweet. I enjoyed developing the deGourgues family, their friends, and their enemies.

My only solace is my new book, *In The Woods: Murder in the North East Kingdom*, and the exploration of new characters, Samantha, Zach, and more. Once again, I created a world for my readers to wander in the setting of the North East Kingdom of Vermont and New Hampshire. Check it out if you enjoy a great murder mystery with a colorful tapestry of characters.

Keep in touch and get updates about new releases by following my website ElisabethZguta.com or EZIndiePublishing.com and sign up for my newsletter.

Thank you for reading the Curses & Secrets serial,
I appreciate your support!

If you could spare a few minutes, please write a quick, honest review of my work. Post it wherever you purchased the story. If you prefer, post a review on any reader's website you visit like Goodreads. A few words can make a big difference and help future readers discover the story.

Thank you for spending time reading my stories.
Your patronage is appreciated.
Elisabeth